AVOIDING MATTHEW

Caroline Bell Foster

Scan for free reads

Publisher: Sunshine Publications
Cover design by: Coral Elliott Endsor
Editor: Alec Hawkes

Dedication
To my mother, Victoria, I will forever feel
your arms around me. I miss you. x

CONTENTS

Title Page

Copyright

Dedication

Chapter One   1

Chapter Two   12

Chapter Three   16

Chapter Four   25

Chapter Five   33

Chapter Six   40

Chapter Seven   47

Chapter Eight   55

Chapter Nine   65

Chapter Ten   69

Chapter Eleven   80

Chapter Twelve   92

Chapter Thirteen   95

Chapter Fourteen   101

Chapter Fifteen   107

Chapter Sixteen   115

Chapter Seventeen   124

Chapter Eighteen   129

Chapter Nineteen   140

Chapter Twenty   144

Chapter Twenty-One   151

Chapter Twenty-Two   158

Chapter Twenty-Three   163

Chapter Twenty-Four   169

Chapter Twenty-Five   175

Chapter Twenty-Six   181

Chapter Twenty-Seven   187

Chapter Twenty-Eight   192

Chapter Twenty-Nine   196

Chapter Thirty   199

Chapter Thirty-One   206

Chapter Thirty-Two   212

Chapter Thirty-Three   216

Chapter Thirty-Four   221

Chapter Thirty-Five   226

Chapter Thirty-Six   230

Chapter Thirty-Seven   234

Chapter Thirty-Eight   239

Chapter Thirty-Nine   242

Chapter Forty   248

LOVE TO BELONG   253

About The Author   267

Books By This Author   269

CHAPTER ONE

Matthew knew he was fortunate, but it was at times like this, when he was alone, walking at the edge of the forest at his aunt's retreat, that he missed certain sounds.

Yes, he could hear most things, but it was the smaller things, the things hearing people probably took for granted, or didn't notice, like the creak of a tree limb, the scupper of a rabbit, hell, even the sound of snowflakes landing.

Yeah, he wanted to hear those tiny things.

Matthew had been sent on vacation. A vacation he didn't want or need. But when the booming command filtered down the sterile corridors, he bowed out with a scowl of displeasure. Vacations were over-rated as far as he was concerned.

He reluctantly left D.C. and drove down to New York to spend time with his stepmother, Greta, and father Charles. His younger brother Ace and new wife Sabrina had bought a place not too far from their parents, so he spent a night with them also, getting to know baby Ace, the newest addition to the family. But two days of all that family bliss and he was itching to get back into the field.

His cousin Kyle saved him, wanting him to follow some guy called Jai. He was the dude Kyle's ex-girlfriend Camille had installed in his house that Ace had told him about.

It was all very complicated. Kyle's life had always been filled with drama, Ace's less so now that he was married and grounded, literally. Kyle was going through some shit that had the whole family worried, so Matthew leapt at the chance to use his skills, and sitting down with the closest people in his life, Kyle and Ace, Operation 'Stalk Jai', began.

The covert operation had seen Matthew track Jai around New York City. Not really the clandestine operation Matthew was used to, with him being an international operative working for the government, but at least it was something.

When Jai met up and had a coffee with the same doctor, Kyle's ex-girlfriend knew things got interesting.

Things were still going off with Operation 'Stalk Jai', but with his cousin's phone being tracked and a routine that Matthew was very much a part of, he knew he wouldn't be needed for a couple of days.

Matthew walked out of the trees and over to one of several piers dotted around the lake. The air was so crisp if you breathed in too deep, it would hurt your nostrils. The whole place was a picture of tranquillity, but he was bored out of his mind.

Kyle's parents owned a retreat on the lake with several log cabins ranging from two to six bedrooms. His aunt, an eccentric but loveable woman, held silent retreats, crystal healing and New Age Reiki, kind of bull–ahem, retreats that people drove two hours up from New York or over the Canadian Border to attend. They were hardly ever empty.

Trust his recent luck to be here when a silent retreat was going on, though. He couldn't even engage in conversation with anyone.

A slight movement from one cabin caught his eye, and he stilled mid-stride, watching and waiting.

He'd walked quite a distance around the circumference and was no longer on his aunt's property.

These cabins were of average height and left empty most of the year by wealthy owners who lived in the larger cities. He knew the one he was looking at was supposed to be empty, as were all of them.

Stepping softly off the pier, Matthew stealthily retraced his steps until his footprints were nothing more than flattened bits of grass as he moved.

He slipped into the trees and walked around the back of the cabin. There wasn't a vehicle, or anything else, to say the cabin was occupied, but Matthew followed his instincts. It was those same instincts, and being the best lip reader in the bureau, that made him the best operative they had.

He crouched down and waited.

***

Lacy was exhausted, but she tried to push it back for just a few more hours.

She had been waiting for the signal for two hours, and still, nothing came.

She was in the right place. The fifth cabin from the secondary road with the blue and white porch swing and split-second step. This was the cabin.

She had driven all night, her eyes were aching and dry, and she was hungry.

She walked around as though haunted. Waiting. She didn't like loose ends. She didn't like when her life was being dictated to, of not having control and this situation was all the above.

Her car was parked a mile up the road, hidden by a natural canopy of fauna and she had walked silently through the trees, appreciating nothing, but focussed on the one thing, and that was getting to this cabin.

She reached up and undid the elastic in her hair to massage her scalp for a second before scooping her curls into one hand, giving the whole thing a quick twist and securing the knot on top of her head again.

It was a bit chilly, and Lacy looked longingly at the open fireplace. It was huge, and she could picture a fire raging there, warming up the entire cabin. She sighed, rubbing her hands together. She couldn't chance anyone knowing that she was here.

She'd already scoped out the neighbouring cabins, and they were all empty. The only residents were practically opposite at the retreat, a reasonable distance away. She was alone.

One thing she could do, she thought with a smile, looking down at her jeans and plaid shirt, she could have a nice hot shower and even wash her hair.

Lacy pulled off her clothes as she went along, and reaching the bathroom, dropped them in a corner.

Hmm, she thought, looking at the claw-footed bath. Hmm? She had nothing but time on her hands for the next few hours and, reaching for the old-fashioned plug, ran a bath for herself.

As the bathroom was at the back of the cabin, she knew she could crack the window to let out the steam. She did just that, peeping out, noticing the lengthening shadows as she did.

Lacy couldn't turn on the lights, but she used the flashlight app on her phone, stuffed the bottom of the door with a towel, to stop the light from filtering through and, with a blissful sigh, stepped into the hot water.

She washed using the half bottle of shower gel she'd found and slid all the way down until she was covered, loving the feel of the warmth as her worries were temporarily forgotten.

***

Lacy was trying to catch a droplet of water from the tap with her big toe when she heard a noise outside.

It could be anything, but her instincts had never failed her yet. No matter what, you checked out what that *'anything'* could be.

Quietly leaving the bath, Lacy secured a large towel around her body. Silent, but dripping, she listened at the door before turning the light off her phone.

It was now dark outside she saw, and stepping soundlessly, went to the window to first peer out and then close it. It was too small for her to fit through anyway, she'd noted when she'd initially mapped the place for any potential escape routes if she needed to get out in a hurry.

A creak from inside the house told her she wasn't alone.

It wasn't the usual yawns of an old house; this was the creak of a floorboard.

Lacy opened the door a little, peering into the darkness. She knew the layout of the cabin, having memorised it and everything in it when she'd first entered.

It was one of her many talents, she'd been told; seeing and

computing anything or anyone in one sweeping glance.

Her sweeping glance now told her someone was in the cabin and trying to blend into the shadows.

Closing the door as quietly as she could, she knew she was going to go out there.

She secured the towel more firmly under her arms and left her hair.

She reached for her gun and opened the door.

***

Matthew had known for definite that someone was in the cabin when the window opened.

From the size of the hand, a teenager had probably broken in, but him being who he was and not because he was bored, decided to see for himself and scare the hell out of the kid and see him off the property.

Wealthy people paid a premium to have a house on the lake. Besides, he didn't want some transient hanging around the family retreat.

It didn't take much effort to go through the front door. His pocket knife and two flicks of his wrist and he was in. Baby stuff.

The place was in darkness, but he followed the smell of lemony soap.

The kid had been careful, Matthew recognised expertly as he slithered against the wall with both hands out so as not to knock anything over.

A door opened slightly down the short hall. Matthew waited. Feeling the thump, thump of his heartbeat as adrenalin surged through his body. Now, this was more like it.

The door closed, and Matthew quickly and stealthily moved to the other side of the door and waited.

He didn't have long to wait. The door opened wider and, at the appearance of a barefoot, Matthew hooked his arm around the kid's neck and pulled him backwards, putting his hand over his mouth to muffle any sounds.

A well-aimed stamp on his foot and an elbow in his throat took Matthew by surprise, and he almost let go, only to grab the kid by the hair, flick him over with ease and sit on his chest.

"Get the hell off me!"

Matthew realised three things.

One, the kid wasn't a boy but a girl. Two, she was a girl that he knew, and three, she had a Glock.

"Wallace?" he asked, amazed, thinking the blow to his throat had starved his brain of oxygen, and his eyes were deceiving him.

She bucked her hips to dislodge him, but he leaned forward, grabbed her forearms, and slammed them above her head.

Her chest was heaving and, oh yes, the towel had loosened.

The soft swell of her upper breasts drew his notice as he appreciated it definitely was Special Operative Wallace Dawson beneath him.

"Get off!" Lacy yelled, bucking frantically and then with a twist to one side, unbalanced him enough to scramble out from under him, kick him in the face, then take off.

"Oomph!" Matthew fell to the side, but recovered enough to grab her ankle. She went flying and hit the floor hard. With anyone but her, he would have felt guilty. But this was Wallace, AKA Lacy. She was tougher than her petite frame looked.

"Behave!" he yelled, trying to evade her other foot as she tried to kick him.

"Get the hell off me, Matthew!"

At least she knew who he was, Matthew thought with dark excitement, grabbing her other leg to still her movements as he crawled up her body. Her smooth, damp body.

He couldn't see her eyes in the darkness, but he knew they were probably spitting fire at him. Her eyes were the deepest brown. So deep and dark, they hid everything from him. She liked it that way. What he didn't tell her was that he could read every flicker and sweep of her eyelashes. Every tip of her eyebrows.

With a deep smirk, Matthew tugged the wet towel out of his

way and settled on top of her.

The fight went out of her as he knew it would.

It had always been like this with them.

At the academy, during a sparring session and in front of their classmates, he would get her on the mat, be over here, and the air would suddenly change. He'd want to kiss her, enter her body and see if she was as smooth and tight on the inside, like the rest of her body. He'd made the mistake of dipping his head and kissing her in front of their coach once, and they had been separated after that. He'd got a warning. His first of several.

With his thigh planted firmly between her legs, both hands held in one of his, Matthew knew she could unseat him if he didn't have all of his weight on her.

She was good. A brilliant fighter. She had trained in Krav Maga but also fought like a street fighter when she needed to. She could and would fight dirty. He was not moving and didn't care if he was squashing her to death.

"What are you doing here?" he asked.

"Get off me, Matthew," Lacy repeated fiercely. She couldn't breathe, but forced the words out.

"Not until you tell me who you're working—"

He didn't know how she did it, but she was out and running for the door before he'd finished the sentence.

"Get back here!" he yelled, storming after her. She was nimble, he'd give her that, as he dragged her into his chest anchoring an arm under her naked breasts as he threw her onto the couch and followed her down.

Lacy knew if Matthew didn't move, she would no doubt embarrass herself in the next twenty seconds.

They had a history. A history that saw them sneaking around right under the noses of their superiors. They'd been sex buddies before being assigned to different parts of the country. Deliberately, no doubt. Their physical attraction was hard to hide.

Whenever their paths crossed, they ended up sleeping together. The last time they had been watching different people from the same gang in Chicago. They had been on the same rooftop and somehow lost themselves in each other for a few minutes before being called back to headquarters. That was two years ago.

Matthew, the only person she had shared any part of herself with. Physically. Being an only child, adopted by an all-American couple who lived and breathed law enforcement, Lacy had learned to keep herself to herself. Once her parents realised her potential, she'd been encouraged to join the bureau when they came knocking as soon as she'd finished high school.

She had enjoyed working for them until recently. She wanted more.

She had yet to know what that 'more' was, but it felt good being a free agent, even if the bureau was still keeping tabs on her and sending Matthew to do it.

***

He never could resist her, Matthew thought, feeling her heartbeat rapidly beneath his chest and knew with a skimmer of male ego she wasn't out of breath from the exertion of running. This was sex. Her heart fluttering was because of his proximity.

She couldn't keep her hands off him, any more than he could off her. It had always been that way, and there was no reason why they both couldn't indulge in one another for a few hours.

Matthew dipped his head and kissed her.

Lacy had no choice but to let him in. From the moment they both lay still, and she could feel the hard ridge of him against her hip, she knew what was going to happen. She couldn't resist him and wouldn't even bother trying.

Lacy felt his hand smooth down her neck, his thumb doing its own thing as he moved down and palmed her right breast.

He knew how sensitive her nipples were and went straight there. Without apology. It may have been two years, but my God, her body had craved him. She hadn't seen him physically, yet every night the image of him tipped her over the edge so that she could sleep.

Matthew dragged his tongue against hers, dancing them together, reacquainting himself with the inner recesses of her mouth. God, Matthew could kiss.

Lacy had once rolled into an orgasm from his kisses alone. She hadn't told him because she didn't want him to know he had that kind of power over her, but having him kiss her was magical.

He moved down her neck and Lacy couldn't help undulating against him. He nipped along her collar bone, and she mewed with pleasure. He skated his rough tongue around her areolas, one then the other, again and again, teasing and playing with her nerve endings until she took control, fisting his hair to direct him where she wanted him.

She felt the rumble of his chuckle.

Bastard.

Lacy luxuriated in his touch but knew in the back of her mind this was not going to be an all-nighter. She was supposed to be on a mission. A private mission, but still important.

She needed to hit her orgasm, and then he needed to be gone.

She moved her legs around his back and locked her ankles before raising her hips in invitation. The waistband of his jeans was rough against her inner thighs, heightening her awareness of him. If she wanted, she could reverse their positions and take him; however, she liked. But no, right now she wanted to be taken care of. It had been a long time.

Becoming desperate with need and trying not to be distracted, Lacy scraped her fingers down his sides and reached for the button of his jeans.

He eased off her slightly, making it easy for her as she unzipped him and held him in her hands. He was hot and heavier than she remembered.

"Tighter," Matthew growled in her ear.

Lacy squeezed him hard and felt his whole-body shudder with need for her.

It was empowering how she could literally hold this hard,

powerful man in the palm of her hand and bring him to his knees. She had that power, and she knew he was aware of it. That's why they didn't get along.

The sex was great, the conversation almost non-existent. They had never made plans. She would see him on an assignment, across a room. Their eyes would meet, and she would lead the way, knowing he would follow. Both of them turning off their earphones and trackers along the way. A dark corner, a bathroom, the gardens, even the edge of a mountain in Switzerland once. They were reckless and unprofessional but would never stop.

Lacy slid down even further, ready to take charge if he didn't enter her body and ease her ache right now. When he did, he filled her to the hilt, knowing she could take him.

Grabbing her bottom, Matthew lifted her high to meet every hard thrust he made. In two places, he kept her locked to him. Claiming what he could from her mouth and her sex.

Matthew was about to lose his mind. It was always like this with Lacy. He had never reached this kind of pleasure with anyone else. The excitement of their sex, unplanned as it always was, drove him to fill her up.

For this moment, the here and now, he would be all she thought about, and he would make damn sure she would never forget it.

He knew when she was climbing, he knew with each tremble, the small sound in her throat telling him she was ready. He wanted to slow it down and savour, but she wouldn't let him, and he thought *what the heck* they had all night. He pushed her over the edge, pounding into her and followed soon after as her body tightened and pulsed around him, taking everything he had.

He was depleted. With anyone else, he could take two breaths and start again. With Wallace, he needed a minute to recover.

They were both breathing heavily, and he moved onto his side, not wanting to crush her, but she scooted away.

"Where are you going?" Matthew asked, flinging one arm

over his eyes. If he smoked, he would have had a cigarette. Their sex was that satisfying. When she didn't answer and edged away from him, he caught her arm.

"To the bathroom," Lacy answered softly, leaning over to smooth his brow with the pads of her fingers. Once, then twice.

Matthew watched her go. She had a beautiful body, long and athletic. Her breasts were smaller than he liked, but the lure of her large nipples made up for that. The shape of her nipples reminded him of overripe grapes in his mouth, and he could lap at them all day. They had all night, and Matthew was looking forward to indulging himself in all things Special Ops Lacy Dawson.

Matthew settled into the sofa and looked towards the corridor. With only a slight difference on the outside, the layout of the cabins was all the same.

He'd called her Wallace on purpose to get a rise out of her. She hated her given name, and actually, it didn't suit her. Wallace conjured images of a hard bitch of a woman. Lacy, he smiled, rolling her name across his tongue. Lacy was feminine, sweet, and pliant, just as she had been, even though he knew she was as tough as they come. Lacy suited moments like this. When she was pissed off, she was Wallace. She'd graduated top five. He had been top three. She had been the only female in their squad. Everyone called her Wallace.

Funny how she had touched his brow, Matthew thought. They'd kissed, had sex. He'd tasted the most intimate parts of her, but she had never *ever* touched him with a gentleness as she had just touched him.

With a start, Matthew jumped up and raced down the corridor and swore loudly, finding all the rooms empty.

She'd gone.

CHAPTER TWO

"God-damn it!" Matthew charged, pulling up his jeans to race through the house, but tripped on something metallic that skidded along the wooden floor. He smiled. She'd left her gun. He picked it up, slipped it into the back of his jeans, and rushed outside.

She had less than a five-minute lead on him, and he stopped.

Darkness had fallen with a rapidness of a summer's night. It was late, and the air was still.

He closed his eyes and waited, feeling the vibrating rush of footsteps hitting the ground fast.

Matthew took off after her. She was heading for the main road, but he knew how she would think. What he would do. How they'd been trained.

She would skim the edges, keeping to the shadows, only going out into the open if she had to.

She didn't have to.

Matthew and his brother, Ace, had spent many weekends up here as kids, and he knew the area well. The forest stretched to the Canadian border. It was a hostile and lonely place if you didn't have any survival skills. Both he and Lacy could survive and live off the land if they needed to.

He knew she'd gone when he hadn't caught her yet, so instead, he walked into the middle of the road and waited, his chest heaving with excitement.

She gave a good chase, he would give her that, he thought, feeling the heavyweight of her gun at his back. He pulled it out and turned it over, remembering one of the few lengthy conversations they had ever had.

They were still training, going through the different weapons and being told to use whatever had felt good in their hands. Lacy had chosen the Glock, much to the admiration of their supervisor.

Matthew didn't remember what gun he had chosen. He just remembered picturing the supervisor's face on the target and putting a bullet right between his eyes. He'd come top of the class for target practice that day.

A car started. Being born deaf, even with his hearing aids, Matthew was able to put his other senses to optimum use.

He turned to see a car, without lights, race towards him.

It was her. It could only be here. There was nothing else along this stretch of road. The only users being other vacationers and there wasn't any this time of year.

Matthew, with his feet planted far apart, raised her gun and waited.

***

Lacy's feet were stinging. She had managed to grab her clothes and phone and bag, but not her shoes or her gun. She felt naked without her weapon, she thought, stepping quickly but softly through the woods to her car.

She knew Matthew. He was chasing her, and for a moment, she allowed a smile to grace her face. She had the advantage.

Getting to her car, she stopped and waited, listening into the silence.

Matthew may be deaf, but he was the best tracker the bureau had, although they liked to keep him close to 'home', keeping track of all the Intel that came second by second from around the globe.

Hearing nothing but the night-time tunes of the earth, Lacy quietly opened her car door.

She sent a coded text with one hand and pulled her jeans up with the other before starting the car and backing out of the bushes. It didn't make sense trying to be quiet now. He would know it was her on the road.

Lacy pressed the gas, and the car surged forward. A powerful engine under the guise of a rusty exterior. With one hand she managed to button-up three buttons on her shirt, before seeing

Matthew in the middle of the road, pointing a gun at her.

No doubt it would be her gun, she thought, pursing her lips.

Frowning deeply and knowing he would move, she kept going. Flooring the gas pedal.

She did up another button.

His hair was shorter than the last time she had seen him, she thought, noticing the burnished red being picked up by her headlights. She went full beam.

He didn't squint as she thought he would.

She watched as he spread his legs wider, aiming the gun at her head, and she narrowed her eyes, driving faster. He would move.

Please move.

Move!

Move, damn it!

He didn't.

Lacy gasped, skidded out of control for a split second before pulling up the handbrake, gripping the steering wheel and spinning the car in the opposite direction.

Matthew was lying motionless on his side in the middle of the road.

"You idiot!" Lacy yelled frantically, coming to a stop and storming out of the car.

Matthew had hit the hood hard, bumped up the windscreen to slide off the side. He'd frightened the life out of her. She watched as he lifted his head, shook it once, then twice, before rolling over and hauling himself up.

She catalogued his slow movements. He'd be sore in the morning, but otherwise, he was okay, she thought charitably. Stupid man.

"Matthew?!" Lacy yelled from a safe distance. If Matthew caught her now, he would want answers. She wasn't giving him, or anyone else, answers, and that included their mutual employer.

"You hit me!" Matthew charged.

"You shouldn't have been in the middle of the road!" Lacy

shot back.

"You're fucking crazy," he wiped his nose with his arm, "do you know that? You could have killed me!"

"Running you over is not the way I plan to kill you." She answered, noticing his small but gaining steps. She edged to the door.

"Oh yeah," he smirked. He couldn't see much of her, what with the headlights trained his way, but he could see enough. She'd buttoned her shirt up wrong and hadn't got to the top buttons yet. He could see the golden slope of her breasts. Breasts he had held in his hands not half an hour ago. "And how do you plan to kill me?" he asked conversationally. She didn't answer, but was looking down at her phone in her hand before throwing it into the car.

"I'll tell you another time," she advised with a laugh. "Duty calls." She told him, getting into her small car.

Matthew jogged towards her vehicle, but she was already driving off. Matthew watched her go with a smirk and the biggest hard-on he'd had in half an hour.

When she was at a reasonable distance, she stopped.

Matthew waited with his arms crossed over his chest.

"Have a hot shower, babe!" she yelled at him with a laugh before driving off.

Matthew laughed and laughed even harder as he picked her gun from the asphalt. She'd be back for it, he knew.

Until next time, sweetheart, he thought with a smirk.

CHAPTER THREE

Matthew was going hunting.

For the first time since he'd been on vacation, five days, he was looking forward to the three months that stretched ahead.

He was going to hunt down Wallace AKA Lacy Dawson, AKA Special Operative Agent Two Six One, before the first frost dusted the ground.

He was already on his way to the city, much to the dismay of his aunt and uncle. But the silence of the lake was no hold compared to the lure of Lacy.

She was up to something. A phone call to the office this morning only confirmed his suspicions.

She had taken an unpaid leave of absence two months ago and hadn't given a date of her return.

She was working outside of the bureau, and he wanted to know what she was up to, why she was hiding in the cabin by the lake and why she had been in such a hurry to escape.

Matthew pulled out his phone because first, he needed to organise somewhere to set up.

He didn't have any reason to have his own place in New York as he usually stayed at his brother's place, but Kyle was there with his on-again, off-again movie star girlfriend, Camille.

Using the Bluetooth, he called Ace.

"Bro,"

"What's up?"

Matthew chuckled at his younger brother's surly tone. "You sound sleepy, baby keeping you up at night?" he teased.

"And I wouldn't have it any other way." Ace said. "What the hell do you want?"

Matthew laughed before saying. "I need a place to stay."

"Thought you were going fishing with Uncle Mitch?"

"Something's come up, and I need a base,"

"What's come up?" Ace asked. "You're on vacation."

"Yeah well, this is my kind of something,"

"What?"

Matthew sighed loud enough to let Ace know he was getting pissed off. "Look, can I stay in the new place?" Matthew gritted his teeth, knowing Ace was silently laughing.

"I'll tell the front desk," Ace confirmed after a moment, "but don't turn it into some out there Star Trek shit," Ace warned. "It's our love nest." He added.

"Yeah, yeah, thanks," Matthew said, knowing Ace had bought the new apartment for Sabrina as her wedding present. It was in that pencil-thin high rise, Four Thirty-Two Park Avenue and overlooked Central Park. "Tell Sabrina hey and kiss the girls," Matthew told his brother.

Matthew was so happy for Ace, finally married to the woman he had met and lost almost eleven years ago. Sabrina was the best thing to happen to his often reckless, adrenalin junkie brother, add their kids, twelve-year-old Heather, and the baby, and Ace didn't stop grinning.

Matthew hung up before making another call. If he was going hunting, he needed the right tools, and he knew just the right person to get them from, off the books.

***

Matthew watched the multiple screens in front of him, searching for the late model foreign car Lacy was driving.

He had access to the last twenty-four hours of all the traffic cameras from the lake in every direction. She was on one of them, and he would find her.

If Ace could see what he had done to the 'Love Nest', he would attempt to throw him out, but to Matthew, this was normal.

He'd passed his field duties for the bureau, but he mainly worked on the inside. Artificial Intelligence was his speciality. He would find Lacy; it was just a matter of when.

He was eating a ginger nut from a tin of Sabrina's British

biscuits, appreciating the taste. Being born in England, he still liked some things, ginger nuts being his favourite.

A flash of red caught his eye, and he threw the tin aside.

"Gotcha," Matthew whispered with excitement, zooming in on Lacy waiting at a stoplight. He zoomed in closer, watching as she held the steering wheel with both hands, her thumbs rhythmically hitting the cracked black leather. She was listening to music. She looked happy and relaxed.

She was still wearing the pale blue plaid shirt she'd had on last night. Where the hell had she been?

This was the first time Matthew could actually drink in her perfect features unnoticed. Lacy looked younger than she was, and because of that fact and what annoyed the hell out of him, the bureau used her as bait for jacked-up Paedos.

Her hair was piled high on her head, and she wore small gold hoops in her ears.

The light changed, and Matthew followed her on the twenty-six screens he had in front of him.

She drove straight into New York, parked her car outside a Bodega, went inside and bought a bagful of groceries before pulling up in front of a nondescript four-storied building.

Matthew made a note of the address. He turned his chair to run the address on his computer. In two seconds, he had the names of every occupant, their date of birth, and what they did for a living.

From a camera at the other end of the street, he watched as Lacy got out, locked her car and, with several bags in her hands, climb the short flight of steps.

She had great legs, he thought, encased as they were in tight jeans that cupped the surprising flare of her hips and ass. You wouldn't expect such a round ass on her slight frame, but Lacy had curves. Curves he liked to cup and stroke and, God-damn it, he needed to get a grip and stay focussed. He would get back to thinking of her ass later when he was in the shower, maybe, but right now, he needed to focus.

He couldn't see which bell she had pressed and changed the

database to zoom in on the building from above. He rewound and noted the number she pressed. Why didn't she let herself in? he thought?

Within five minutes, he knew a foreigner had purchased the apartment six months ago, with cash.

He looked at the time. She had been there a little over six hours.

Matthew moved swiftly, pulled on his leather jacket, and found his brother's motorbike helmet.

Adrenalin was pumping through him. He loved the feeling, relished it in fact as he rode the elevator down.

His brother Ace collected anything with wheels, and Matthew took his pick, going for the lime green Kawasaki Ninja parked beside the 'His and Her' black and gold motorbikes that had been wedding presents.

Matthew rode across the city at speed, weaving in and out of the lines of traffic with ease, reaching Lacy's street within ten minutes. He pulled up a few doors down, parked behind a utility van and, astride the powerful bike, reached for his phone from his pocket.

He called the land-line to the apartment she was in and hung up, just as she picked up.

Watching keenly, he noticed the curtains on the top floor twitching.

Matthew smiled.

***

It was a rookie error, Lacy thought as soon as she picked up the stupid phone. She could blame it on very little sleep these past few days, but really, why would she answer the land-line in a house she didn't live in?

She quickly hung up, and went to the window, slowly sliding the curtain aside to peer out.

The street looked normal. The few people out and about minding their own business. The utility truck up the road looked suspect and, thinking on her feet, sending another text, she grabbed her bags, opened the door, stepped out and before she could react, was propelled back into the room by a tall figure clad in leather.

She was not a screamer, but a high-pitched sound lodged in her throat as she was lifted off her feet, a leather-gloved hand clamped over her mouth, and a hard muscular arm held her tightly from under her breasts.

She was about to throw her weight forward and hopefully dislodge his hold when her body started that annoying tingle of awareness. She knew it was him just as his aromatic aftershave of sandalwood and lemon gave him away. Matthew.

"Are you going to behave?" Matthew whispered in her ear and felt her nod. He stayed on high alert, knowing just how highly trained Lacy was.

He moved his hand from her mouth and waited a second. Good, he thought, lowering her cautiously to the ground, but not releasing her, instead, nudging the gun he had into her lower back to let her know he meant business.

"Yes," Lacy answered, now over her initial fright and the instinctive fist she was going to land in his Adams Apple.

She had known Matthew would follow her, she just hadn't thought he would find her so quickly, especially as she now knew he was on vacation and supposedly didn't have access to the advanced tech of the bureau's computer system.

"Good girl," Matthew praised. "Now walk slowly to the couch, sit down and face me." He ordered.

Lacy followed his instructions, moving slowly, before sitting as demurely as she could and facing him.

Why oh why did he have to look so damn good, she thought, taking in the jeans that edged over the tops of his black Timberland boots, a white T-shirt that moulded his pecks, a black leather bomber jacket and riding gloves with the knuckles cut out.

His hair was flat, and she quickly realised with his current attire, he'd ridden here.

Matthew was a suit and tie kind of man. To see him looking

all biker hot was making her flustered, and she slowly clenched her legs together, hoping he wouldn't notice. He did if the flash of green in his eyes were any indication.

He had hazel eyes, a mixture of earthy greens and browns with flecks of vivid golds. His eyes gave him away every time she thought, watching as they were currently tracking over her chest, moving in an insultingly slow way down her body, staying at the juncture of her legs far too long before pinning her in place. Lacy gritted her teeth, trying not to reveal how turned on she had become.

It was ridiculous, she thought. He'd scratched the itch she had been living with for two years, given her one of the best orgasms of her existence not twelve hours ago and one smouldering look from him and she was ready to fall on the floor, spread her legs wide open and yell 'take me!'

"Who are you working for Wallace?" Matthew asked quietly, looking into her eyes. They gave nothing away, but he already knew she was not on assignment.

"As you are not on assignment."

Matthew's head shot up, hearing her words echo the thoughts that had just been in his head.

"How do you know I'm not on assignment?" he challenged, leaning against the door and folding his arms. He needed to keep her at a distance until he had at least got her talking or else he'd be buried balls deep inside her within the next fifteen minutes. She was wearing a simple ribbed white vest, no bra, pink boy-short styled panties and her feet were bare.

She ignored his question. "As you are not on assignment," she repeated. "You have no right to interrogate me."

Matthew smirked. "We are just having a conversation darling," he said lightly. "You know? As we're friends with benefits. I just want to know what you're working on. Curious is all."

"We aren't friends, Matthew," Lacy scoffed. She felt her phone vibrate against her bottom where she had tucked it inside her panties and knew she needed to read it and reply. She moved to the edge of the seat as casually as she could and smiled. "I need the bathroom. I'm just going to–"

"Sit down," Matthew gritted, remembering the last time she had said that. He was not going to be hoodwinked again.

She ignored him and moved as though about to get up.

"Sit down!"

Hearing the steel in his voice and biding her time, Lacy scooted back into the sofa.

"Who are you working for?" Matthew asked again. He usually had a mild easy-going temperament, but Lacy was testing it. "You're working for someone, and I want to know now, who they are."

"No."

His eyes narrowed as he said softly. "What did you just say to me?"

"You heard," she repeated, rolling her eyes, "you are not my superior, and I am not employed by the bureau at this time." She lifted her chin defiantly when she spoke.

"Fine," Matthew unlaced his arms and walked purposely towards her, "I'll take you in."

Alarmed, as the last thing she needed was to be hauled up to, D.C. Lacy shot off the sofa to evade his arms and scrambled around the room, putting the sofa between them.

She had to give him something. "It's private."

"What is?"

She licked her lips, liking as his lovely eyes dropped to witness her innocent act and she did it again, not so innocently.

"I'll fuck you when I'm ready," Matthew stated quietly, watching as a tide of red swept into her cheeks. "What are you working on and who for? You've been off-grid for two months."

"I'm helping out a friend," Lacy admitted, still feeling the heat in her cheeks. Darn it. He was the only one who could slip under her defences with just a few words and what he just said about having sex with her? Well hey, she could easily picture him doing that too.

"What friend?"

"You won't know him."

"What's his name?"

"You're crazy if you think I'm telling you that?"

"You will tell me, Wallace," Matthew took the safety off his gun, and casually stepped around the sofa, watching as she backed up against the wall.

"What are you going to do Matthew," she asked, looking at his hand, "shoot me?"

His laughter was but a huff. "There are lots of things I can do to you with a gun," he challenged lightly, "want me to remind you?" He offered with all seriousness.

Lacy swallowed and shook her head.

Alone, after gun practice one day, Matthew had rubbed the nozzle of his gun between her breasts, her legs and all over her body. It was one of the hottest moments of her life. The steel nozzle, the scent of his sweat mixed with her arousal. That incident was another memory that helped her fall asleep at night.

"No thanks, I remember." She admitted reluctantly. She'd prefer to get shot right now than go through that torture again.

His laugh was small and low, but his eyes were pure gold as they trained on her.

"Stop playing games, Wallace," he was getting tired of this, "tell me what you're doing, why you're in a house owned by a Russian, or I'm taking you in for treason."

She gasped. "Are you insane?!" she exclaimed. "How could you even think I would betray my country?"

"Tell me!"

"Okay, okay," Lacy began reluctantly. "I am working for a friend," she admitted. "I don't know who owns the house, but what I'm doing is legit."

"Working? Doing what?"

She shrugged.

Matthew took a step closer. "Doing what, Lacy?"

Matthew seared her with his deep frown again. He was so distractingly sexy with his good looks. It was ridiculous how turned on she was, Lacy thought. He would never hurt her, take her into the office, hmm maybe, but he would never hurt her. She couldn't and wouldn't tell him any more.

The silence stretched, and before she could say another word, the door was smashed in, and two people dressed all in black came bursting through with their guns trained on Matthew.

"No! Don't hurt him!" Lacy yelled, diving in front of Matthew with her arms out wide.

"Lacy get back!" Matthew ordered, trying to push her behind him, but she wasn't moving.

Matthew picked her up and threw her over the sofa. When he turned back, a fist hit him in the face, and he saw flashes of light as his gun sailed across the room and went off as it hit the wall near Lacy.

"Lacy!" he yelled frantically. "Tell me you're okay!"

He wore a tiny hearing aid in one ear, and it went flying.

Knowing he had to keep his wits and get her out of here unharmed, Matthew dived at the two men, throwing his fists as he tackled them both. They were good. One slightly smaller than the other, but both quick on their feet, obviously trained.

The fight was brutal, the men coming at him at the same time. If Lacy wasn't in the room, he could have enjoyed this a bit more, but he had to get her out of here.

In the corner of his eye, Matthew saw movement, and when she neared, he managed to hit one guy out and kicked the other in his stomach so that he went flying across the room, smashing into the table before falling on the floor.

Matthew grabbed Lacy's hand, and together they ran out of the apartment, down the dingy stairs and out of the building.

Reaching the bike, he shoved the helmet on Lacy's head, got on, and roared off when he felt her arms grab his waist.

CHAPTER FOUR

Being picked up and thrown over his shoulders was totally unnecessary, Lacy thought when they entered the plush elevator. She knew where she was, but had never been inside New York's most upscale high rise. Four Thirty-Two, Park Avenue.

The apartments here were expensive, and the higher up you went, the likelihood of encountering Royalty was a real possibility.

They exited mid-way, and from her upside-down position, Lacy noted the marble floors that were so glossy her p'd off expression bounced right back to her.

When they entered the apartment, her view was replaced by highly polished oak herringbone floors.

"That was completely unnecessary," Lacy said to Matthew when he'd put her down, and she'd pushed her hair out of her face. The blood rushed from her head, and she closed her eyes for a moment to orientate herself.

Matthew was looking at her lips. She knew he was clinically deaf in one ear and had partial hearing in the other, but there really wasn't any reason for him to be reading her lips, as he wore hearing aids.

"Where are your hearing aids?" she asked puzzled, using sign language. She saw his eyes widen in recognition. He hadn't known she could sign, and it was something she'd kept from their mutual employer. Some things they were better off, not knowing.

"You can sign?" he asked, using his hands.

She grinned and swore at him with her hands.

He said nothing for a moment before signing. "Make yourself at home, you won't be leaving any time soon." He signed, giving her a fierce look before turning away.

That's what you think, Lacy thought to herself.

Lacy watched when he rapidly punched in a long code by the door, and she heard several security locks bolt into place. She sighed, knowing she really wasn't going to be leaving any time soon.

Matthew walked off down a side corridor.

That's how he'd found her, Lacy thought, seeing the multiple screens and the frozen image of her at the door of the apartment building.

He was good, she thought, silently praising his resourcefulness and expertise. It was no wonder he was the bureau's wonder boy.

The apartment was beautiful, with massive windows that dominated the room yet tantalised your senses, Lacy noted, walking over to them to take in the view and smiling as Central Park lay sprawled out way below. She could stand right here forever, she thought, feeling a peacefulness settle on her shoulders. She sighed before turning her thoughts on today's events. Matthew had now interrupted the change over twice. They wouldn't like that.

She had been hired by a global organisation, doing nothing shady like spying on her great nation, no, she was more like an international baby sitter. She temporarily cared for the children of dead sex slaves, refugees and other horrific situations where children were left behind and needed to be saved before they too disappeared. Sometimes she only had a child for a night or two, others for a week or more.

These children had been traumatised. Had seen things no child should ever see. Their families killed in front of them by militants or pimps or drones.

Lacy didn't know who'd hired her as she'd been approached one day while out running late last year.

An American man, all thick shoulders and blond buzz cut had pushed an envelope into her hands and continued to run.

At home, she had followed the instructions written on a yellow Post It entered an IP address into her private laptop, and within seconds a proposal was issued.

The message pixilated and another was sent offering her a tremendous amount of money and that pixilated too, scattering the message to leave a blank screen. These people knew of her skill.

The money wasn't the pull. It was thoughts of those poor kids, casualties of war and greed, that made her agree, she could help and be able to see the difference she was making in the world.

She had known for a long time life at the bureau was not how she wanted to spend the rest of her days. It was too clinical and riddled with red-tape, authority and backstabbing. Her own shadow even took off when she walked into the building, it was that corrupt. She didn't want that for the rest of her life, she didn't want to feel stifled and restricted, forever given instructions as the bureau played games, sometimes against their own people.

She said yes as they had asked her to, by placing a vase of yellow roses in her bedroom window. Maybe she should have thought about it some more, ask who she was working for, especially as more and more subterfuge was being used and the missions became more and more complicated.

Most of the children didn't speak English, and the last little boy she had was from Crimea. That was alarming as everyone knew Russia wanted Crimea back.

Lacy reached into the back of her panties where she had stashed her phone when Matthew had stormed into the apartment, but it wasn't there. Either she had dropped it, or nimble-fingered Matthew had it.

Where were her wits? Lacy scolded herself, walking over to the hall she had seen him disappear down and glanced in the opulent rooms along the way. She found him in an enormous bathroom, but her gaze skidded right past him to take in the room.

Like the rest of the apartment, it was huge and made of natural stones. She would love to have a bath in that round sunken tub, she thought, picturing herself looking out into the skyline, relaxing with a glass of red wine, vanilla scented candles and some Otis Redding.

She was pulled out of her musing when her eyes hit on Matthew, doing something at one of the three sinks. His top half was bare and, who knew? He sported a massive tattoo of a falcon on his back. It wasn't the run-of-the-mill type of tattoo, she realised, walking into the room uninvited, whoever did this was a top-class artist. She looked closer. The work was perfect, and without thinking, she traced her finger over the wingspan of the bird. It was beautiful. *He* was beautiful. His back was wide and solid, the skin beneath her fingertips smooth and hot. She stepped closer, feeling her nipples pinch as his masculine scent washed over her. They had a lot to discuss, but first, she wanted to have sex.

Matthew spun around and grabbed her hand.

"No." he said simply.

***

Lacy felt a furious tide of heat slam into her cheeks. He never had, in all the years they had been sexually involved, ever, told her no.

With her back ramrod straight, she spun on her heel and left the room, thinking of all the different ways she could kill him.

Lacy went into one of the bedrooms and locked the door. She was feeling antsy and turned on, tired and, damn it, turned on.

He always did this to her when he was around. Tied her up in emotional knots that wound tighter and tighter until they had sex. That's why he was so dangerous because he knew what he did, made her aware of her femininity and forget herself until she was sated.

There was an en-suite attached, and Lacy made use of the bath. It wasn't as opulent as the other bathroom, but it was just as luxurious in champagne coloured tiles, gold fittings and huge mirrors.

She turned on the taps and water gushed designer like, from

hidden recesses. Looking at the beautiful cut-glass bottles placed conveniently beside the bath, Lacy danced her finger over the extensive array, picked the purple one, opened, sniffed, smiled, then upended half the bottle into the water. She wanted bubbles. Lots of them. With another smile, she walked into the bedroom and undressed.

People would be out searching for her, and she really needed to check-in, but she didn't have her phone, or her laptop and Matthew wasn't going to let her out any time soon either, so why not have a bath?

She was Matthew's captive, and honestly, she really didn't mind, as long as he gave her what she wanted and that was another orgasm or two.

How had she become so basic in her wants, she thought to herself, stepping into the hot water. It was the warning tick-tock in her head that was getting louder and louder as her eggs started to disintegrate, she reasoned.

She wanted children. Lots and lots of them. She'd always wanted a family of her own and fostering these lost children fanned that flame into a blaze.

Her adoptive parents were decent people, but not the hug and kiss, hang a Christmas wreath on the front door, type of parents.

Lacy wanted stability. Doing this outside job meant she could at least try to buy herself out of the bureau–if that could be done–and move to somewhere hot and raise a family of her own. She didn't need, nor had even thought about sharing her lif–

"Hey!" Lacy screeched, seeing Matthew watching her from the doorway.

The problem with him was that he was as good as her with picking locks. She shouldn't be surprised to see him lounging there with his hazel eyes swirling with desire, although the rest of his face remaining stoic.

They had things to discuss. She knew he was going to interrogate her about the people in the apartment, but he was taking his time about it. Tactics, maybe?

He was on vacation, and he knew she was on leave. He had all the time in the world, and it showed.

He was still bare-chested, she noted, appreciating the small scattering of reddish-brown hair across his chest. A long thin line of hair ran from his deep navel, disappearing into the band of his jeans.

She could see the heavy ridge of his arousal pressed against the denim and, under her hooded gaze, watched it grow and thicken.

Lacy looked into his eyes, wondering what he was thinking. They didn't know each other outside of assignments when their paths crossed. They had never gone out to dinner, had a conversation about a movie or played poker. No, they had sex and then got on with whatever it was they had been doing before bumping their privates together. Sometimes they didn't even kiss.

She didn't know Matthew, and he didn't know her.

She watched heavy-lidded as he uncrossed his ankles and watching her, slowly undid the snap on his jeans.

She waited.

Hooking both thumbs into the waistband, Lacy watched as Matthew pulled his jeans down and shrugged them off his feet. Naked, he was stunning. His body hair a deep burnished red. His arousal stood straight, proud and pointing directly at her, aggressive with its intention. But she was ready.

Lacy noticed a slight bruising on his ribs where he must have been hit earlier today or maybe when she'd run him over yesterday. The thought of hurting him made her feel all sorts of things she didn't want to explore, guilt being one of them.

He moved forward, grabbing his arousal in his hand and sauntered towards her.

Lacy fought the urge to lean forward and kiss him, take him in her mouth and love him, but it was a hard battle, and besides, she'd never done that before.

He went behind her and without a word got into her bathwater.

She scooted forward and waited.

***

Matthew hadn't been this relaxed in a long time, he thought as he lay in the water, his head resting on the conveniently placed padded nook. The water was too hot, and he'd come out smelling of lilies, nevertheless, this was nice.

Lacy's smooth back was pressed against his chest, and he rested one arm along the side of the bath, the other was under the water lying on her thigh.

He sighed, not really having a plan. They were going to talk, but not tonight. He'd had every intention of sitting her down, tying her to a chair if he had to, and questioning her. But then to see her lying in the bath, her hair plastered to her head, the water lapping at her breasts and with that dreamy smile playing at the corner of her mouth, before she knew he was there, made him change his mind.

Lacy, Matthew mentally sighed. He didn't know what he was going to do with her. Actually, he corrected swiftly, he knew. She wasn't leaving his sight. She was involved in some shit, and he wanted to know what. Something wasn't right.

Whatever it was, he was going to help her get out of it. She was too small for jail, her skin too soft for the roughness of flannel. No, he was going to help her, and she was going to repay him, and his bed was a good place for her to start.

Happy with his thoughts, Matthew moved his hand up her thigh, and she automatically opened her legs, giving him access. He moved in, stroking the thin strip of curls before seeking and finding that little nub that would make her tremble and sigh in his arms.

He touched her gently, playing within her folds as her head lolled against his chest.

Her breathing quickened in seconds. Lacy was a passionate woman. She gave all of herself when they had sex. He knew what she liked, how to play her body to undulate against his. Her kisses alone were sometimes all he craved, and many times it

31

was visions of them having sex that helped him please himself. It was only Lacy who had ever featured in his dreams.

Lacy was pure sex, and he didn't understand why she hadn't been snapped up yet. Not that he was complaining.

In training, he had watched her. She excelled at everything. Was one of those high achievers, but quiet with it. Their squad had been genuinely happy for her. Yes, she was a good operative, but she wasn't a killer.

Everyone at the bureau was supposed to have some sort of killer instinct, he knew he did, but Lacy? No. Her hips were meant to cradle a baby. Her breasts meant to nurse a child. There was just something about her that was calling to motherhood, he saw it every time he looked into her eyes.

Feeling her hips rock back towards him, he used his other hand and swept his flat palm across her nipples, before tweaking one in time with the rhythm he was using between her legs.

She couldn't keep still as he played her body, and using his teeth, nibbled the side of her neck before moving up to swirl his tongue in her ear, stoking her fire as she made small mewing sounds.

Her body tensed, and even in the cooling water, he felt her warm silkiness bathe his fingers, and her body lifted, pushing her nipples above the bubbles when she came. She was beautiful. Just. Fucking. Beautiful.

With another nip to her ear, Matthew eased out of the bath, grabbed a towel and left her to shower off the bubbles, pleased with himself.

CHAPTER FIVE

Lacy was so soft and pliant you could pour spaghetti sauce on her and have her for dinner, she mused, brushing her teeth with her finger.

Look at that she thought, I'm staying in a million, plus plus dollar pad and there isn't a toothbrush in the bathroom.

She tutted, rinsed her mouth and leaned close to the mirror to peer at her face.

Her skin was still red from the bath, but her cheeks were flushed from the orgasm, compliments of Matthew. He was good. So so good, she thought, feeling her body tingle at the memory of their shared bath and the view of his naked body as he'd walked out of the bathroom.

His body was rock hard. His back wide and defined, his waist narrow and his bottom and thighs solid.

Tucking a huge white towel around her body, Lacy tackled her hair. She had none of the hair oils she liked to use on her natural coils, so reached for the conditioner, squirted a large dollop into her palm, rubbed her hands together, then spread the cream all over her hair, paying close attention to the delicate ends.

Then, using her fingers, combed it through her curls, grabbed a handful of her damp strands and twisted it into a knot. She repeated until she had seven tight Bantu knots on her head.

She wasn't nervous to go out there to Matthew, she was just a little weary. Same thing she told herself silently; nervous, weary, anxious, they all came under the same umbrella, she reasoned, knowing she was delaying the inevitable. She was not about to cower in the bedroom. Confidence could be faked and fake it, was what she was going to do.

She strode out of the bathroom but wobbled in her stride as her clothes weren't on the bed where she had left them. Then, lifting her chin and flinging back her shoulders, Lacy marched into the body of the apartment.

Matthew was lounging in a chair, one leg thrown over the arm and holding a bottle of beer loosely in his hands.

His face gave nothing away as he watched her walk into the room. However, his eyes dipped to her legs as she sat in the chair furthest from him.

"Are you hungry?" Matthew asked with his hands, dragging his eyes from the delectable curve of her calves. He'd never seen so much of her skin on show before and knew he was going to enjoy the next few days no end.

"Yeah, I could murder something hot for once," Lacy answered without thinking. Oops, she thought quickly, she needed to be more careful with what she said around him. He wasn't just anybody and had probably just computed the fact she hadn't eaten hot food in a couple of days.

"Something hot coming up," Matthew said cheerily, getting up and stretching his arms high over his head.

Lacy tried not to watch him, but it was so hard. Again, he surprised her with his casual clothing. Soft black tracksuit bottoms and a plain white T-shirt which hugged his chest. When he stretched his arms high like that, she could see a tanned strip of skin above the elasticated waistband of his pants.

"Are you going to order something in?" Lacy asked, trailing behind him to the kitchen. "And where are my clothes?"

He didn't answer.

The kitchen was so high tech, the fridge door had a huge LCD screen built-in, and she could see inside without having to open the door. There was nothing inside. She sat on a stool at the granite island and repeated the questions as he was facing her.

"Which question would you like me to answer first?" Matthew asked.

Lacy watched as he bent low to look into a cupboard and pull out a griddle pan.

"From the looks of it, I guess you're cooking?" Lacy stated instead.

"Sounds about right," he looked at her.

"So where are my clothes?"

"In the washer," he answered, turning to the cupboards.

She hadn't expected that. If their roles were reversed, she would probably keep him naked or in a towel or his underwear, just to add a bit of vulnerability to his situation, and some eye candy for hers.

"Oh, okay, thank you," she said.

Lacy watched, noticing he opened several bags on the counter. Salad stuff.

She really wanted a hot meal and said as much when he looked at her. Why make his life easy?

"Where have you been where you couldn't get anything hot, Lacy?" Matthew asked, giving her his full attention and leaning against the counter with his hands hooked on the rounded edge.

"I've been camping," she said smoothly.

Matthew looked at the widening of her eyes, he wasn't sure if she was lying or not, but he wasn't in the mood to question her tonight.

"Enjoy it?" He enquired instead.

"Yes, very much, thanks." She answered, slamming a smile on her face and realising he was still reading her lips. "Where are your aids?" she asked, noting the flash of gold lightning in his eyes before his brows lowered, shielding his gaze. She had annoyed him, and she wasn't the least bit intimidated by the dark look, he slashed her way.

"None of your business," Matthew answered sharply.

"Okay fine," Lacy put her hands up, stepping backwards. She shouldn't feel hurt at his dismissive brusqueness, but she was. "I'm sorry."

Matthew watched her back away from him, feeling all sorts of terrible for upsetting her. He didn't know what the hell was wrong with him. She annoyed the crap out of him, yet he wanted to touch her and see her smile every chance he got.

Lacy got under his skin, always had, and he liked having her around like this. He just didn't like that she was still lying to him and playing games.

He watched her go, just as he felt his phone vibrate, signalling a text message. It was from the concierge, as expected, and he went to the entrance. He disabled the alarm after checking Lacy wasn't behind him, opened the door to the apartment, walked around the decorative table in the outer lobby, before opening the front door. The security in this place was perfect. Perfect for keeping Lacy hidden until he was ready to let her go. He'd caught his mouse and was going to enjoy the games he had planned for her, he chuckled silently to himself. Vacation had never looked so good.

Picking up the bags, Matthew locked the doors and went back to the kitchen.

He didn't like discussing his deafness with anyone outside of family and his friend, Rhodes, at the bureau. Rhodes was a genius and had invented the tiniest hearing aid for him. But it was more than just a hearing aid. Unfortunately, he'd lost it in the fight and instead of replacing it with the conventional type that shouted to the world that he had a disability, he preferred to lip read in his own home. If Lacy didn't like it then tough.

He unpacked the bags, wondering what she was doing. He wasn't concerned as he had her phone and her clothes. She didn't have access to the outside world and couldn't get past the security system in his makeshift office.

For the first time since she came into his life, he could relax, and relaxation to him meant cooking.

He liked to cook, his stepmother, Greta, had been his teacher. When his brother Ace was busy chasing girls and freebasing off buildings, Matthew had been learning how to cook. Greta was the best cook in the world, and he was a close second.

His own mother had died when he was nine, and his father had brought them up. He'd been doing a pretty good job of it, and then he met Greta and her four daughters. Greta and the girls had been on vacation in England, and his dad had literally run Greta over with his bicycle.

Within months, his father had moved Matthew and Ace to

America, and for a while, Matthew had been lost. A teenage boy, moving across the world, living with a bunch of loud Italian American women and his disability. He used to take refuge in the kitchen or behind his computer, but things got better, and he could appreciate how lonely his father must have been. Moving to America was the best thing for all of them. Matthew loved Greta and his step-sisters.

Feeling a hand touch his shoulder, interrupting his silent thoughts, Matthew instinctively swung around and grabbed the person, flipping them over his shoulder and slamming them on the floor before he computed it was Lacy.

"Shit Lacy," he apologised guiltily, quickly leaning over her. She was breathing heavily, and her eyes were closed. "I'm sorry."

He touched her shoulder and was caught in her warm brown gaze when she opened her eyes. For once he could see her pupils, he could watch as they expanded with awareness or pain as she looked at him.

Lacy hadn't expected to find herself sprawled on his kitchen floor, but on the floor she was. She had put her guard down and looking up at him, was guiltily aware he hadn't heard her coming.

She smiled brightly and hauled herself into a sitting position, but a stinging pain streaked across her tail bone, and she winced.

"I hurt you," Matthew said, watching her closely, seeing her body jerk when she moved.

"No, I'm fine," Lacy assured him, ignoring his hand to haul herself up. She dipped her head so that whatever he was searching for in her eyes couldn't be confirmed.

She'd taken a fall last year on assignment and hurt her back. Badly. It wasn't on file, as the bureau would have taken her off the case and she wasn't having that. So instead, she would have long warm baths, use a heat pad, and lay flat on the floor every chance she got.

"Can I help?" she asked, wanting to change the subject. He was still watching her, and she turned to look at the food on the counter. Two raw steaks were already seasoned with salt and cracked black pepper on a plate.

He'd taken out a deep fryer, and fat chips lay waiting in the wired basket to fry beside it.

Steak and chips English style, she thought, smiling over at him.

Lacy watched when his chest expanded once then twice as he breathed in and out, his relaxation technique, she guessed. With a nod, he indicated the salad stuff and gave her a knife.

"Don't kill me with it Lacy, or I'll haunt you for the rest of your life." He warned with all seriousness.

Lacy laughed and played with the knife with her fingers at his look. Together they prepared dinner.

It was nice. She hadn't enjoyed herself like this in a very long time. In fact, she didn't think she ever had.

As soon as she'd graduated from high school, the bureau had come calling with all kinds of promises. She'd been fast-tracked and trained in a special programme for the gifted. Mental training, or rather, psychological brainwashing, as she liked to call it, began straight away. She hadn't enjoyed reading a book in years.

Then the field training had begun, and assignments soon after. Her times of freedom and fun had been fleeting, but almost all of them included Matthew.

"Can I have my clothes back now?" Lacy asked after she had washed the dishes. There was a dishwasher, but she enjoyed washing plates. It was such a normal domesticated thing to do.

Matthew shook his head.

"What do you mean no?" she asked, going to stand in front of him.

"I like your hair like that," he said instead, touching one of the knots.

Lacy leaned her head back. "I want my clothes,"

"How do you do it?"

She gritted her teeth, knowing he was playing with her and ignoring her on purpose.

"If you don't give me my clothes, I'll–"

"You'll go naked," Matthew interrupted. "I'm not giving you your clothes."

Lacy didn't know why she did it, but she stamped her foot, which made no impact at all being as she was barefoot, and what made it worse was that he laughed and walked off.

Lacy dried their plates with furious swipes and sat looking narrowly at his computers when she had finished. She was just about to unplug the whole lot when he came back, holding a white T-shirt out to her.

She looked at it, stood in front of him, lifted an eyebrow and dropped her towel. Instead of reaching for the T-shirt, she sidestepped him and walked naked to the bedroom she had assigned herself, and got into bed, knowing there wouldn't be any point in locking the door.

CHAPTER SIX

Lacy lay in bed looking at the bedroom door and hoping the moving shadow of Matthew would somehow be ungentlemanly enough to kick the stupid thing down and carry her off to his bed.

She thumped her pillow. What was she thinking? She scolded herself. She should be figuring a way out of her predicament, not lying in bed in a fancy apartment, waiting for a man. She hadn't even thought about checking in. She was supposed to send a text and check in every four hours.

Lacy turned her pillow over, thankful for the coolness and lay back down.

She couldn't sleep and had been tossing and turning all evening. This is what you get when you flounce off in a huff when it was barely nine o'clock in the evening, she reprimanded herself.

She was hot, and her skin was on fire with awareness. It all came back to Matthew. That tall reddish/brown-haired stubborn man with the hazel eyes and freckles over his shoulders.

Determined to fall asleep, Lacy rolled onto her stomach, punched her pillow several times and started counting sheep.

***

Lacy tip-toed into the living room and went to the bank of windows. It was summer, and there was still a shimmer of warm excitement and bar-be-que smoke in the air, seen even from this distance.

Haunted, Lacy walked around the apartment wrapped in a sheet and fiddled with the ornaments. Matthew had gone to bed at least two hours ago, and it was about three in the morning. She didn't know exactly what time it was, but she thought around three.

Finding the TV remote, she muted the sound and flicked through the stations, noticing it was after four in the morning, which was even worse than three.

She rarely watched TV, preferring to listen to music as she couldn't read leisurely. The bureau had taken the joy out of reading by making her do reading challenge after reading challenge for months on end. How to fast read and absorb two hundred and fifty words? Less than ten seconds.

Curling up in the corner of the suede sofa that was so deep and plush she sank into the cushions, Lacy tucked her legs beneath her, lifted a cushion to hug to her chest and settled in to find something to watch.

She channel surfed up into the high numbers and came across the foreign films, zooming past the dark Swedish dramas to settle on the beautifully exotic Indian films where the women wore gorgeous clothes, and the acting was refreshingly overdramatic. India made more films than any other country in the world, with Nigeria a close second, she knew.

She had heard all the hoopla about the current actress she was watching, Camikara, although this was one of her earlier movies. She was stunningly lovely with dark skin and clear grey eyes.

Before long, Lacy was crying along with the actress, and she sniffed and wiped the corner of her eye with the sheet.

***

Matthew stayed awake knowing Lacy would probably try to escape and watched her from the security screen on his TV.

She stayed by the window for a while looking out. She looked like a model in a perfume campaign, wrapped in the white sheet, the back dipping dangerously low to the curve of her ass. Her hair was still in those crazy knot things, although one had come loose and dangled onto her bare shoulder like a wayward corkscrew.

She was so beautiful, Matthew thought, watching her and

wondering what she was thinking, as she rubbed her lower back. She had hurt herself when she'd surprised him in the kitchen earlier, he realised guiltily. Tomorrow he'd ask her about it.

She turned towards the room. She didn't go to his computers as he thought she might, and curiously, instead, curled up on the couch, picked up the TV remote and surfed through the channels before settling on one.

Before long she was engrossed, and Matthew, feeling the pull of sleep got up and went to the kitchen to warm some milk for them both.

Lacy hadn't heard Matthew leave his room, but she moved her feet so that he could sit beside her after he handed her a large mug of something frothy. She took a sip and smiled. She hadn't had hot milk since second grade. He'd grated nutmeg on top, and she inhaled appreciatively, hugging the mug in her hands.

When he sat down, and without asking, she put her legs across him and snuggled deeper into the chair, feeling a contentment she hadn't felt in years.

Was this what domestic life was like? She asked herself without looking at him. Was this craving to share the smallest of things like crying in front of the TV with your lover, what love felt like?

She had never been in love. She respected her parents, but she didn't love them. Nor did they love her. As a little girl, she had once asked them why they had chosen her out of all the other children in the home, and they'd never answered. Even now, she remembered the look that had passed between them. Usually, it didn't bother her, thinking about her parents and her life, but tonight, with domestic normality, it did.

***

Lacy felt a hand at her shoulder and opened her eyes with a start. She must have fallen asleep.

"Time for bed," Matthew said, using his hands.

She nodded and accepted the hand he held out to help her up.

He didn't move back, and they stood close, with Matthew looking into her eyes. She could feel his breath fanning her face as they stood almost touching.

Lacy knew what she wanted and licked her lips. His eyes dropped and zoomed in on the movement.

She couldn't have been more obvious, and when he didn't move, she reached up and wrapped her arms around his neck, intending to pull him down to her, but without a word, Matthew picked her up and walked her to his bedroom, and followed her down when he placed her on his tangled sheets.

Then he did the strangest thing. He lay beside her, pulled her into the curve of his body, wrapped his arm around her waist and fell asleep.

With a smile touching her lips. Lacy joined him.

***

Now was her chance. Lacy wasn't going to let Matthew sleep beside her without them having sex she knew, waking to feel the intoxicating closeness of his hard warm body cupping hers.

She turned slowly, damning the sheet that was wrapped tightly around her as though she were a caterpillar and she tried to wriggle free as slowly as she could.

Giving up, and to a moan of objection deep in his throat, Lacy turned in the circle of his arm.

She looked at him for the very first time deep in sleep. His face was so relaxed she could drink in his strong features without having to guard her own.

He had lovely full lips, bracketed by one line that was deeper on one side. Matthew was a smirker, he rarely smiled, or even laughed for that matter. He was intense, and the frown lines between his brows told their own story.

His brows were a deep reddish-brown, matching his long eyelashes. His nose was straight and very European, and now she could see that his entire face was covered in faint freckles. He was a beautiful man, a man she didn't mind cooking for, or pleasing... *Hold on, what?*

He was the closest she had ever come to a relationship. An hour here and twenty minutes there over several years. It was sad really, looking for and getting sex from him whenever she saw him. But it had worked for her.

She wondered how he felt about her. They'd never talked about what they did or how carnal their relationship actually was.

Lacy lifted her head and supported it with her hand. She moved in closer and smoothed her lips across his, once then twice, ever so softly, before flicking her tongue to tease along the seam of his lips.

When she pulled back, she was caught in his gaze. In the morning light, she could see equal tones of autumn browns, rich golds and deep forest greens. He was perfect.

"Good morning," she said and watched as the colour of his eyes changed, the green dominating as his breathing quickened.

He didn't smile, but his cheek did tick when he blinked.

Encouraged, as he hadn't pushed her away, Lacy leaned in again and skimmed her tongue across his mouth.

He was letting her have her own way.

She rose above him and nipped at his lips, asking permission to be let inside, and when he opened his mouth, she went straight in, swirling her tongue around his, feeling his warmth and how his body trembled when she skimmed the roof of his mouth with the tip of her tongue.

He reached up and with his hand at the back of her head, pulled her even closer and took over, deepening the kiss.

They kissed for long moments, un-rushed like a Sunday morning while sipping and nibbling each other's lips.

Frustratingly, he was tangled in the sheets, but she was able to feel the hard ridge of his arousal dominating his form.

She pushed her hips into him, inviting him to take her. But he didn't move.

Frustrated at the pace, Lacy shoved the sheet from him and groaned in annoyance feeling his pyjama bottoms. When had he put these on? She could have taken a moment to appreciate the silk pants he was wearing in moss green, but she wasn't in the frame of mind to wait. She pushed them down and over his feet to throw them across the room. His knowing smirk soon disappeared as she stretched out on top of him again.

It felt so good. He felt so good, and again and again, she moved her hips, simulating what she wanted. He didn't help her, in fact, when she looked into his eyes, she could see the playful challenge lurking there.

She could do this, and with a smirk that would rival his, she went exploring.

His body was magnificent. For a nerd he was ripped, his abs cut so sharp she traced her tongue along each slab of hard muscle.

She twirled a finger in his belly button and pinched his nipples none too gently. She felt when his breathing fractured and when he drew in a deep shivering breath. Then she moved down to explore the bright mound of short, wiry hair. They had never been this vulnerable or open with each other.

They'd always had to rush, one of them usually fully clothed, with only the necessary parts undone. Today they had reached a new place.

Lacy nuzzled her way through the coarse hair, breathing in his musky scent that should be bottled for her enjoyment alone.

Then she gripped him in her small hands, looked up to make sure he was watching, but his eyes were closed, and she pulled him. Hard.

His eyes flew open, and she frowned, telling him with her own petulant expression that she wanted him present and watching.

He smirked and put his hands behind his head.

I'm all yours, his expression said.

Lacy licked him once and then twice. Going from the tip of the smooth head, tracking the long veins underneath and then up again, all the while her hand smoothed him up and down.

When she took him in her mouth, she pumped her hand,

developing a rhythm that had him lifting his hips off the bed and breathing harshly.

Smiling on the inside, knowing this was a power she was going to enjoy and do to him time and time again, Lacy brought him to an orgasm that made him shout her name out loud. *Damn right,* she thought smugly.

She kept going until he softened in her mouth, and she licked him clean before crawling back up his body, taking the sheet with her to snuggle in the crook of his arm to fall asleep.

CHAPTER SEVEN

The next few days were the best Lacy had ever experienced in her life. All she wore was one of Matthew's shirts–she was okay with that–stayed holed up in the flat with him, cooked, shared long baths and had dinner by candlelight.

They spent most evenings watching Bollywood movies, with the famed actress Camikara featuring in a lot of them. They had sex in every room and on every surface of the apartment, and she was okay with all of that too.

They'd had turkey bacon, eggs and a shot of kale juice for breakfast this morning, and Matthew was working out in the weights room. Lacy had been ordered to stay away as the last time she'd worked out with him, they'd both got so turned on, they'd had sex against the mirrors.

When she'd pointed out the imprint of her body, Matthew had spent a long time cleaning it off. She had laughed so hard; he'd thrown the paper towel at her and chased her around the apartment.

Lacy smiled to herself and flopped onto the sofa to listen to the audiobook of a best-selling romance author Matthew had recommended. It was called *The Beholden* by a British author called S.M. Forrester and Lacy was enjoying it.

This was the best way for her to read, Lacy now knew, and wondered why she hadn't thought of it herself. Matthew had hit on the idea, and so far, it was working. For the first time in years, she was able to lose herself in a novel and enjoy it, although she had declared no thrillers because she had enough espionage and deception in her real life, she'd warned him playfully. He hadn't returned her smile.

He hadn't tackled her about what she was doing, but she knew it was only a matter of time. Nor had she checked in and there was no telling how her new employers were going to react about her disappearance. But right now, she really didn't care.

Matthew was waiting for something though. He was antsy, checking his phone every minute and sending off text messages.

She didn't know what he was up to, but she was watching and waiting. Sadly, subterfuge was second nature to them both, she thought, watching as the man of her thoughts walked into the living room dressed in shorts, a black muscle top and a small white towel over his shoulders. He flicked her a quick glance before going to the fridge, reaching for a bottle of water and drinking most of it, before placing the bottle on the counter.

Lacy watched under her lashes as he checked his phone, disabled the security alarm, walked to the first door and then the outer door, to pick up a package someone had left there.

Flicking another glance in her direction, he went to his room.

Lacy followed, only to hang back as his bedroom door was open. She wasn't spying on him technically she told herself, she was merely trying to stay one foot ahead of him, she reasoned, watching him rip off the brown paper and open a hand-sized box.

Whatever was inside was wrapped in tissue paper and just as she was going to walk nonchalantly into the room, he looked up, smirked, reached out and slammed the door in her face.

So much for being invisible, Lacy chuckled, not the least bit offended.

She went back to her favourite spot, where the sun hit the chair, and lost herself in the complicated love life of the heroine in her book.

***

"Want to go out?"

Lacy looked up startled, seeing Matthew dressed in black jeans and a jade green button-down shirt that did amazing things to his eyes. He was wearing boots and a watch with a large black and gold face.

Lacy sat up and yawned. "To go where?"

Matthew shrugged. "A drive?"

"I'll need my clothes," she stated, looking down at his vest she was wearing. He'd given her access to his clothes, and she helped herself. She wanted to keep his eyes on her and had succeeded. A vest that was too large showcased the sides of her boobs and skimmed the rim of her bottom was today's choice.

Lacy had never considered herself to be a siren, but she wanted eyes, Matthew's eyes, on her at all times.

"Pity," Matthew murmured softly, his eyes swirling with colour.

Something was different about him, Lacy thought, but she couldn't put her finger on it. She followed him into his closet and caught the folded clothes he threw at her.

"Hurry up." He ordered.

Matthew was a man of few words. Maybe it stemmed from his disability Lacy mulled dressing quickly, but he really wasn't a conversationalist.

They would eat and work out in silence, but it wasn't a painful silence. His eyes spoke for him. She was beginning to read all that he wasn't saying in his eyes. When he was relaxed, they were browner, and when he was annoyed, they would flash bright gold and when they were green, her favourite, he was aroused and about to make her body sing.

Full of excitement, Lacy dressed in her white vest and his shorts and immediately felt restricted after days of wearing hardly anything. She unwound her hair, bent at the waist to shake out her curls then finger-combed it away from her face. She didn't have any make-up with her, so made do with pinching her cheeks for a little colour, then walked out.

Matthew was busy typing into the computer, but he shut the whole thing down at her approach, she noted.

"We have a problem," Lacy told him.

"What's up?"

"I don't have any shoes."

They both looked down at her bare feet.

"No worries," he pulled out his phone. "You're a what? Six?"

he asked and sent a text with her confirmation.

"Whoever you're texting, can I get a pair of jeans or leggings and maybe a jacket too? It looks a little cool outside." She looked out over the cloudy sky with bulging clouds that looked as though they were about to burst.

"Anything else?" he asked.

"I could do with some lip gloss, but you can kiss me instead," she said with all seriousness, seeing his lips twitch, and as soon as he sent the text, Lacy wrapped her arms around his neck, went up on tip-toe and let him kiss and nibble colour into her lips.

They only pulled apart when his phone vibrated a few seconds later.

"That was fast," she said when he returned from the entryway with several bags.

"There's a couple of stores' on the fifth floor for occupants only."

"So, all this time I could have had clothes?" Lacy asked, with her hands going to her hips.

"Why? You like wearing my stuff," he answered with a one-shouldered shrug. "Don't even deny it."

Looking in the bags, Lacy ignored him because it was true. She pulled out a pair of black skinny jeans, a brown leather jacket that was as soft as butter, white sneakers, a handbag, a small make-up bag, that upon further investigation, held translucent powder, eye-liner and two shades of lip gloss a nude and a red. When she pulled out a wispy lace bra and matching panties in dove grey, she looked at him.

That small smile was tugging at the corner of his mouth again and feeling devilish, Lacy raised a brow.

He wanted to play games, oh boy, was she going to play with him.

Within seconds she pulled off her top and, smiling at his hooded look and smouldering eyes, she hooked her thumbs in the waistband of the shorts and tugged them down, stepping out, to kick them at him.

He caught them with a laugh that halted abruptly when she licked her lips and stepped out of her panties.

Lacy pulled on the sheer bra as though she had all the time in the world and arranged her breasts within the delicate cups. She walked towards him, swinging the panties around her finger.

Turning her back, and with her bottom in the air, she glided the silky wisp of nothingness over one ankle, glanced over her shoulder to make sure that he was watching, before wriggling the fabric up her legs to settle on her hips, only she didn't get that far, instead, screaming in surprise as Matthew tackled her from behind, pulled her around to face him, and lifted her high so that she could wrap her legs around his waist as he walked to the nearest hard surface, which just so happened to be the column that divided the living-room space from the entrance.

They had sex right there. Hot, rushed, guttural sex that finished in the shower with him on his knees, paying homage to the tiny button and swollen lips that had given him so much pleasure.

It was mid-afternoon before they finally made it out of the apartment.

In the garage, Matthew took his time looking at several cars.

"You don't own all of these, do you?" Lacy asked him, for the first time allowing her curiosity to show. She'd bitten her tongue these past three days, not wanting the bureau to own the apartment and ruin her fantasy.

"My brother," Matthew answered.

"This is all your brother's?" she asked, flinging her arms out to incorporate the building as well as the expensive cars and motorbikes.

"Well, technically the apartment is Sabrina's,"

"Who's Sabrina?"

"My sister-in-law,"

"I didn't know you had a brother," Lacy said, as he chose a white four-wheel drive. She wasn't into cars, but she knew the vehicle was up there in the luxury ranks.

"Why would you?" he asked, getting into the vehicle.

"Why would I what?"

"Know that I have a brother," Matthew clarified, watching as she put on her seat belt before driving up the ramp to street level. "You've never bothered to ask."

He sounded almost angry, she thought, picking up the tight edge in his voice.

Lacy laughed it off. "You know zilch about me too, Matthew. It's not like we're friends or anything. We have sex and that's it. We don't *need* to know anything about each other."

"Your full name is Wallace Rosemarie Dawson," he began as he drove through Manhattan. "You were adopted at two and a half, your parents are white and work in law enforcement. You weigh one hundred and eight pounds and have to get an iron shot every month because your periods can be heavy. Your birthday has just gone, and pickles give you a rash on your neck." Matthew volunteered. "How am I doing so far?" he asked.

"Have you gone through my file?" Lacy spluttered, angry that he knew so much about her, even the intimate stuff.

"You don't sleep around," he went on. "Although you do sleep with me every chance you get." The glance he levelled at her was hot and deliberate. "You don't like skirts or dresses. You spend a lot of time walking around baby stores, and you hate your parents."

"Now you hold on! I don't hate my parents! And how would you know I walk around in baby stores?!" She asked, beyond angry now. That was too much. It was her secret escape.

After an assignment, especially if it was a particularly harrowing assignment, she would go into a baby store to decompress. Seeing the tiny furniture and clothes, all the innocence of soft colours and textures brought a sense of worthiness to what she did. She cleaned up the world to make it a better place for all the babies that would be born. It made it all feel worthwhile.

"And I do have sex!" She shouted when they cleared the city. "Lots of it!"

"I hope you're on the pill,"

"Matthew!"

He shrugged. "I haven't been using anything when we make love."

"We don't make *love* we have sex!" Lacy yelled. "No emotion is involved! You could be anyone!"

"Keep telling yourself that sweetheart." He drawled around tightly clenched teeth, swiftly changing lanes.

"I'm right, and why are you even getting mad?" she charged, hearing the edge in his voice again. "I should be the one getting mad, you looked into my background!"

"Do you want a baby?" he asked instead, after a deep breath.

"Not with you, I don't," Lacy snapped. She wanted a baby and a husband. She even wanted a porch swing and a people carrier to use for carpool.

Matthew swerved the car to the side of the road with a chorus of car horns objecting behind them.

"What the hell is wrong with you?!" Lacy sputtered when he tore down a side street lined with Silver Maples. They were out in the suburbs she noticed, seeing a couple of sprinklers watering lawns, a red tricycle laying on its side in a driveway, and an older man washing his car, in one sweeping glance. Matthew stopped under the shade of a large maple.

He grabbed the back of her neck and tipped her head so that she was looking at him.

"One, we make love," he growled. "We do not have sex. Understand?" he gritted. When she didn't answer quick enough, he got in her face, his hazel eyes blazing fire into hers. "Understand?"

She nodded.

"Two. You want a baby?" he didn't wait for her to answer, but flexed his fingers at her neck. "I will give you a baby." He promised angrily. "And three," he took a deep breath before continuing. "If I *hear* you have been with another man, I will fucking kill you both. Have you got that?" He snarled.

Lacy nodded again. She wasn't scared, Matthew would never hurt her no matter what he said. But to see him like this, all possessive and he-man'ish did all sorts to her insides, and she surreptitiously moved her hands to the inside of her thighs and pressed down.

He pulled her forward and kissed her hard. Lacy felt the laden heat pool at the juncture of her legs and quickly clambered over the centre console to sit on his lap to ease the pressure. His tongue swept into her mouth, and one hand swept under her top to seek and pinch her nipples as she sighed her agreement in his mouth. He knew. He knew how she was feeling. He knew what he did to her.

They were in broad daylight but didn't care. Matthew's hand was already inside her jeans, rapidly dipping in and out of her, as she muffled the sound of her whimpers into the base of his thick neck until she fell apart.

When her breathing finally settled, Matthew stroked her cheeks with his thumbs, wiped away her tears and kissed her gently once, then twice, before touching his forehead to hers and smiling.

A smile that for the first time, made both brackets around his mouth deepen.

Lacy smiled back as her heart tripped over. She scooted over to her seat and with her hand on his hard thigh, leaned back as he drove them to wherever. She didn't care where.

CHAPTER EIGHT

Matthew pulled up some twenty minutes later in front of a mid-sized clapboard house with dark green shutters. It was very pretty with an abundance of rose bushes rioting around it.

"Who lives here?" Lacy asked curiously, shutting the car door to walk towards him.

He didn't answer but took her hand and walked to the side of the house. They passed a weather-beaten wooden bench and pots of miniature roses. It was a romantic space, and for some reason, Lacy felt the sting of tears.

She wanted this. The house with the bench placed in the sun, ready for her to relax in the evenings and sigh contently as she drank tea and watched her children play.

Matthew rapped two times on the partially open back door before entering.

A woman wearing a frothy bright pink, polka dot shirt, and orange leggings ran forward beaming.

Matthew's cheeks were clasped by be-ringed fingers before he was engulfed in a tight hug and rocked left and right.

When the lady pulled away, Lacy received the same treatment, and she closed her eyes as the scent of security and love enveloped her. Gardenias.

"Son, why didn't you tell us you were coming and who is this beautiful young lady?" she asked, firing the questions at Matthew, before taking Lacy's hand to introduce herself. "Hi, I'm Greta, Matthew's mommy, although he still calls me *Mum*. Can you imagine? He's lived in America more than half his life and insists on sticking to such a silly sounding word. Mum," she went on. "It reminds me of mumps." She tapped the underside of her jaw as though checking her glands weren't swollen. "Come on in, sit, sit." She ordered briskly indicating the floral sofa.

Matthew let go of Lacy's hand, and she sat down.

"My husband, Charles just went to get some milk, he'll be back in two ticks."

The lady, Greta, was bubbling with excitement and the magnitude of what Matthew had done was not lost on Lacy. This was huge. He had taken her home. What did this mean for them? No-one in the bureau really shared their personal lives, especially at their level, wanting to keep work at work and their personal lives as far away from it as possible. Her being here, in his family home, meant he was beginning to trust her, and she wanted to weep.

"Oh Matthew," she whispered, looking at him. But he was busy signing to his mother.

Lacy couldn't follow what he was saying as he was turned partially away from her. His mother was beaming, her eyes bright as they talked between themselves.

Lacy looked around. This was the family hub. Built on love. There were groups of pictures everywhere, and she wanted to look closer but didn't want to appear rude. Instead, she concentrated on the five frames beside her on the round coffee table. There was a photograph of Matthew grinning with two other men. One older, the other younger–who Lacy knew from somewhere, but didn't want to focus on that right now. They had to be Matthew's brother and father because of the strong family resemblance.

There was a picture of his parents looking down at a newborn. That had to be recent as Greta was wearing the same shirt. A picture of Matthew's brother with his arm around a pretty brown-skinned girl, a baby and a teenager that looked like them both. Another frame featured Matthew, his brother, a good-looking blond-haired man and several girls, all with their arms entwined and grinning at the camera. Lacy could just imagine the photographer ordering them to say 'cheese'.

Matthew came from a strong, loving family, Lacy mused looking across the room at him. Why was he working for the bureau surrounded by cold steel corridors and people who really didn't give a hoot about you? The bureau changed you and not for the better.

Matthew's father returned from the store and soon after, followed by Matthew's brother Ace, who Lacy now recognised from the internet. He was famous, and when she told him she'd also illegally climbed Shanghai Tower, they'd laughed at Matthew's snort of disapproval and bonded over their escapades.

Lacy spent a wonderful afternoon with Matthew's family and as the day progressed more and more people came. She met his step-sisters, his half-sister Kelly and nieces and nephews. When someone asked how Kyle was doing, they all fell silent and changed the subject.

Lacy filed that away, for no other reason than she wanted to know everything about Matthew and his family.

He was currently laying on the floor helping his niece, Heather, with her maths homework. She was around twelve and also deaf.

Lacy helped with dinner and made a batch of double chocolate brownies and a quick Victoria Sponge cake with cream and strawberry jam in the middle. Everyone was impressed, and Matthew saved two slices for when they got home 'later' he said, much to everyone's amusement. Lacy warmed at his words and felt heat touch her cheeks when Heather and her cousins made kissy noises when he leaned over the dinner table and kissed her cheek in front of them all.

Everyone aside from Ace and his family left after dinner. Lacy and Matthew were alone in the kitchen with Matthew following orders from his mother to wash the dishes. Lacy had been told to relax, but she stayed to help him, falling easily into the domesticated bliss of the past three days; him washing and she drying, as they stood side by side, in companionable silence.

"Your family is amazing," she told him, smiling as she dried a saucer.

He looked down at her, his hazel eyes gold and intense for a moment, before he relaxed, and his mouth tipped upwards. She knew it was a big deal for him to bring her here. It just wasn't done.

"Yeah, but don't let them hear you say that," he winked down at her.

"Did your hearing aid come in the package this morning?" Lacy asked suddenly. That was what was different. He was replying to her without reading her lips. For three days he'd been reading her lips and using sign language and then suddenly, he wasn't. She didn't mind what he used as long as he was talking to her.

"Yeah,"

"Specially made?"

His eyes cooled, but he did answer. "Yes."

"By the bureau?"

"Why the questions?"

She shrugged one shoulder. "Curious," she answered. "You can buy hearing aids from the drug store nowadays, and you went without one for days. Three days." She pointed out.

"So?"

"So, I can't see it,"

"I have a friend who custom makes mine."

"Is it only a hearing aid?" Lacy asked curiously, well aware of the technology that wasn't available to the public but was to them.

"I can't shoot people with my ear Lacy," Matthew said with a tinge of amusement. "My name isn't Bond."

That reminded her.

"I didn't know you were British,"

He stared into her eyes, holding her gaze and said. "You were born in Germany."

Her eyebrows shot upwards, "What?" then her brows dipped low. "Germany?"

He was silent, watching as she digested what he had revealed. He thought she knew, but the shock in her eyes told him she hadn't.

"They lied?"

He nodded.

"Why would they lie?" She blazed, upset, but really not that surprised.

Matthew was about to answer when Greta and Sabrina entered the room and started asking him questions about the rest of his vacation.

Some of the glow was sucked out of Lacy's day with Matthew's announcement. She wasn't American? She was born in Germany?

It didn't make sense, yet it did. The lies continued. She was adopted as a toddler. She had no baby pictures, although she always felt as though something was missing, that something wasn't right. She had images, reflections of herself that didn't add up. Almost like a broken mirror. Her life was like a jigsaw puzzle, but with every piece that slotted into place, another piece went missing. The lies were like fragile wiry coils within coils. Many of them unnecessary.

So, she was German. Did the bureau think she was going to go off and look for her birth parents or something? She had no desire. She was going to have her own family.

She flicked away a tear as she sat alone on the bench by the side of the house. As lovely as Matthew's family were, she needed a moment to herself to digest what he had said.

Germany. She'd been to Europe many times but wasn't exactly enamoured by the old dark place. Besides, she couldn't live in a place with so much history when she had none herself. Illogical but true.

***

Matthew suddenly changed lanes and Lacy jerked into the door. She looked at him, but he was looking in the rear-view mirror.

"What is it?" she asked with increasing alarm. They had left his parents' house about ten minutes ago and were heading back into the city. "Are we being followed?"

"I think so."

"By who?"

59

"I don't know," he answered tightly. "Hold on." He tore into the fast lane and sped off, although constantly checking his mirrors.

Lacy turned in her seat, not seeing anything out of the ordinary and said as much.

"Maybe it was nothing," Matthew said, switching lanes and reverting to average speed, not wanting to bring attention to themselves by getting pulled over.

The navy sedan he thought had been following them was nowhere to be seen, but he didn't relax. His gut instinct had never failed him yet, and it was currently telling him something was up.

Matthew had waited until he got his hearing aid before tackling Lacy about what she was doing and who she was working for. He was a pro lip reader, but sometimes he missed things, and he didn't want to concentrate on the wrong stuff.

"Who are you working for Lacy?" he asked quietly.

She sighed. "I don't really know," she admitted, knowing how foolish he was going to think she was.

"What the hell!" he blazed. They had been taught to ask questions, double-check the answers and be suspicious of everyone. It was supposedly second nature to them.

"I know," she giggled at the look of outrage he flung at her. "Risky, isn't it?"

"Jesus, Wallace," he gritted, before reining in his temper. "How did they approach you? You could be working for the mafia."

She tutted her objection and rolled her eyes. "I'm not." She didn't know for sure, but did the mafia save children from around the world? She didn't think so.

Lacy told him about the time she was out running and the instructions she'd received via email.

Matthew said nothing, obviously mulling over what she had told him. But as the silence stretched, Lacy felt the need to fill it in.

"I want out of the bureau," she admitted quietly for the first time out loud to someone other than herself. She did want out, but you couldn't just walk out. You were a member for life, even if they imprisoned you in the cellars below ground for the rest of your life.

"Lacy," Matthew said softly, feeling her pain. He'd been right all along. She may be a genius, but she wasn't made for this shit.

He reached out and stroked her denim-clad leg, wanting to see the smile back on her face. He would find a way for her to live a normal life if it killed him. Being in the bureau, that was indeed a strong possibility. Death. They didn't mess and didn't suffer what they deemed 'outside nonsense' easily.

"Did you enjoy yourself today?" he asked, wanting to change the subject. They would talk about her assignment when they got to the apartment, and afterwards, he would reach out to his friends and see what else he could learn about her past and her future.

"I love your family," she beamed, turning in her seat as far as the belt would allow. "And the baby is just precious." She cooed, going on and on about how cute Baby Ace, the newest addition to the family was.

Matthew listened, hearing the love and excitement. He liked Lacy, he liked her a lot, and he knew he wasn't letting her go. There was just no way. She had become important to him. Three days of her hanging on his every word, making love, cooking, laughing and watching TV together, he'd never had a woman so close. When his car drove itself to his mother's house–because that's what it was, he hadn't consciously driven there–his mother had been ecstatic. He'd never brought a woman home either. Hence, most of his relatives making their way to the house to see for themselves. He should be mad at his mom for broadcasting it, or at least nervous as hell for what it meant to them and to him, but strangely enough, he wasn't. It was almost a relief.

"When we get home, can we–"

Matthew didn't hear what she was about to say, as a large black panelled van rammed into the back of their vehicle, sending it hurling through the lanes, as Matthew fought to keep control.

Lacy screamed and automatically reached in the glove compartment for his weapon.

"Where's your gun?!" she yelled when shots rang out, pinging the asphalt beside them.

"Here," Matthew pulled his 9mm from the side of his door, and she grabbed it. "Ready?" he asked, knowing what they were going to do.

Lacy took her seatbelt off and with her back braced against the dashboard, aimed through the back window and pulled the trigger.

Glass shattered, clearing her view and with her hand steady, aimed at the van that was bearing down on them. She hit it. It swerved. But it kept coming.

She fired several rounds, but the bullets bounced off.

Matthew raced towards the city, but the van stayed with them. Shooting at them. The right rear tyre was hit, causing the vehicle to lose speed and wobble on the road. Matthew fought with the steering wheel, trying to keep control.

"Lacy no!" he yelled a split second later, grabbing her jacket and dragging her back inside. She'd pushed her upper body out of the window to fire behind them. She was too vulnerable like that, and pure panic hit Matthew square in the stomach.

"Shit! Brace yourself, Lacy!" Matthew charged, knowing what was about to happen, but unable to do anything about it when he saw several black vans racing towards them in his rear-view mirror. Matthew floored the gas pedal as he swerved through the lanes, but they were gaining fast.

A Sedan in front of them suddenly slammed on its brakes causing Matthew to clip its rear-end.

"Hold on, sweetheart!" Matthew yelled, flinging his arm out to at least protect her as the truck rolled out of control for what seemed like endless minutes, but was, in fact, three seconds, before careening into the crash barrier, bouncing off it to slide almost gracefully on its side into the middle of the road.

"You okay?" Matthew asked, looking over at Lacy, relief flooding through him when she nodded. He looked behind him seeing a bunch of men in black, their faces covered by balaclavas, rushing down on them. Guns pointed.

"Give me the gun Wallace," Matthew demanded urgently. They had seconds, if that much, to get away.

"I've got this," Lacy said instead, taking aim.

Matthew yanked the gun from her. "On three, get out and run, Operative," he ordered through clenched teeth. "I'll cover you."

"No." Lacy challenged. "I'm not leaving you."

Matthew turned to her, his hazel eyes blazing with fire and something else. He grabbed the back of her neck, forcing her to look at him.

"I need you to run sweetheart," he said, softening his tone and moving his hand to cup her face and run his thumb over her bottom lip.

The two of them looked at each other, connecting on a level other than sexual, as a wealth of feelings, and all that they hadn't said over the years, danced in the air between them. They weren't done.

Lacy took a deep breath, moved her head to kiss his palm and silently mouthed words she wanted him to know in case they didn't make it. Then she nodded.

Matthew counted down, and Lacy hauled herself up and over him, to scramble out of the shattered window-screen.

Shots rang out, but she didn't look back as she weaved through the traffic that had come to a standstill. The air was screaming with sirens and gunfire.

Out of nowhere, she was grabbed from behind. A beefy arm hauling her off the ground when she desperately tried to kick out and find some leverage.

She was shoved into the back seat of a blue Sedan, and he got in beside her. She lurched to the other side, but another man got in, pinning her between them as the car sped off.

"No!" she screamed, knowing this was not good. You fight

to the death, never *ever* go to the secondary location. "Get the hell off me! Let me go!" she screamed frantically, trying to look behind her, scratch their eyes out and escape at the same time. "Matthew!" She yelled, managing to elbow one captor in the face, as she screamed for her lover.

She felt a prick at the back of her ear, and as much as she fought it, darkness seeped into her mind, and for a strange blurry moment, she saw a mirror image of herself looking straight at her. Then nothing.

*****

Three things registered with Matthew at once. One, they weren't shooting to kill him. Two, they had Lacy and three, he'd busted his right arm.

He took off after the car, running as fast as he could, but the Sedan gained speed, and the distance between them grew longer and longer. His chest was burning, sirens were squealing, and Matthew knew he had to get out of here.

He pressed the button on his watch again, leapt over the highway divide, dodged vehicles and ran to the other side. He scrambled over a steep grass verge, under a graffiti-filled ramp and jumped down a high wall to street level.

He wiped the sweat from his face, pushed his gun into the back of his pants and started walking as he blended with the smiling evening shoppers. He found a Chinese restaurant, ordered tea and waited.

CHAPTER NINE

"Where the hell is she!" Matthew yelled, frustrated beyond belief that Lacy had simply vanished. It had been two days since she'd been snatched from him, and nothing. Not a damn thing. It was as though she'd dropped off the planet.

He couldn't find her. He'd used all the resources available to him, and many that shouldn't be. His friend Rhodes had tracked the blue Sedan to an underpass, but it never came out the other side. It had disappeared almost as though the road had opened up and sucked it in. Matthew had even ridden out there to check the area out but found nothing. Not even a damn cockroach.

They'd checked the airports, ran her image on every damn facial recognition database they could think of and still nothing.

"We'll find her," Rhodes promised, not for the first time.

"I don't get it. Where the hell is she?"

"I'll keep looking."

Rhodes rang off.

Matthew looked at the bank of screens that were still set up in Ace's apartment until his eyes burned.

After he'd been picked up, he'd come straight back here and had barely left. She'd disappeared, and he damned himself for being so distracted by her gorgeous legs and pouty mouth, that he hadn't tied her to a chair that first night and interrogated her.

The people who took her were professionals, and Rhodes was able to ascertain they weren't any of their guys. The bureau was messed up and wouldn't have a problem staging a kidnapping of one of their own if they thought it necessary, but it wasn't them. It wasn't the FBI, CIA or any other known organisation.

His phone started ringing again, and he glanced at the screen. He was wearing a cast on his right arm, due to the cash, so snatched the device up with his left.

"What's up," he answered.

"Any news?"

"No."

"I'm sorry." Ace was well aware how much Lacy meant to his big brother and, alongside The Captain–their father–watched as Matthew became increasingly frantic when they'd lost track of the blue Sedan and all the men who had followed them that night. They'd simply left the vehicles on the highway and disappeared. "Want some company?"

"Nah,"

"We're here for you, bro."

"Yeah."

Matthew hung up and threw his phone down. He leaned back in his chair and twisted to his right to look at the image of Lacy lying on the sofa. She was wearing his sleeveless T-shirt, the side of one boob taunting him. Her long legs were bare and crossed at the ankles as she listened to her book with a dreamy smile touching her lips. She looked so relaxed and happy. Matthew turned away, feeling physically sick. Where the hell was she?

He hadn't been able to glean anything more about who she was working for and had even broken into her small apartment in D.C. for any clues.

Her apartment was all Lacy. The walls papered with a floral paper of soft pastels that should look old fashioned and granny'ish, yet didn't. There were soft rugs on the floors and large cushions on the crushed velvet lilac sofa. The whole place screamed comfort and homeliness, peace and security, and there wasn't a trace of life as a government operative in evidence.

Matthew had tinkered with her stuff, sniffed her perfume, looked in her drawers, and that night, prayed like he'd never done before. He'd fought the urge to sleep in her bed. He had to find her.

***

Matthew rode the elevator down to the car park, knowing he couldn't look at those screens another second without breaking one of the damn things. He was going for a ride.

He zipped up his leather jacket, pulled on his gloves and mentally prepared himself to tear up the road and hit some high speeds. Ace was the professional speed junkie in the family, but Matthew could outride him any day.

As Matthew stepped out, he was blindsided by a punch in the face, and before he could recover, a sack was pulled over his head.

"What the fuck!" he yelled, trying to break free of the thick forearm that pressed into the back of his neck, anchoring him up against a wall. An elbow pressed into the centre of his back, and he felt another pair of large hands pat him down, finding and removing his guns, before quickly binding his hands behind his back with a zip-tie.

The man moved then and pushed Matthew's face into the concrete before punching him in the side.

"Leave her alone," an accented gravelly voice uttered quietly in his ear. "Keep looking for her, and she disappears."

"She's already fucking disappeared," Matthew charged through the blinding pain as he was punched again at the same place. It felt as though his right kidney had been torn from his body.

"Disappear permanently," the voice warned before pulling him forward.

Matthew was viciously kicked at the back of the legs, and he went down, hitting the ground hard. The bag on his head was pulled tighter from behind. He couldn't see for shit.

"Where is she?!" Matthew yelled into the silence. "Who the fuck are you people?"

Another punch to the face knocked him on his side, and a kick to his stomach made him curl inwards. He could take them on, but he couldn't see a fucking thing.

Instead, he listened.

He heard a huff of laughter behind him. The scrape of boots on the ground. The rustle of a jacket.

"You hurt her, and you die!" Matthew promised hearing

footsteps. There were maybe three or four people here, but only one assaulting him. "Do you hear me?" he goaded. He needed more time. "Touch her, and I'll hunt you down, peel your fucking skin off, then pour acid on you, you fucking little shit!"

He heard laughter, and maybe, was that the lighter tinkle of a woman? He cocked his head to the side, yelling and swearing, trying to get a reaction from them as he used his other senses to catalogue whatever he could.

They were professionals, that much he knew. They could have killed him, but didn't. That meant they had orders not to. They hadn't shot him that day either, and he'd been right in the open.

He was dragged up by the arm, onto his knees again. For a terrible second, he thought they just might execute him after all, and waited. He could feel his heart racing, blood or sweat, he didn't know which, trickling down the side of his face. He thought of the last words Lacy had mouthed to him, the soft look in her eyes before she'd smiled and scrambled out of the car.

He had to fight.

His captors were whispering now, maybe ten feet away. Were they leaving?

Matthew cocked his head this way and that, trying to hear what they were saying and what language they were using. It sounded swishy and harsh and guttural, Eastern European, maybe? Russian?

He was going to kill every single one of them, he promised himself.

Footsteps neared. The booted step of a heavy-set man came towards him and pulled the bag tighter on his head.

Matthew felt the heavy nuzzle of a gun at his temple and braced himself.

"I love you, Lacy." He whispered and waited for the end.

CHAPTER TEN

Lacy didn't understand why her body was so sore. She ached all over and felt as though she'd fallen down a mountain, got back up and rolled down it again.

There was a large purple bruise on one shoulder, a few grazes on her arm and she felt as though she'd bruised a rib or two. Add to that, a blistering headache that was pounding relentlessly behind her eyes, making her feel like she'd been paralytically drunk and in a bar brawl last night.

She didn't understand why she felt so battered and for the life of her, didn't remember hurting herself.

Lacy looked around the shadowed interior of the log cabin. She'd been assigned to this location and sent a text message to stay and await further instructions early this morning. The fifth cabin from the secondary road, with the blue and white porch swing and split-second step, and she'd found it easily enough.

She'd hid her car a mile away, under the bushy canopy of dense forest.

She used to own a small compact car that conned the world with its guise of a rusty exterior but had, in fact, a brand-new engine. Unfortunately, it was missing this morning, and just when she was about to investigate, an envelope with a vehicular key inside was delivered by messenger. She'd walked outside, pressed the unlock button and the flashing lights of a brand-new black SUV blinked like a welcoming beacon at her. It was a dream to drive, but she still wanted her old car back.

Lacy sighed, feeling a wave of discontent for not being in control of her life career through her again.

It wasn't very late, and, from experience, Lacy knew they would only bring her latest charge once darkness had fallen. She had around four hours. She'd been warned not to make her presence known unless absolutely necessary, so that left her with very little to do as she couldn't yet go for a walk to explore the area.

Feeling the effects of her bruised body, Lacy looked longingly at the open fireplace. It would have been nice to start a fire, curl up and sleep for a while if she couldn't go for a walk, but knew she couldn't take the risk.

She walked around, making sure all windows and doors were secure, before looking through a window to take in the enormous expanse of gently rolling water and the row of log cabins opposite.

She'd been informed that side of the lake was owned by the Manninos', a wealthy family originally from Boston, who ran Wellness and other New Age retreats all year round. Mrs Mannino wasn't a threat, but Lacy was to be wary of Mr Mannino and the rest of the Mannino family.

This area of wooded forest was the perfect place to come and unwind. Near to the Canadian Border, it was still close enough for New Yorkers and other big city residents to travel for the weekend and relax.

It was very pretty, Lacy mused, appreciating the clean air and quietness, and could well imagine how beautiful it would be in the summer, teeming with families playing on the lake and fishing from the piers dotted around. She'd noticed a sign saying no motorised boats or jet skies were allowed. The whole place was idyllic, and Lacy would love to explore further. But first, she had a job to do.

The cabins on this side of the lake were privately owned and, with winter approaching, were all locked up by the wealthy owners who probably came up here over the summer. She had at least a mile of waterfront property to herself.

Lacy rotated her shoulders, and grimaced as pain shot across her ribs, she really didn't understand why she hurt so much and, checking the time, decided to have a bath to help relieve the aches.

Her last charge, Mikhail, was a boy from Russia she remembered fondly, padding to the bathroom. He'd been a pale skinny lad of eleven, with dark, soulful eyes and an erect carriage and mop of sandy brown hair.

He'd been with her for ten days and for the first two didn't say a word. She knew he understood English as he'd followed her instructions for bedtime that first night. 'Wash your face and brush your teeth' and he did so watchfully, but without objection. When on the second day she asked him what he would like to do and he said he would like to go camping, she thought what the heck and took him to a campsite that wasn't too far out of the city. Usually, her little charges, wanted to play on the games console or go to the mall, but Mikhail wanted to go camping.

They'd had a great time, setting up camp, using the large pop-up tent she had rented. Unfortunately, the camping stove she had didn't work, so they made do with cold beans and eating the array of cold sandwich meats she'd brought along, with their fingers. Mikhail loved it.

He'd grinned, and the sadness behind his eyes faded. They'd tried fishing in the man-made lake, although not catching anything, yet he'd seemed happy. Lacy was under the impression he didn't get out much, and when she'd gently asked him about his favourite things to do, he'd clammed up.

She knew these kids came with a lot of baggage, and it saddened her. But it wasn't her job to help them unload it. They weren't with her long enough, and quite frankly, she wasn't emotionally capable of distancing herself from them if she knew what they had gone through. She'd keep every single one of them with her forever.

When their time was up, Mikhail was genuinely upset to leave her. He'd cried and cried, holding her tightly with his skinny arms wrapped around her waist, as he begged and screamed in a dialect she couldn't decipher.

That had been wretched. It was all getting wretched. She enjoyed looking after the children, but she hated to see them go.

Seeing Mikhail, his serious face crumpled with tears had torn her apart. But then he'd collected himself, almost as though he'd heard an inner command ordering him to man-up. He'd stepped away from her and walked stiffly to the black SUV that was idling at the curb for him. He didn't look back when it pulled away.

Lacy had worked hard to keep her own tears at bay because she didn't want Ulvis, the driver, to report back to the 'higher-ups'; how attached she was becoming to the children.

She missed Mikhail and wondered not for the first time, what happened to the children once they left her care.

Wrenching herself from her maudlin thoughts, Lacy entered the bathroom, immediately noticing the shallow puddle of water around the drain in the bath. Strange she thought, frowning, the cabin was supposed to have been standing vacant for months. With a shrug, she quickly rinsed the tub before finding the plug and running herself a bath.

The bathroom was dark, so she turned on the torch App on her phone, put it on the floor and angled it so that the beam was low and throwing shadows into the corners.

Lacy then stuffed a towel along the small gap at the bottom of the door, undressed and stepped into the water with a deep sigh.

Using a sleeping bag for a few nights could not have caused all these aches and pains, she knew as she held her breath and slid under the water, she just couldn't figure it out and, my God, her head hurt.

She liked what she was doing, but it was taking its toll. She was too emotional for all of this she acknowledged, opening her eyes under the water and slowly releasing a stream of bubbles through her nose, controlling her breathing. She was too emotional for working as a government agent too. She didn't belong in this life, any of it.

If she hadn't met Special Ops Matthew Edwards, she probably would have quit the second day of training, but every day she looked forward to sparring with him, watching him, beating him at any task and having sex with him. It was his fault.

He'd been in her squad, and they'd learnt everything they needed to know together. She'd never had a proper boyfriend, but she did have Matthew. He was beautiful, tall and solid with dark red hair. His eyes were her favourite feature, they were an unequal mixture of browns, greens and golds, and they changed colour with his emotions. Lacy had enjoyed learning what the flash of green meant, or the swirl of golds. He was just so beautiful.

They hooked up every chance they got. Pity the last time had been almost two years ago on a rooftop in Chicago, Lacy remembered fondly.

She had been with her squad of five on the south side of a roof surveying a gang that was selling synthetic drugs that had been killing teenage clubbers. Matthew had been on the eastern side of the roof with his team. Following her intel, Ground Ops had swooped in and arrested all members of the gang, and confiscated millions of dollars' worth of pills. Everyone left the roof to celebrate. Everyone except Matthew and Lacy.

They'd walked towards each other, and stopped a hair's breadth apart.

Lacy remembered the way he'd looked at her, the slight tilt to his lips, that couldn't be called a smile or even a smirk. His stare had been hungry. She'd reached over to run her finger along the lines of his bulletproof vest. He'd caught her fingers, yanked her forward until she'd collided with his hard chest and kissed her. Softly.

Without releasing her lips, he'd pulled her Glock from her belt, checked the safety and put it on the low ledge beside them. She had done the same with his two semi-automatics. He'd pulled off her vest and tossed it aside. She'd run her hands around his back, pulled his shirt out of his pants in search of his skin. She'd been like a heat-seeking missile, homing in on his back. Even now, she remembered the satisfaction of feeling the hard ridge of his spine under her fingertips.

Giving up on the gentleness, Matthew had palmed her breasts and nipped along her neck, walking her backwards until she was pressed against a wall. She'd tugged urgently at his pants, telling him what she'd needed, and he'd obliged. He'd turned her around, yanked her pants and undies out of his way and tunnelled inside her, immediately easing her ache.

The sex they'd had on that roof had been unbelievable. Matthew had grunted deep in his throat as he'd pounded into her. When her whimpers became screams, he'd covered her mouth, and she didn't know why, but him doing such a carnal act had sent her rapidly over the edge, her screams caught in his palm.

He'd gone into a frenzy, and she'd come again, joining him as he'd pulled her even closer, his hot breath fanning her hair as he'd pulsed inside her.

Moments later, still breathing hard, his radio had cackled and so had hers. Within seconds, they had both been summoned back to their respective bases.

Lacy relived the memory of that night whenever she needed to relieve her sexual tension. Funny, she didn't feel the need to do that tonight, she thought, releasing her breath with a massive bubble and pushing upwards in the cooling bath water.

Lacy leaned her head on the towel she had rolled for that purpose and wondered when she would see Matthew again. She'd never had a proper boyfriend, the bureau really wasn't conducive to normal relationships, but she did have Matthew.

How had her life come to this? She never thought she'd still be unmarried at her age. She remembered career day back in High School and how everyone had laughed at her. What did she want to become? They'd asked. Martha Stewart, she'd answered truthfully. Her parents had been livid and upped extracurricular activities to also include boxing, chess and a running club. She'd forgotten to stay true to herself over the years.

She had decisions to make. She didn't want to go back into the bureau, she knew that for a fact. And what she was doing working on the side like this would cause all sorts of problems, if they ever found out. But she really didn't care. She liked what she did, but it wore at her heart.

Flicking away a tear, Lacy quickly washed, then using the lemon-scented shampoo/conditioner she'd found in the cupboard, washed her hair before getting dressed to wait in the darkness for the next set of instructions.

And so, it begins again.

***

A few hours later, Lacy walked from the kitchen where she was making a sponge cake in the microwave, to look out of the window, when she saw the sweeping headlights of a vehicle pull up outside of the log cabin. She didn't go to the door but held her aching body taught and looked out.

Ulvis, her only contact, had arrived, and she watched as he opened the back door and reached inside to take out a sleeping little girl, who he cradled in his arms and then strode to the cabin.

Lacy opened the door and ushered him inside, walking ahead of him so that he could place the child on the long sofa.

He lay her down gently, and Lacy covered her with a blanket.

"Hi Ulvis," Lacy greeted, straightening, slowly.

Ulvis was huge, at least six foot seven and big with it. He was originally from Lithuania; he'd once told her in one of the few conversations they'd had.

"Miss Dawson," he answered with a slight smile. Then sneezed.

"Bless you," Lacy said automatically, and Ulvis looked at her in shock, almost as though he hadn't heard the phrase, or he'd never been blessed after a sneeze before.

He dipped his head in acknowledgement and Lacy spied his slight smile.

Ulvis had a shaved head, and Lacy was aware he didn't have the telltale shadowed semi-circle of hair signifying hair loss. He deliberately shaved off his hair. His eyes were pale blue, almost grey, which usually twinkled with friendliness but was currently red and watery. He moved softly, slightly effeminate, and everything about him was contrary to a man of his size. To be honest, he didn't look very well, Lacy thought, noting the mottled flush across his cheeks.

He turned to go back to the SUV as she knew he would, and Lacy took a moment to look at the sleeping child. She wished she was awake as it was going to be very unsettling for the little girl to wake in a strange place with a stranger.

Ulvis returned silently with a small pink suitcase and a black leather tablet case. Lacy took the suitcase from him.

He walked to the small table and set up. He sneezed again.

"Bless you Ulvis," Lacy repeated with a smile and laughed when he went into a series of sneezes.

She went to the kitchen and turned on the kettle. She had a packet of non-drowsy cold remedy in her bag, and she prepared one for him while he set up the tablet.

"Miss Dawson?" he held out the tablet to her and Lacy reached for it and read. Less than sixty seconds later, she had absorbed the three pages of information on the child and the background story for them both. Her name was Soleil, she was six years old and originally from Syria. Her family had been killed, and they were trying to trace an aunt who lived somewhere in North America. To anyone who asked, Soleil was her niece.

Lacy handed the tablet back to Ulvis.

"Finished?" he asked.

He always asked that as though he didn't quite believe she could read so fast.

Lacy nodded and turned to the counter to pick up the mug of lemony cold remedy. "Here you go," she said, holding it out to him.

Ulvis looked at her, then at the mug and then back at her again. He didn't move.

"It's just for your cold Ulvis," she teased, seeing the suspicion in his eyes. She rolled her eyes at him, understanding. "Look," she took a sip. "Not poisoned, you aren't going to die, and you won't even fall asleep as it's non-drowsy." She told him.

Ulvis nodded to himself and reached for the mug. He gulped down the hot liquid, smiled his thanks then put the empty mug on the counter.

"Thank you."

"You're welcome," she answered, turning to wash the mug out, but a flash of pain had her gasping and holding her side.

"You are hurt, yes?" he asked with concern.

"For the life of me, I don't remember hurting myself like this." She laughed at herself, although catching a flash of something in his eye. "What?" she asked.

Ulvis turned away and walked to the door.

"You have new phone in bag," he said, looking over her head.

"Wait!" Lacy said, striding towards him and grabbing his forearm. His skin was hot, and it distracted her. "Ulvis you're burning up!"

He shook off her hand. "I am fine,"

"You are not fine," she stated. "Do you want to wait for a while at least until the medication kicks in?" she asked with concern.

"Thank you, but no."

"I won't tell," she said with a wink. "I promise."

His lips twitched, but he released the doorknob and followed her to the kitchen.

"Would you like some cake?" Lacy offered, turning to the microwave.

He never stayed around once he dropped off the children.

"I must go,"

Lacy ignored him and reached for the plate with the bowl turned upside down. Steam was pouring like waves from the joint between the bowl and the plate.

"Hot, hot, hot," Lacy sang, quickly placing the plate on the counter. "Grab that cloth for me please?" she ordered without looking at the giant who was taking up space in the small kitchen, watching her intently, but she didn't mind, at least he was still here.

He held out the cloth to her and watched keenly when she gently twisted the bowl from side to side, inching it off, until a perfect dome of sponge cake was revealed. Lacy clapped her hands.

"What a beauty, Ulvis," she grinned over her shoulder at him. "Perfect."

He was frowning at the cake and then back at her. If she were to hazard a guess, she would think it was in wonderment.

She walked to the grocery bag on the floor and pulled out a tin of golden syrup.

"Come here, big guy and open this for me," she grabbed a table knife and held it out to him. "You're looking better already." She said, watching as he wedged the knife under the tight rim of the tin. She always bought original British golden syrup from the European store, and it lasted months with it being so thick. A little, really went a long way.

Ulvis turned the tin, lifting the lid with the knife as he went along, and had almost got it open when it slipped off the counter and shot across the kitchen to roll to a stop on the floor. They both looked at it and then burst out laughing.

Lacy laughed so hard tears streamed down her face, and her ribs took exception, but it was just so funny.

Ulvis picked up the tin, opened it and placed it in her hands.

Still giggling, Lacy spooned out the golden syrup on top of the cake, and they both watched intently as it slipped down the sides.

"What did I tell you Ulvis. A beauty."

"*Grazus,*" he said, looking at her and not the cake.

Lacy had the distinct feeling he had complimented her and not the cake in his language. "Come on big guy, let's eat and then you can have a little rest before you go."

***

It had been several days since they had spared his life. Knocking him out with the heel of his own gun instead of killing him, and next thing Matthew knew, his father Charles and his men were helping him up and taking him back to the apartment.

Apparently, his tormentors had known about the distress button on his watch and pressed it before leaving.

It made little sense. They looked and behaved like thugs, yet cared enough to spare his life and help him?

From the security footage of the building, they were able to see them enter the building via the underground parking gates. They had their own security code. There were four of them, and by the stature of one, Matthew had been right, there was a female in the group who only came into view when he had been waiting to die.

She'd said something and the big man, who, with his finger on the trigger, stepped back with obvious reluctance and gun-butted him instead, knocking him out. The female then said something sharply to the man who stiffly nodded his head and flashed his hands in the air, before striding away.

The entire exchange had taken less than ten seconds. It was the female, using her gloved hand, who'd pressed the distress button on his watch.

Frustratingly, they'd again lost them once they got onto the road. They were professionals because only professionals could lose themselves in one of the most surveillance orientated cities in the world.

Matthew was going out of his mind. His family were trying to help, his father, a man, once known as The Captain, had his old colleagues out looking for Lacy and still nothing.

But Matthew knew one thing for sure, he would never give up searching for her.

CHAPTER ELEVEN

"You won't believe who just walked in." Ronald Rhodes said in disbelief, into the mic on his headset. He'd watched the operative he'd been searching for walk casually past him, giving him the same finger wave and half-smile, she always did, before she flashed her badge at the security guard, say a few words to him, that made him laugh and forget himself. Then watched as she pressed her hand on the palm-reader to walk through the sliding glass doors and deeper into the enclave of the building, out of sight.

"Who?" Matthew asked. He hadn't slept for days and was feeling the effects.

"Wallace."

"Wallace who?"

"Special Ops Wallace Dawson. Bloody hell mate, I thought I was seeing things."

Matthew shot upright in his chair and put the noodles he'd been eating–because he had to eat something–on the floor. "At the *office!*"

"Yeah, man."

"How did she look?" Matthew spoke as he rushed down to his bedroom. "Was she hurt?" he pulled a long-sleeved T-shirt over his head, a sweater, his jacket and shoved his feet into his boots. "Was she hurt?" he repeated.

"Nah, she looked–," Rhodes paused to rewind the footage of Wallace walking across the parking lot into the building, in a pair of tight blue jeans and a white sweater that fell off her shoulders. Her hair was loose and blowing in the wind. He zoomed in closer, noting the light make-up and natural flush to her cheeks. "She looks rested."

"What?" Matthew halted in his stride, thinking he hadn't heard right. "*Rested?*"

"Yeah, mate," Rhodes expanded. "She looked like she always does, hot as a mother–,"

"Watch it," Matthew growled. "I can still fuck you over,"

"Dream on Wonder Boy," Rhodes teased, using Matthew's nickname at the bureau.

"Where'd she go?" knowing the office was indeed an oxymoron. They worked in a mini-city with miles upon miles of underground facilities.

"I don't know man, there was a certain something in her eye. Bounce in her step. She went downstairs."

"Keep her there, I'm coming."

"You know I can't keep her here. Keep your phone on you. You got the aid in?"

"When would I not have my hearing aid in?"

"When your bloody arse gets knocked about."

Matthew laughed for the first time in days. He needed answers, but at least Lacy had surfaced, none of the nightmare images that had played on repeat in his head this past week had materialised, she hadn't turned up bloody, beaten, bruised, or God forbid, dead. She looked *rested*. What the hell did that mean, anyway?

He slammed out of the apartment with questions tripping off his tongue.

***

Lacy drove away from the office with mixed feelings. She was still on unpaid leave and turning up there hadn't been the best idea, but she wanted to put some feelers out and speak to her boss, Ian Franklin.

He was a reasonable man, in his late seventies with bright silver hair and sharp grey eyes that looked straight to your brain and told you what you were thinking.

She'd walked into his office after a quick knock and sat in front of him with a smile.

"No," he'd said, with just a glance in her direction, before looking at his laptop.

"But I haven't asked you anything yet,"

"You come here, happy like a Sunday School teacher who just got–" He'd stopped abruptly and cleared his throat. "I haven't seen you in eight weeks four days and," he'd looked at his phone, "twenty-three minutes, looking all refreshed. The answer is no."

"Is that for real?" Lacy had asked, pointing to his phone.

He'd waved it at her. "Yep, you're my favourite operative, and I want you home."

Lacy had bit the side of her lip then. She knew he looked out for her, always did. Lacy remembered repeating the things she'd practised on the drive over in her head and just blurted it out.

"I'm thinking of migrating,"

That had got his attention. He'd leaned back in his chair and placed his hands behind his head. "Oh yeah, to go where?"

"Europe,"

"Again, to go where?"

"Exploring."

"Europe's a big place. I've already given you all the time you want, to *'go find yourself'*," he'd made quotations marks with his fingers. "Go explore, take a trip on a gondola or something, but I want you back here," he'd stated. "And before you do or say something that will get you in trouble, remember this. Special Ops for Life is not just a phrase."

"Yes, Sir."

Ian had sighed, leaned forward and closed his eyes for a moment before saying. "I've known you since you were a little scrawny thing with pigtails, Wallace, you're like a daughter to me." He'd shaken his head. "Read between the lines, there are no choices here."

"Yes, Sir."

"Now leave my office."

"Thank you, Sir." She'd stood then and walked away knowing she'd been right.

***

Lacy shouldered her way into her apartment. She hadn't been here in, she thought back to what Ian Franklin had said, eight weeks four days and however minutes, so had stopped at the grocery store and ended up wandering up and down the aisles.

It had felt good to walk along aimlessly and pretend to be a normal person with normal worries like paying the mortgage, and if she needed to buy hair dye for her roots. Funny thing, she'd stood in front of the boxes of semi-permanent for a moment, before realising she didn't even dye her hair.

Was this her state of mind now?

She'd had an idyllic time at the lake with Soleil the little girl delivered to her and forming a surprising bond with friends Camille and Dirk who were staying in a cabin close to hers. Lacy didn't have any friends outside of the bureau, and it was nice to laugh and joke over the silliest of things.

Camille was a Bollywood actress and Dirk a famed hairdresser. It had been comical to see the expectation of recognition in their faces the night they'd shared their secrets, but she hadn't recognised them and said as much.

Lacy had built a small fire on the beach and, wrapped in blankets with Soleil asleep in her arms, they'd talked into the night. It had gone deep quickly, with Dirk almost in tears as he talked about acceptance and his family. Camille had talked about the father of her child and Lacy had revealed what she did for a living, both jobs, who Soleil really was and needing to escape this life. Her new friends had promised to help her. They'd made a pact to each other that night.

They'd travelled back to New York together, and Dirk had invited her and Soleil to stay the night and meet his husband, Duncan.

While the chicken and chestnut meal they'd cooked was resting, Dirk had declared he needed to go to the store for fresh flowers. Camille had gone with him. That had been the last time

Lacy had seen them. She'd received a call to pack everything and get out.

It had taken her four minutes.

A blue Sedan took her to a hotel that night, and they'd taken a crying Soleil from her this morning. Lacy had then been ordered to return to D.C. and lie low until further notice.

So here she was. Home.

Lacy kicked the door shut and walked to the kitchen, sniffing the air and wrinkling her nose. She put her bags on the counter and opened her cupboard for her scented candles. First things first, she thought, get rid of this musty smell.

She placed vanilla scented candles on the small island that divided the kitchen from her living space. Another in her bedroom and a third on the windowsill in her bathroom.

She still ached and put her bruising down to falling off the bed in the middle of the night and not remembering.

Lacy had a quick shower, put on her comfy clothes and went about preparing a light dinner. Salmon on toast. She was just settling in and going online to look up Camille and Dirk when there was a knock at the door. Lacy checked the new phone she had been given by her employers on the side this morning, but there weren't any messages.

She decided she would not answer. She was on vacation, after all. A real vacation.

Then the banging started.

Lacy reached for the gun she kept taped to the underside of the table. Who the hell...?

"Lacy! Open the door!" A voice yelled.

Lacy rushed to the door, not believing what she was hearing and yanked it open.

Matthew Edwards stormed across the threshold before she could stop him.

"What the hell are you doing at my house?!" Lacy screeched, beside herself. Her work and home life did not mix. "And how the hell did you know where I live?" she never, *ever* shared her private space with her colleagues.

Lacy waited for him to answer but became aware he was busy looking her over, from the Bantu knots she'd put in her hair, over her pink cami and shorts set, down to her bare toes and back again.

Lacy watched as his large chest expanded before letting his breath out in a whoosh. "Are you all right?"

"Answer my question first Operative," she asked quietly, trying not to notice how good he looked in black jeans, black V-necked sweater with a green T-shirt underneath and black jacket. "What are you doing here?"

Matthew ignored her question only to frown darkly as she backed away from him. "Where the hell have you been!" He exploded suddenly.

Lacy lifted her gun and widened her legs. She would not sleep with Matthew Edwards ever again. That night at the lake she'd decided to clean up her life. How could she gain an ounce of normality, *date*, when she slept with him every chance she got?

"You have five seconds to answer my question, Edwards, or I'll blow your brains out."

"What the hell is wrong with you?" Matthew asked in disbelief, the lines between his eyes deepening. He'd spent the better part of two weeks searching the god-damn world for her, and she turns up looking hot and sexy as hell, but looking at him as though he was pond scum!

He was enraged and without thought, stepped forward and pulled the weapon she still had insultingly trained on him from her hands and tucked it into the waistband of his jeans.

"Hey!" Lacy yelled about to tackle him for it, but he put his hand up.

"Don't," he warned.

Now that he was here and seeing her for himself, the last dredges of energy he'd been running on rapidly dried up. He was exhausted and hungry for her.

Matthew grabbed her waist and yanked until she was plastered against him. When she opened her mouth to protest, he shoved his tongue inside, intending to take over her mind.

This was her punishment for not greeting him how he'd envisioned. Kissing him at the door. All smiles and shit, not all angry and holding a gun. A gun for Christ's sake!

Lacy pushed at his shoulders and stepped away from him, wiping her mouth with the back of her hand as she glared at him. This was her home!

"Who do you think you are coming to my apartment and pawing me like that? I've not seen you since Chicago, and you think I'm going to have sex with you in my *home*! Are you out of your mind?"

Matthew looked at her sharply, his eyes green and intent. "You saw me two weeks ago,"

Lacy tipped her head back to laugh. "I know time flies when you're having fun, Matthew," she rolled her eyes. "You're good, but not that good." She sneered.

Matthew stepped closer, his head canted to the side and after a moment asked. "When was the last time you saw me, Lacy?"

"Don't worry, operative, the sex we had was memorable on that roof, but I'm not about–"

Matthew gritted his teeth. "Shut the hell up Wallace and answer my question,"

"Or what?" she challenged, tipping her head back.

He stepped into her space and grabbed her naked shoulders. "Or I'll remind you just how much you like me inside you."

"Dream on big–"

Matthew ran out of patience and shook her. "When?!"

Lacy grimaced as pain shot across her ribs.

"You're hurt?" Matthew immediately let her go to bend at the knees and look into her eyes. When she avoided his gaze, he ran his hands gently but firmly over her shoulders and down her smooth arms.

"Hey, what are you doing?!" she screeched, swatting at his hands.

Matthew stepped back to look at the rest of her body, staring intently as though he could see beneath her skin. He noticed the faint smudge of a bruise on her shoulder and felt a pang of regret chase through him. He reached over to trace it, but Lacy took a step away from him.

"You must have hurt yourself in the accident," Matthew revealed grimly.

She swung around to him. "What accident?"

"The same one I got this," he lifted his broken arm, covered in a navy coloured cast.

"I wasn't in an accident."

Something was very wrong here, and Matthew knew to first defuse the animosity.

"Can I get a glass of water?" He asked. "Please?"

She looked at him first, as though not trusting him in her space which pissed him off, but he looked away, not wanting her to see his face.

"Sure,"

When she walked away, Matthew looked at her. She was favouring her left side. She looked the same, her legs, long and smooth in the tiny pink satin shorts with lace trim. She wore a matching top with narrow straps and no bra. Not so long ago, he would never have guessed she was so feminine.

She returned with his water, and he deliberately drank half down and went to sit on her sofa.

She followed suit, across from him.

"Two weeks ago, you spent the better part of four days with me,"

"Why?"

"We agreed to give this thing we have a chance,"

Lacy blinked twice as she looked at him, and he could see her trying to remember.

"And?"

Good, she was curious.

"We'd spent days in bed," he smirked at her gasp. "And went for a drive, visiting my family," he added swiftly. "And before I knew it, my car was rammed, we were in a gunfight, we crashed, and you were kidnapped."

"Kidnapped? By who?" Lacy asked, although storing away his

reference to visiting his family. That just wasn't done. What did it mean?

"I don't know."

"This is ridiculous. I'd remember being shot at and kidnapped, Matthew."

"I know," he confirmed. "What is the last thing you remember?"

Lacy thought about Soleil up at the lake. The quiet little girl with huge dark eyes filled with sorrow. She remembered her tears just this morning and how bereft she felt, having to let her go and before that there was Mikhail, the boy from Russia.

Lacy looked at Matthew, who was watching her intently. She wasn't about to tell him any of that.

"Well, I don't remember spending any time with you," she stated. "I wouldn't do that to myself."

"Is that right?"

"A two, maybe three-minute romp is all I want from you."

"Is that a fact?"

"Yes, sex is all we have," she looked at him then. "Besides, how do I know you're not making all this up to get into my pants?" she asked.

His eyes flashed bright gold and Lacy could see him gritting his teeth. Even as angry as he was, she was becoming increasingly turned on. A dancing wave of delicious tingles spread from her nipples straight to her core, and she tightened her muscles to intensify the sensation.

Matthew stood and walked casually over to her. "We both know all I need to do is this," he snapped his fingers in the air. "And you'll come running."

Lacy laughed, drawing up her legs to tuck them beneath her. She desperately wanted to touch herself.

"That was then," she conceded, wanting to turn him off. He wasn't hiding the heavy ridge of his arousal pressing against the snaps on his jeans as he stood in front of her. Too close. "I have a boyfriend."

Matthew laughed, he couldn't help himself, seeing her

looking as she was, her chin tilted in defiance. The situation was serious, he had things to say, and she had things to tell him, but first, all he could focus on was the way her pretty nipples pointed through her top, taunting him and the way she was fidgeting in her seat. Boyfriend? He huffed; she was going to be sorry she even said the word out loud.

Matthew dropped to his knees in front of her, grabbed her folded legs, shouldered them apart, scooped her bottom to the edge of the chair and placed her legs over his shoulders before burying his head between her legs, within seconds of her angry gasp.

The scent of her arousal was unsurprising, and he breathed her in, missing her all over again.

He moved her shorts to one side and pressed his lips against the small button he knew he could control her with.

Lacy closed her eyes as Matthew kissed and licked her sex. This wasn't right, she'd gone back to a habit of a lifetime, she scolded herself but as she rode a gentle wave of pleasure. Whenever Matthew Edwards was around, she forgot herself.

His tongue fluttered against her and her back lifted against his mouth as another wave rolled through her again.

He reached up with both hands to cup and knead her breasts, skimming his open palms across her nipples, before pinching and rolling them between his fingers.

She gasped and, giving up the fight to remain motionless, grabbed his hair to direct him exactly where she wanted him.

Matthew sucked and licked her, setting up a sensual slow dance as her body undulated to the rhythm of him tweaking her tight nipples.

Then, with quick efficiency, he got rid of her shorts altogether, opened her legs wider and tongued her until her whole body trembled and tightened when she screamed his name. *His* name. As she came.

Matthew sat back on his haunches to watch her. He had never seen anything so beautiful as her golden skin, now flushed a pretty red colour all over. The swollen lips between her legs pulsed and glistened, her head rolled back against the frilly cushions as she rode the last of her orgasm.

Yes, Matthew thought smugly, mentally thumping his chest, he did that.

He went to the bathroom to wash his face and rinse his mouth. Then he finished the bottle of water she had given him and watched her straightened her clothes.

Now that Matthew had got *that* out of the way, that, being her stubbornness about just who she thought she was playing with. They needed to figure out what had happened to her. She had lost those days that included him, the same days that had changed their entire relationship. Something had happened. Those foreign bastards had done something.

It was time for the game playing to stop. But first, he needed to get them out of here.

"Get dressed. I have something to show you." He said when she continued to look everywhere but at him.

Her head snapped over to him. "I just got here."

"From where?"

She looked at him then, and he could see her about to lie to him again. This fucking stopped right now!

"Don't think about lying to me this time Wallace, I know you even better than you know yourself and I've just proved it," he gritted swiftly. "Something is going on, you're involved in some shit that got me shot at more than once, assaulted and threatened to stay away from you or else."

"Then why are you still here?" She dared to ask, not ready to put herself in his hands. They didn't really know each other outside of the bureau. They had sex, and that was about it.

"Don't," he growled. "You have two choices," he'd been here before, and hadn't got very far. This time the distraction of her arousal was out of the way. He'd taken care of her. "Get dressed, or you come as you are." He stated, folding his arms over his chest.

Lacy looked down at herself. She'd put her clothes to rights, but there was an embarrassing damp patch between her legs.

Matthew was right, though, something had happened to her. He had no reason to lie about being in a car crash, and she definitely felt as though her body had been tossed around, not to mention that vicious headache she'd had. She didn't trust anyone from the bureau, but she had to know what Matthew was talking about and for that she would *temporarily* put herself in his hands.

Lacy sliced him with a scathing look when she walked past him, as she was still feeling insulted by him snapping his fingers at her, and she, fool that she was, had proved him right.

CHAPTER TWELVE

Two and a half hours later, Lacy found herself standing in the middle of a luxury apartment after an uneventful flight in a private plane.

They hadn't talked much, but she had felt his eyes on her as she pretended to sleep.

Taking her coat, Matthew returned to look at her expectantly.

"Do you recognise the apartment?" he asked.

Lacy looked around, wanting to go to the windows and look out, but first things first. She didn't recognise it and shook her head.

"Who owns it?" she asked.

"My brother,"

"I didn't know you had a brother," she stated and watched as Matthew smiled to himself. "What's so funny?" She asked.

"You said that before, about my brother," his smile widened. "Then we'd argued, and had kinky make up sex on the side of the road."

"We did not!"

He laughed. "We did, but you'll have to take my word for it." He turned to the bank of computer screens in the middle of the room. "Come here." He pulled out a chair for her, then started tapping away as she sat watching.

"What are you doing?" she asked after a moment. Patience wasn't one of her strongest points.

"I want the truth, Lacy, and I want it tonight." Matthew pinned her with a look, rolled her chair to face him and pulled her close. Their knees were almost touching. He kept his hands on her armrest, caging her in. She had nowhere to look but at him.

"I've told–"

"Stop," he stated grimly. "Let's get one thing straight, I hate liars," he stated. "But I care about you and don't want to see you hurt. Tell me the truth, Lacy."

He cared about her, Lacy wasn't sure if she wanted to perform cartwheels or run for the hills. But he was an operative.

"I'll help you along," he encouraged softly. "I know you are working outside of the bureau. I know how these people made initial contact with you. I know Russians own the apartment I tracked you down to. I know you like whatever it is that you do, and I know you want out of the bureau."

At her gasp, he stopped to give her a second to digest all that he had said before continuing. "I know you have a back injury as you let me massage it for you. I know you like to take long hot baths and listen to Motown, especially Otis Redding. You make a killer Victoria Sponge, and I know you care about me too."

"I–"

He shook his head at her, leaned forward and kissed her gently on the lips. Her lovely eyes had become glassy with tears.

"You have to trust me, Lacy."

She sniffed, trying to collect herself. She didn't understand why she was so emotional.

"I won't let anything happen to you," he took her hands and folded his fingers around hers. "I need you to tell me what's going on, sweetheart."

Lacy pulled her hands away and rolled the chair back so she could stand and put some distance between them.

It was all too much. She was floundering and knew that he knew it too. How did he know all that stuff about her? Her back? She didn't talk about it, but then again, the things he said could be gleaned from anywhere, really. He was called Wonder Boy for a reason. He was a brilliant IT specialist, she knew, and did he just call her 'sweetheart'?

"You could have found all that stuff out," she pointed out.

"I could," he acknowledged with a shrug. "But I didn't. Let me show you."

He pressed a button, and all twenty-eight screens had images of Lacy, or him, but mainly of the both of them, wearing little or no clothes.

Lacy gasped and stepped closer. She saw images of herself thrown over Matthew's shoulder and standing at the same window behind her. There was a shot of the two of them eating a meal by candlelight on the floor. There were images of her with headphones on with her eyes closed, and she was smiling.

In most of the images, she looked relaxed and happy. Matthew looked relaxed and happy too.

Matthew pressed another button, and those images were replaced by one large image of them having sex in bed. Lacy, seeing herself, was entranced. Her breasts were bouncing as she moved over him, her head thrown back, Matthew's large hands on her hips, guiding her and the sheer look of pleasure on their faces.

Lacy felt heat surge into her cheeks.

"Turn it off!" She yelled.

He didn't turn it off, but he did reach over to freeze them all.

"Three days we spent here, Lacy," Matthew said calmly. "Three days, you gave your body to me. You told me you loved me."

Lacy looked at him, feeling all sorts of chaotic emotions surging within her. She had never used those words to anyone.

"I don't remember," she cried, feeling the sting of tears and stopped fighting, letting them fall.

"I know you don't." Matthew walked over to her, picked up one hand and carried it to his lips, before gathering her close and holding her. He felt the trembling of her body and made wide soothing, circular patterns on her back as she held him tight and cried into his neck.

"What happened to me?" she asked, eventually.

"Come, let's talk,"

Matthew led her over to the sofa and arranged her so that her back was against his chest and their legs entwined.

"Tell me everything."

CHAPTER THIRTEEN

Matthew took a languishing moment to watch Lacy, where she was busy whipping pancake batter in a metal bowl. Her back was to him, and she was humming to herself and wiggling her hips to the rhythm of the whisk or the tune in her head, he couldn't figure out which.

She looked as she always did in the mornings, and for them, their morning was after one in the afternoon.

They were both practically nocturnal, staying up most of the night watching movies, talking and of course making love, until the sun was almost up.

They'd eventually get up, hang out in the apartment, work out, have a lazy breakfast, and Matthew knew he had never been this settled and content in his life.

He felt himself harden, as was normal around her. If she wasn't wearing his T-shirts, she was walking around in her panties and tiny satin tops in soft colours. Like now.

"Oh! You made me jump!" Lacy exclaimed before grinning as, still mixing the batter, she stepped barefooted over to him and angled her head for a kiss.

Matthew obliged, using one hand at the back of her head to keep her in place when she would have moved away.

Matthew took his time kissing her, and played with the idea of some slow, afternoon lovemaking, but thought better of it. He'd worked her out most of the night, and she might be a little sore, he thought, not that Lacy would ever tell him.

Because it was so plump and inviting, Matthew sucked her bottom lip into his mouth and swept his tongue across it one last time before letting her go.

Her eyes fluttered open, and she smiled the kind of smile that made him feel as though he were the king of the castle.

"I have a surprise for you," he said, watching as she wobbled over to the counter. One kiss and she was wrecked. Her coordination was off, and she could barely function, he mused with pride. "Well, two." He amended.

"Oh yeah," she smiled over her shoulder, putting the bowl down to turn to him.

Matthew reached behind his back for the first surprise. "Here."

Lacy looked at her gun in his hand. She hadn't seen it in weeks and hadn't missed it. Strange how, for years not having her gun had felt as though she had a limb missing, but now the thought of it practically repulsed her.

"We really need to work on your gift-giving, Matthew," she said without humour, however taking her Glock from him. She turned it over in her hands, not liking the weight of it and the sheer ugliness of its power, before placing it on the island behind him. "What's the other surprise?" she asked reluctantly and if it was her bureau ID or badge–as she'd tossed them in a bag somewhere–she'd be really upset.

Matthew noted how the playful gleam had left her eyes. "I think it's just gone to three," he said instead and watched keenly when her shoulders relaxed. "How about a new gun? Something a lot less–" he searched for a word to describe her weapon. "A lot less gun'ish?"

She laughed. "Gun'ish?" she walked towards him and wrapped her arms loosely around his waist, to dip her fingers into her favourite place–the shallow curve at the base of his strong back. "Is that even a word?"

He angled his head for a quick kiss. "It can be ours," he answered against her lips.

"Okay," she sighed, sweeping her tongue along his bottom lip. "A new gun."

"And the third? We're going out."

She didn't look as excited as he thought she might. He'd concluded that Lacy really was a living, breathing, 'homebody'. She was happiest doing something at home, whether it be cooking, or baking or dreamily going online and perusing property websites around the world. If the decades rolled back to the 1950s, she'd fit right in.

"I was thinking about ordering some venison and trying out a new recipe," she informed him sulkily.

"Another day," he dipped his head for another kiss. "You'll like this surprise, I promise."

"Promise?"

His smile was indulgent. "Hmm-mm,"

"What should I wear?"

Matthew palmed the surprising fullness of her ass. He loved how each globe overflowed in his hands. He used to be a breast man, now all he wanted to do was palm Lacy's fine ass. He nudged her up and Lacy, knowing what he wanted, jumped into his arms to wrap her legs around his waist.

"What about our pancakes?" she asked, even though her tongue was already swirling around in his ear.

"Later," Matthew growled, walking rapidly to their bedroom.

Lacy chuckled. "What about my surprise?" she whispered, deliberately nibbling his earlobe. She knew it drove him crazy when she did that and smiled when he stumbled, so she did it again.

Laying her quickly on the bed, Matthew's head went straight between her legs, pulled her panties aside with his teeth and then, using the tip of his tongue, teased her along her already deliciously wet folds.

***

Much later, Lacy found herself bundled up in a thick coat, jeans and boots, with Matthew dressed similarly.

Leaving the apartment after having cereal, because the pancake batter had turned too thick, they went gun shopping, and Lacy spent just five minutes choosing a gun, that if any of her operative colleagues saw, would laugh themselves silly.

She chose a silver .22 pistol with a pink Mother of Pearl handle.

Matthew had been horrified.

Now they were walking around a tropical paradise with their coats thrown over their arms, right there in New York, with the winter sun baking the heavy planes of glass in the conservatory.

A butterfly sanctuary.

It was a stunning place, filled with leafy foliage replicating the tropics perfectly.

Paradise, Lacy thought, holding her hand out as a brownish-grey butterfly with spots that looked like owl eyes fluttered close, but didn't land.

She watched as it brushed close to Matthew, and when he put his hand out, it settled.

"Typical," she said with amusement.

"What can I say?" he chuckled, as they both peered at the delicate wings before it flew away.

They spent a lovely afternoon at the sanctuary, exploring the different domes, walking hand in hand through the meadow of long grasses, protected from the winter elements by glass windows and ceilings, before having an early dinner of burgers and fries.

They took a taxi back and when Lacy saw Matthew look behind him a second time, she nudged him in enquiry. "What is it?"

"See that car over there?" he pointed to a shiny Sedan, being driven by a white man with a bald head.

"Yes."

"It's been following us all day."

"That's Ulvis," Lacy said with a shrug, after waving to the man.

Matthew turned to her as though she had sprouted wings. "Ulvis?" he sputtered.

"Yep," she replied lightly. "He's my contact."

"You *knew* he was following us?"

"Yep," Lacy answered and watched as his eyes flashed bright gold. She knew he was getting mad even before he lashed her with his tongue with his next words.

"We're being followed, and you didn't think to warn me?" his words bounced around in the confines of the taxi. "They might want to hurt you! Kidnap you again!" Matthew yelled.

Lacy, aware the driver could hear, turned to Matthew and used sign language to answer him instead.

"If they wanted to hurt me, they would have done so weeks ago," she signed. "Remember I don't work for them anymore?" she reminded him lightly. The night they'd returned to New York, Matthew had insisted she contact them, via text, and say she was no longer available to them. They'd replied that they'd respected her wishes.

"Are you out of your mind?" he signed rapidly. "They took you from me. Drugged you. You lost all memory of me!"

Lacy touched his face and smiled gently, hoping to calm him. They hadn't talked about their feelings towards each other, but the blinding panic in Matthew's eyes told her more than he'd ever said with his body.

"It's okay, they won't hurt me."

"How do you know?"

"Because they've had ample opportunity."

"Then what the hell do they want? Why have they got–?" he looked at the car behind them, seeing the huge man staring back at him. "Why have they got *The Tree*, following us?"

Lacy giggled at Matthew's description of Ulvis, he was a big man and the description fit. She shrugged. "I really don't know."

Matthew was beside himself. He wanted to get out and haul, Ulvis, Elvis or whatever the hell his name was, out of that car and ask all the questions that Lacy was dreamily ignoring. What the hell had happened to her instincts? Her training? She was taking this as though it was normal when it was fucked up.

"I'll take care of it," Matthew gritted out loud. "Of him."

Lacy shrugged again, tucked her arm around his and snuggled close.

"Okay."

***

When they got to the apartment, Matthew physically put her old gun in her hand and lectured her on her safety. Then he showed her where the panic room was, where Ace's weapons were hidden around the apartment and made a plan for if she ever got into trouble.

He was mad that Lacy wasn't taking this seriously. He was mad at himself for indulging her *Ivory Tower* tendencies, but enough was enough. She was a trained operative. She had an IQ above his–although he had never divulged that. She was being used by a group of confused Russians, confused because they shot at them, manhandled him, told him to leave her alone or else, yet had left them alone until now. He was going to sort this shit out.

CHAPTER FOURTEEN

Matthew's blood was boiling and surging through his veins like hot lava. He'd just received intel from Rhodes, and he still couldn't believe it. He was only glad Lacy wasn't with him right now as he would likely wring her damn neck!

She was down on the fifth floor, no doubt running up his credit card at the residents shopping mall. Not even an hour ago, he'd gladly handed it over, telling her to treat herself. Go to the spa or something while he got lunch sorted. He'd planned to make mustard and rosemary pork chops with mashed potato on the side. She'd already made a batch of double chocolate chip brownies for dessert. Then he'd got the call. He still couldn't believe it.

Bitch. That bitch.

Matthew scrubbed his hands over his face, and when he heard the ping of the expected email, he reluctantly walked over to his computer and opened it. He'd wanted proof, and here it was. Damn it!

What he saw obliterated everything he'd ever thought of her. Wiped it clean. Snuffed it out and whatever fucking analogy he could use in the face of her lies. She'd taken him for a damn fool. Somewhere between enjoying her smiles and her kisses, he'd forgotten she was Special Ops, top five in her class, Special Ops for Life, first and foremost.

He shut the video down ten seconds in, unable to watch any more.

She'd lied to him, again. He thought she'd told him everything. They'd started afresh the night he'd brought her back from D.C. all those weeks ago.

After her tears and talking about the children, he'd picked her up and carried her to bed, where he'd made gentle love to her. He'd been making fresh memories for them ever since.

The night of the butterfly sanctuary, he'd made Lacy call them, but they didn't answer. She'd sent a text message telling them to call off Ulvis. They'd replied with a simple okay. But Matthew knew there was never a simple 'okay' in their world. So without Lacy's knowledge, he'd put a tracker in her bag and in a pair of earrings he had given her last night, just in case.

They went for long walks, and it felt natural to hold her hand. He took her to the movies. They went running every evening and did everything together, without being followed.

What she'd done for the Russians wasn't as bad as he'd imagined. Yes, she called it international babysitting and he and Rhodes were checking it out–but hadn't come up with anything–but it could have been worse. In a way, it suited her if you took out the foreign element that is. But honestly, she wasn't made for any of this shit, or so he thought. But seeing what he had just seen made him question all that he knew about her. How had he got it so wrong?

Lacy came home an hour later, all smiley and shit and she walked over to him where he was sprawled on the sofa. She was wearing a deep red dress that hugged her curves lovingly and flirted above her knees. She was even wearing black heels, and Matthew bit his tongue to distract himself from reaching for her. She looked sexy as hell. Bitch.

She'd had her hair done, he noticed, seeing the absence of curls as it swung around her shoulders in a glossy, lightly scented curtain that brushed his face when she leaned down to kiss him.

"What's the matter?" Lacy asked, frowning when her lips landed on his cheek, and he moved away so violently she had to step back.

The look he sent her way chilled her to the bone. His eyes were dead. The swirling colours flat and muted like paste.

Lacy dropped her bags by the chair and reached for him, but he moved away, deliberately shifting his arm to walk to his computers instead.

"Is there anything you want to tell me?" he asked quietly,

giving her one last chance to tell him the truth.

"Like what?" She shook her head, puzzled. "No."

"You sure?" He asked again lightly.

Lacy stepped cautiously away from him. "Matthew, you're scaring me. What is it?"

He turned his back and fiddled with something.

"Come here, Lacy." He ordered.

Lacy stayed where she was. This past six weeks had been the best she had ever spent in her life. She had fallen in love with him, and she knew, she just knew, if she went over there, her life was going to change.

"Come here!" he shouted, flexing his hands as though trying to stop himself from throwing or smashing something.

Lacy jumped. "I don't–"

Matthew stormed over to her, grabbed her wrist and pulled her with him. He stabbed a key and stepped back to let the video play.

It was only twenty-nine seconds long, but what was there killed him.

He looked at Lacy, but only because he had to.

"What were you doing?" he asked quietly.

"I don't know what that is,"

"Don't fucking lie to me!" he charged. "What the fuck were you doing on that roof?"

She pushed away from him.

"I don't know!" she yelled. "That's not me!" she charged.

He laughed in her face.

"There's no denying it's you Lacy!"

"It's not me, I don't remember doing anything like that!"

"How convenient," he sneered.

"It's true!" she cried. "I don't remember. When was it taken?"

"Don't try it," he warned. "You aren't who I thought you are!"

"It's not me!" she cried, scrubbing at the tears that now fell. "Matthew?" She implored with her arms out wide, begging him to listen to her.

"What happened to justice?"

"I didn't do it!"

"There's footage of you on a fucking roof! Don't lie to me!"

"I'm not lying! I've never lied to you!"

"Were you," he gritted. "Or were you not staying with Camille and her friend Dirk?" he asked quietly.

The night they had talked, and he thought she had come clean, she'd told him about going to the lake and meeting Camille and Dirk. They'd watched the movies of the famed actress again because she didn't remember or *claimed* not to remember watching them the first time around. Lacy had been giddy with excitement, knowing she was friends with the famed actress. The same actress who was involved with his cousin. It was all a lie. All a damned lie!

The silence hung. To confirm or deny would be to break a promise to her friends and Lacy couldn't do that.

Maybe Matthew saw something in her eyes because his next words blew her away.

"Get the fuck out."

Lacy gasped. "Matthew?"

"What? I'm not speaking Russian." He sneered at her.

"Huh?" she said in confusion. What did speaking Russian have to do with anything?

Matthew turned and strode to the windows, his back stiff with rejection. "Get out Lacy."

Lacy looked at him in disbelief. What was he saying? Didn't what they have mean anything to him? He knew her. He claimed that he knew her better than she knew herself, yet he could still think she could do something like that. Where did that leave them? Her? With her head held high, Lacy walked out of the apartment with only the clothes on her back. He didn't have to say it a third time.

Out on the street, Lacy looked around, feeling numb. People were going about their business, walking around her as though she were a vacant space suspended from the ground.

It wasn't that cold, but she felt the wind lift her hair and whip it across her face. She wished it hurt. Anything to feel again.

Lacy couldn't believe what had just happened, and she scrubbed at the tears that continued to fall.

She began to walk, vowing to never leave herself open to this kind of hurt again. Never would she open up her heart and let a man close. She would go back to how she was. She was an operative before she was a person, she scolded herself, trying to gather her courage. She was a survivor. She was trained to survive anything, being lost in the Amazon or nursing a broken heart, she would get through this. She would survive, but first, she needed to–The obnoxious blast of a car horn drew her attention, and she looked over her shoulder.

A car rolled gently beside her. The passenger window slid down.

She hadn't heard from her other employers, and Matthew had said he would deal with it. And she, fool that she was, had left him to it, happy to let the 'man' take over. She was a stupid, head-in-the-clouds, kind of fool. Living in his apartment like they were some sort of couple. One argument and she's out on the street. Never would she leave herself so vulnerable again. Never—

"Miss Dawson?" An accented voice called out.

Lacy looked inside the car, recognising her one link. Ulvis.

She walked over and bent to speak to him.

The last time she had seen him, he'd picked Soleil up from the hotel and told Lacy to go home to D.C.

"You are sad, yes?" he asked, to confirm his suspicions. He had been given strict orders; ensure Miss Dawson was safe and to take out any person, or remove her from any situation, whichever came first if he thought it necessary. She was crying.

"You could say that," she sniffed and wiped her nose with the back of her hand.

Ulvis reached into his pocket and gave her a folded handkerchief. It was ridiculous, as it was heart-warming to see this six-foot giant, with a white cotton handkerchief, shaved head and gentle smile.

"I have news," he said after she blew her nose.

She sniffed. "Oh yeah,"

"Mikhail,"

"Mikhail?" That got her attention, and she felt the blood drain from her face. "Oh God, is he okay? Has anything happened to him?" All her 'kids', as she called them, held a special place in her heart, but there was something about the serious little boy who liked camping.

"I give you good news, yes?"

"What?"

"His family, they want to meet you,"

"I thought he didn't have a family,"

"He has family. They want to meet. You come, yes?"

Lacy hadn't been on that roof, for that she was almost sure. Almost, because she'd already been drugged, not by Ulvis, he didn't have it in him, but by his people. To go with him would be a risk, but something was going on and to clear her name, she needed to speak to someone higher up on the chain of command.

Lacy looked behind her. She had walked quite far and could see the fancy building that had been her slice of heaven in the distance. Slice of heaven, she sniffed again and wiped her eyes. She needed to plan, but right now she would go and meet Mikhail's family, forget Matthew Edwards ever existed, try to find out what's going on and not live her life as though she was a normal person. She was a government operative. She needed to start acting like one and take charge of her life again. That meant no working on the outside, no playing house and definitely no Matthew Edwards.

Ulvis leaned over and opened the passenger door.

Lacy got in.

CHAPTER FIFTEEN

Matthew almost tripped on Lacy's bags as he went to answer the door.

She must have left her key, he thought, striding through the first set of doors to the main entrance.

He was still mad but had calmed down enough to at least listen to what she had to say. They'd figure it out, he reasoned, knowing he had completely lost it and shut her down. Very few people actually knew how nasty his temper got, and regretfully Lacy had learnt it to her peril today, but he was sorry and would say as much.

He'd finished cooking their lunch and was just waiting for her to calm down and come home.

Pulling the door open with his apology and smile at the ready, Matthew was surprised to see his twelve-year-old niece Heather standing in front of him instead.

"Hi, Uncle Matthew,"

"Hey what's up Beetroot."

She giggled like he knew she would at the nickname he'd given her. He was her favourite uncle, and she'd made him pinky swear not to tell anyone. Heather and her mother, Sabrina, had recently come into their lives, because Sabrina had raised her daughter on her own in Derbyshire, England. His brother, Ace, hadn't known of Heather's existence until bumping into Sabrina when she'd been doing a book signing in New York last year. Like him, Heather was also deaf.

"Mum and Daddy are coming with the baby." She said, looking over her shoulder just as her parents stepped from the elevator with baby Ace in a carrier. The baby's name was Abigail Charlene Edwards, the same initials as her father's real name, Alister Charles Edwards, hence them both sharing the nickname, Ace.

"Hey, what's all this?" Matthew asked. He loved his family, he really did, but he didn't want to see them right now. He needed to sort shit out with Lacy first before welcoming visitors. Never mind it was their house.

Lacy had been gone twenty-one minutes now, and something must have been written on his face because Ace smirked and gave him the finger as he trailed behind his wife and daughter.

"Didn't I tell you not to mess with my place?" Ace charged as soon as Matthew closed the door.

Ace was standing with his hands on his hips, looking at the bank of screens and table full of computer paraphernalia that spilt onto the floor.

Sabrina giggled, went over and kissed Matthew's cheek. "Leave him alone Ace, he has to keep the world to rights from somewhere, even if he is on holiday."

"Yeah, Ace," Matthew smiled over her head. "I have to keep the world to rights." He echoed his sister-in-law, giving her a hug and then bending to take the carrier from her. "Thank God she takes after you, Sabrina." He teased, peering at the baby with her warm skin tone, reddish curls and cute button nose.

"Fu-ahem," Ace coughed to cover his almost blunder. "Give me back my daughter." Ace grabbed the baby carrier and looked around with displeasure, shaking his head at the hi-tech mess. "Where's Lacy?" he asked.

Matthew shrugged and felt a tide of heat hit his neck and surge up his face.

Naturally, his brother noticed. "What did you do?"

"Nothing."

"Like hell. What the fu–"

"Ace," Sabrina said, sending a warning look in their daughter's direction. There was a swear jar in everyone's house with Ace's name on it.

"Heather, honey, let's see if the baby needs changing," Sabrina ushered briskly, knowing the brothers needed to talk.

Heather sniffed the air. "She doesn't."

"Let's go see anyway,"

"Why?" Heather replied mulishly, looking down at her iPad. "She doesn't."

Matthew tried to hide his smile, Heather was just like her dad in temperament; hyper and stubborn as hell.

Sabrina took the baby carrier from her husband and grabbed the baby bag. "Let's go," she ordered, nodding towards the bedrooms. "Now!"

Heather dragged her feet as she followed her mother.

"Don't say it," Ace warned before Matthew could say anything.

Matthew looked at him, wide-eyed, but his lips were twitching. "What?"

"Nothing." Ace changed tack. "You were saying? Lacy?"

Matthew scrubbed his hands over his hair, down his face then looked at his watch. She'd been gone twenty-eight minutes. "We had an argument."

Ace waited with his hands on his hips again, knowing Matthew liked to roll over his words in his head before they came out of his mouth. It was frigging annoying sometimes, and when the seconds dragged, Ace tapped the face of his watch.

"I told her none too gently to leave," Matthew admitted, feeling all kinds of stupid.

Ace felt as though his eyes were about to pop out of his head. "Leave?"

"Yeah,"

"What did she do?" Ace asked in wonder. As far as he knew, things were going good for his brother. "If she has another man, I won't fucking believe it. That woman sees you and only you. The only other person who looks at you with hearts in their eyes is, well," Ace tapped his chin with his index finger. "No-one."

"Screw you Ace," Matthew warned. It was raining outside, he finally noticed. "Did you see her in the lobby or something?" He asked, remembering she didn't have her coat.

"No, what happened?"

Matthew took a deep breath and walked over to the computers.

"Look," he started the video for his brother and turned away.

Ace watched, startled, rewound it, watched and paused it, to peer at it, before letting it play to the end again.

"Have you seen it?"

"Of course, I have dip-shit."

"So?"

"What?"

"What did she say?"

"What is there to say? The evidence is right there. She's been working outside of the bureau, running around with Russian mobsters. They're killers!"

"Daddy?"

Both men turned to Heather.

"What's up babes?" Ace asked.

"Mummy said sorry to bother you, but she thinks the baby has a temperature and if you can come and check too please."

"I'm coming. Keep your uncle company." Ace quickly strode out of the room.

"Hey, Uncle Matthew," Heather said.

"Hey,"

"Did you go shopping?" she asked.

Matthew looked over at the pile of bags Lacy had left. She'd been gone thirty-three minutes now.

"Not me, Lacy."

"Can I call her Aunty Lacy yet?"

Matthew looked at her puzzled. "What do you mean?"

"Daddy says I should only call the people we accept into the family aunty or uncle. It's about respect, he said. I don't have to respect everyone just because they're older 'cuz not every older person respects us kids." She advised before continuing.

"Lacy is nice, her cakes are yummy, and I heard Daddy tell Mum she's the best thing to ever happen to you and that you'll make really cute babies." She beamed over at her uncle before walking to the bags and sitting on the floor. "Can I call her aunty?"

Matthew was completely thrown by everything Heather had

said.

"Uncle Matthew?" she waved her fingers to get his attention. "Can I?"

Babies? Yeah, he could easily see Lacy swollen with his kid. "What?"

"Can I call her aunty yet and look in the bags?"

"Sure," Matthew replied, slightly dazed. "Whatever you want, Beetroot."

Matthew went to the table and deleted the video. He didn't want to see it ever again. He needed to get rid of everything that could get her arrested.

He heard rustling behind him and Heather ooh'ing and ahh'ing. It was hard not to turn around and see what Lacy had bought. He knew it should have been a special moment for the two of them, but they could have it later, he assured himself.

"Erm Uncle Matthew?" Heather called out. "You know you're my favourite uncle, right?"

Matthew smiled, he and Heather had made a secret pact. She was his favourite, and he was hers. "Yeah,"

"Well, I think you're gonna want to see this."

He rolled his chair backwards and turned slightly to look over his shoulder. His niece had a pile of clothes beside her and was wearing a pink satin teddy–Lacy had obviously bought for later to tantalise him with–over her jeans and red hoodie. But what really caught his attention was what she was holding in her hand.

"What you got there, babes?" Matthew asked tentatively. Heather was never at a loss for words, but instead of saying anything, she dipped her head and held the box higher, almost like a sacrifice.

"Remember what I said about? Erm, look?" She said quietly instead, looking at the floor.

Matthew felt a pang of something he couldn't name shoot through him.

He strode over to his niece, feeling as though he was having an out-of-body experience. Everything slowed down, even his steps. He reached for the box.

Prenatal vitamins!

What the hell?

***

Matthew went straight to his computers and hacked into the security feed to the building. He expertly navigated to the fifth floor with the shopping mall and looked inside the boutiques and restaurant. Then he went to the gym. No Lacy. With a gathering sense of doom and panic, he moved to the lobby and watched people come and go, but she wasn't sitting in the leafy section with the plush-chairs, where he'd originally thought she was.

Then with a few clicks of his fingers, he did what he should have done in the first place and tracked her from the apartment into the lift.

There she was with her head bent low, her shoulders hunched into her chest. Matthew felt the muscles tense in his stomach, seeing her tears.

He felt Ace stand beside him as he pulled up the images of every floor. He heard Sabrina and Heather talking in one of the bedrooms.

Lacy got out at street level, wiping her eyes with her fingers, but the tears still flowed. Then she went outside and stopped for a moment as though contemplating where to go. When she turned to her left, Matthew could track her for a few seconds and then hacked into the traffic cams.

From the lights at the intersection, he saw her walk away from the building. It was raining, but she walked on, the shoulders of her dress turning darker from the raindrops.

She stopped again, and Matthew watched her look over her shoulder. A car pulled up beside her and slowed. He felt sick, watching as the window slid down. He couldn't see inside the car, but he could guess who was inside.

**

The night of the butterfly sanctuary, he'd slipped out when Lacy had been in the bath and went downstairs. It hadn't taken him long to find The Tree, Ulvis. The man had been leaning against a wall smoking a cigarette and seemed unsurprised to see him.

"Why the fuck are you people still around?" he'd yelled, getting in the man's face. "Why are you following us?"

The man drew one last time on his cigarette, flicked it to the ground beside Matthew's feet before answering.

He took his time.

"I have my orders," he'd said.

"From who?"

He'd smirked.

Matthew had grabbed his shirt and pushed him into the wall behind him.

"One day, you will see. But for now my friend, you take your hands off me, yes?" He'd said looking down at Matthew's fist filled with his shirt.

"You hurt her, and I'll hunt you down." Matthew had warned, before turning away.

There was a laugh behind him, and he'd heard the other man say. "Peel my skin off, yes?"

The foreign bastard was letting him know he was the one to gun butt him in the garage all those weeks ago.

**

Lacy walked to the car.

"Don't do it, sweetheart," Matthew whispered, feeling a mist of darkness penetrate his mind. "Don't do it."

He felt Ace's arm go around his shoulders.

Lacy wiped her eyes and blew her nose as she talked to the driver. Then she did something strange, and Matthew was very much aware of the significance of it. She stood up straight and looked towards the building. He felt as though she were looking right at him.

Matthew zoomed in closer, seeing her red eyes and tear tracks on her beautiful face. Then she took a deep breath and right before his eyes, he knew she had pulled herself together and made a decision.

He had lost her in more ways than one in that moment.

She got in the car.

"Damn it!" he yelled, slamming his fist down on the table.

"What do we do?" Ace asked quietly, beside his brother.

Matthew didn't answer right away; instead, he pulled a keyboard closer and began to type rapidly. Several of the screens changed to multiple streets. "Keep track of that car."

Ace watched the car drive along, while Matthew continued to type, pull up data and do other stuff. After a few minutes, Ace realised where the vehicle might be heading.

"I think they might be going to a private airport."

Matthew stopped what he was doing, his fingers suspended over the keys as he looked at the screen with the car speeding along.

"Shit, if she gets on a plane..." Matthew said out loud.

He started typing again, "Tell me where they are," he ordered, after a moment. He knew they wouldn't be able to track them for much longer. Once they hit the highway...

"I've lost them," Ace said, peering at the screens. One minute it was driving behind an eighteen-wheeler, the next, gone.

CHAPTER SIXTEEN

The newness of leather tickled her nose, and Lacy sniffed loudly as she settled into her seat, and wiped the last of her tears away.

The heavens opened, sending down sheets of rain loud enough to drown out her thoughts.

"Thanks for the handkerchief Ulvis," she said, as he pushed his way into the line of traffic.

He glanced at her but remained silent.

She was all sorts of foolish, she berated herself, feeling the tears behind her eyes again and willing them away. Enough. No more tears.

With a deep breath, she opened her eyes and looked out unseeingly as bits of the city was revealed by each swish of the window-screen wipers.

"Where are we going?"

"Not far," Ulvis advised, before changing lanes and accelerating. He drove faster than he usually did and pressed the brake hard, making them jerk to sudden unnecessary stops. She frowned over at him, but he looked to be enjoying himself. Normally he was a relaxed driver, and she could close her eyes and unwind. Not today.

"Ulvis?" she began cautiously as he drove along. They had come a long way in their relationship since the lake, he was less formal and even cracked a smile, and she really didn't want him to go back to the uncommunicative grunts that he used to do. But she needed to ask him about what she had seen on that video.

She took a deep breath before starting again. "Ulvis, we're friends, right, and this stays here," she began cautiously. "Did they drug me to make me forget Matthew?"

"I cannot say,"

"Can't or won't?"

He stared silently ahead.

"Who can tell me?"

Silence.

"Okay, tell me this," she turned in her seat. "Will I get answers, and what's the name of your boss?" Now was the perfect time for her to learn more about the organisation.

"I do not like to talk when I drive, Miss Dawson,"

She chuckled. "Oh, come on now," she teased. "It'll stay between us. What's the name of the head honcho?"

"I do not understand this saying,"

"Your boss. The person you report to. What's their name?"

"We have many above us,"

Lacy sighed. This was going to be hard. "Your immediate superior then. Male or female?"

"Female,"

"Older or younger than me?"

He glanced at her quickly before looking ahead with his jaw jutting out.

"You must wait, Miss Dawson," he advised. "You will see for yourself."

"Did you drug me?" she repeated.

"No,"

"Do you know who did?"

Silence.

"When I was drugged, did they make me do things?" She thought about the video, seeing herself on that roof wearing unfamiliar clothes and shooting into the street below with a semi-automatic rifle. Not her weapon of choice. From the angle of the video she couldn't see who or what she had been shooting at, but there had been screams. "Things I–" She was a trained operative, trained to kill, but had never needed to. She took a quick breath and blurted it out. "Did I kill someone?"

He remained silent.

Lacy sighed and changed tactics, not liking what his silence could mean. Something twisted in her gut, making her nauseous.

"Why do Mikhail's family want to meet me?" she asked, concentrating on the swish-swish of the wipers. "What did I do that was so special?"

Ulvis shrugged his huge shoulders. In all the weeks she had known him, she had never seen him shrug his shoulders or wave his hands around so much.

"Then how do you know they want to meet me?" She pressed.

"Orders."

"And if I didn't want to come?" Lacy asked. It did seem very convenient for him to be casually driving along as he was.

He shrugged.

Lacy lapsed into silence, aware she wasn't going to get much else from him. They drove on, the rhythm of the elements the only sound until Lacy couldn't take it much longer.

"How's the cold?" Lacy asked if only to stop herself from drifting into thoughts of Matthew. She missed him already. Now, how contrary was that? She scolded herself.

"The cold?" Ulvis repeated.

Lacy looked at him frowning. "Remember you were sneezing up at the lake and being all brave about it when you were obviously suffering."

"Yes yes," he took one hand off the steering wheel and waved it around dismissively. "It was nothing."

"Nothing!" she exclaimed sharply. He'd all but collapsed at her feet, and she'd made him lie down. "You were burning up!"

Silence.

"Did you enjoy the cake?" she asked instead, watching him from under her lashes.

"Yes,"

"All that jam?"

"Yes, yes, nice," he nodded. "Strawberry jam." He added, flashing his hands again.

He was so rude, Lacy thought, going over their conversation in her head.

Reading a sign, she finally noticed they could be heading out of State.

"Where did you say we were going?" She asked, forcing a light note into her voice.

Silence.

Something was off. So off, the car stank with it.

Lacy eased closer to her door and slowly tried the handle. It was locked.

She looked ahead. There were two sets of traffic lights she could see swinging up above. The closest was glowing red, and the other just went from amber to green. She slowly slipped her seatbelt buckle off but held it in place. Mentally counting down, Lacy yawned widely and catching Ulvis's look, relaxed into her seat. Approaching the traffic light, Lacy lunged at him and with all her strength, used her elbow and rammed it into his throat.

"Oomph!" he grunted quickly, clutching his throat with one hand as he fought to keep control of the vehicle, before trying to grab her with the other.

Lacy scrambled away from him, pressing all the buttons she could reach to get the doors and windows open.

Ulvis grabbed the front of her neck and lifted her from her seat, choking her as he did so. He was so strong.

She scratched at him, going for his eyes, but he pressed harder, cutting off her oxygen and stars danced across her eyes.

"Stotelė!" he yelled. "Stop!"

For endless seconds he held her aloft, his eyes boring into hers and Lacy was very much aware of the coldness in their depths. He'd never looked at her like this. This was the stare of a true killer.

Lacy pulled down with both hands, trying to dislodge his hold, but he was so strong, and she was becoming more and more light-headed. His large hand practically went around her neck, his thumb crushing her windpipe. He squeezed and squeezed.

"Okay, Ulvis!" she croaked, putting her hands up and spreading her fingers in defeat. "Okay."

He'd gone into another place. A distant place that allowed

him to detach himself from what he'd been doing. Ulvis was a killer.

Bright green light bathed the inside of the vehicle, and to a chorus of impatient car horns blaring behind them, Ulvis let her go, bore his eyes into hers in warning, before calmly turning in his seat to drive.

Lacy gulped in some much-needed air. Her throat was burning, and her eyes were streaming. He would have choked her to death, Lacy was sure, knowing she had to get away from him.

She waited for him to be midway into the intersection and dove into the back seat, kicking out at him, when he made to grab her bare legs.

He said something guttural in his language when her foot viciously connected with his face.

With the car swerving violently and car horns blaring from all directions, Lacy kicked out at him while stretching across the back seat. She had to get out because she knew he was going to kill her.

Bracing herself against the seat, Lacy hiked up her dress and positioned herself to land a blow. She kicked him in the neck just as he turned to grab her. Blood spurted from the wound from the stiletto, and he grabbed at it, blood pouring through his fingers as the vehicle-mounted the sidewalk and crashed into something metal. They were both thrown forward.

Lacy's breath whooshed out of her as she hit the floor and jolted her back. Pain ripped through her, making her gasp, and she fought the enveloping blackness to propel herself upwards.

The driver's airbag went off hitting Ulvis full in the face, and as he fought with it, using her other shoe, Lacy hammered at the window with the heel. She covered her eyes with her arm and gave it a massive thump. Pieces of glass rained down on her, going into her neckline, but she ignored it and hauled herself out of the window.

Barefooted, she tore down the middle of the rain-soaked street, not looking behind her as she put as much distance between her and Ulvis as she could.

Lacy ran between two cars and into the fluorescent glare of a twenty-four-hour shop.

She had a sweeping impression of chequered floors, rows of potato chips, a tower of soda cans and a wall of refrigerated milk.

"Help me!" she yelled frantically. "I need your phone!" she said to the young Asian man behind the counter. He pointed to a payphone at the back of the building. Who the hell used payphones? She thought.

She leapt over the counter. "Don't." She warned, seeing the teenager inch closer as though about to tackle her. "I was in an accident," she explained on a rush. A damsel in distress was always a better cover story than being hunted by a killer. "I'm a government agent, and I need your help." She advised, repeating her bureau I. D number, minus one digit.

The teenager nodded and pulled himself up to his full height of five foot five or six. "You want me to lock the door?" He asked eagerly.

"Yes," Lacy said, searching under the counter and finding the gun she knew was under most shop counters across America.

She watched as the boy locked the door. "Thanks. I'm not going to hurt you. My name is Wallace Dawson," she soothed. The boy didn't look skittish, in fact, he looked as though he was enjoying himself. "Lend me your cell."

"Here," he moved to the counter and handed his phone over.

"What's your name?" Lacy asked.

"Akash,"

"Do the security cameras work?" she asked, looking above her head seeing the camera and another one pointing at the door.

"Yes,"

She looked down at the trendy phone in her hand. "The security pin, Akash,"

Akash went through his phone then handed it back to her.

"Matthew!" she yelled with relief, clutching the phone with both hands when he answered. "Yes, yes," she answered his questions. "Listen!" she interrupted his lengthy tirade. "Listen!

I'm in trouble," she rushed. "I'm at–" she looked over at Akash for the address, but before he could answer, there was a mighty crash.

With splintered wood and glass flying, Ulvis shouldered his way in. Blood covered his face and stained his shirt, and his nose was puffy and disfigured. In a flash, he seized the teenager by the hair and held his gun at the boy's temple.

Lacy grabbed her gun and pointed it at Ulvis's head with one hand.

They stood watching each other, both breathing hard as the standoff lengthened.

"Put the gun down," Ulvis ordered eventually and waited for Lacy to place the revolver beside the packets of candy and chewing gum on the counter.

"The phone," he nodded towards the device in her hand. "Throw it down." He said, rearranging Akash so that his arm was across the teenager's neck.

Lacy knew Akash wouldn't be able to get out of the choke-hold. She didn't want him to. The Ulvis in front of her differed from the one she knew and liked. This one was dangerous. The warm twinkle replaced by shards of ice.

Lacy threw the phone beside the gun. It was still on, and she knew Matthew could hear everything that was happening, and he'd be able to trace her location.

Ulvis shuffled over with Akash and awkwardly picked up the gun with one hand, quickly shoving it into the waistband of his pants. Akash wasn't making it easy for him, Lacy noted, but she didn't want the young man to play the hero.

Ulvis picked up the phone, looked at the screen and snickered before whispering into it.

"She dies." Then he threw it on the tiled floor and stamped on it.

"I'm coming." Lacy surrendered with her hands in the air. She had no choice. "Leave the boy alone."

She could fight, but she couldn't risk Akash getting hurt. Ulvis had the gun pressed so hard into Akash's temple, Lacy could see the teenager's skin pulling taut.

She stepped around the counter. Akash was trying to catch her eye, and she avoided his gaze. She knew he wanted to do something, save the day, but this was not a game. She had no choice but to go with Ulvis.

"Let go of the boy," she requested calmly.

"Come closer,"

She went, her eyes focussed solely on Ulvis.

She steeled herself and stepped on the broken glass. The splinters cutting into her feet.

"Let him go, Ulvis please," she begged. She flicked a glimpse at the boy and shook her head, seeing the alarming glint of bravery in his brown eyes. "He's innocent in all of this. Leave him out of it."

A car screeched to a halt outside, and she prayed it was Matthew.

Ulvis looked over his shoulder and smiled. He pushed Akash into the shelves of potato chips and cookies so hard the entire aisle swayed snake-like, sending produce crashing to the floor. Then he grabbed her arm and yanked her into his chest.

His arms were like steel bands across her neck and ribs, and he lifted her easily off her feet.

Lacy wouldn't risk Akash's life by fighting the giant and remained pliant in his arms.

"Come quietly Miss Dawson, or the boy dies," Ulvis warned nasally in her ear, training his weapon on Akash.

"It's okay Akash," she soothed the teenager, who for the first time looked scared. She smiled reassuringly at him. "It's okay."

Ulvis walked backwards, his weapon trained on the boy as he moved, his boots crushing the shards of glass. When he cleared the entrance, he glanced left and right before spinning around on the sidewalk and shoving Lacy into the waiting vehicle, getting in beside her and slamming the door.

He said something in his harsh language and the vehicle sped off with a screech of tyres.

"What the hell?" Lacy said in confusion, seeing the driver.

He turned to her, his twinkly eyes apologetic. "Do as he says please, Miss Dawson," he warned.

Lacy turned to the man beside her. He pushed his gun into the underside of her jaw as she looked into his eyes. Eyes that were cold and deadly.

Ulvis was an identical twin.

***

"Fuck!" Matthew yelled frantically. The call from Lacy had disconnected before he could triangulate the signals and pinpoint her location. "She's in trouble, Ace," Matthew said unnecessarily because he had to say something into the brittle silence left behind by the smashing of glass.

"I'll get dad," Ace said.

"Take the girls home," Matthew advised, hearing Sabrina talking to Heather in the bedroom.

"I won't–"

"You will do what I say," Matthew warned. "I don't know who these people are. Keep your family safe, Ace."

He could see that his brother was torn and reached over to touch his shoulder.

"I've got this." Matthew turned to his computers and started typing quickly.

Then his phone started ringing again. He grabbed it, feeling his heart beat heavily against his chest.

"Lacy?"

"No, my name is Akash."

CHAPTER SEVENTEEN

Matthew rode across town and got to the shop seconds before his father.

He was met at the broken entryway by a dark-skinned Asian boy with jet black wavy hair that flopped into his eyes. He looked to be around sixteen or so.

"Akash?" he asked, striding towards him with his hand extended, aware he would gladly owe the kid for the rest of his life.

"Matthew?" the boy asked, shaking his hand and turning into the shop. "I didn't touch anything." He advised, watching Matthew look around.

"She didn't have any shoes," Akash explained quickly, seeing the other man pale at the sight of all the blood on the floor.

Matthew nodded.

"Tell me again what happened," Matthew asked when his father and four of his men strode in.

Akash explained and then showed them the video footage. "Miss Dawson asked if the cameras worked. They are voice-activated, I programmed them myself." He added with pride.

They all peered at the six screens, Lacy and Akash featured in two of them.

"Did he say anything?" Matthew asked calmly even though he wanted to hit something or someone, preferably the man, Ulvis, holding Lacy. He should have killed him when he had the chance. But Lacy had said he was harmless and her friend. Some fucking friend, Matthew thought darkly.

There were scratches on her chest and bruising around her neck. That foreign bastard was going to die, Matthew promised himself silently.

"He spoke in a Lithuanian dialect," Akash revealed and grinned sheepishly when all the men turned to him. "I study languages and spent a year in St. Petersburg for college." He explained.

"Like I said, I took the license plate, and I saw the driver look at me from the wing mirror. The men are either closely related, or they are twins, and before they drove off, I heard them say they were going home, and the driver said Tanya is not going to be happy."

"Tanya?"

"He said, Tanya. It's a common name in Eastern Europe." He advised wisely. "I took a picture of the vehicle and the license plate. Here." He plucked a phone from his pocket and placed it beside the smashed one on the counter. "I cloned it, so I can scare any sons of bitches if it got stolen." He informed them, missing the look Matthew sent his father over his head.

Matthew patted the boy's narrow shoulder. "You did good kid," he praised, knowing the information the boy gave and trusting him enough to not call the police when he had asked, would go a long way with them all.

He watched as his dad, always on the lookout for new recruits, put his card in the kid's hand.

"How old are you Akash?" Matthew asked.

"Almost twenty-one," then added, shaking his head and rolling his eyes. "It's hard to get girls looking like this, man." He looked down at his skinny frame.

All the men chuckled.

Matthew patted him on one narrow shoulder again. "You did good ki–Akash. We'll get someone to fix the door and clean-up." Matthew turned to his father.

Akash watched, wide-eyed, as the group of men in front of him took out devices that looked like phones, but seeing the screens knew that they weren't just phones. He was no fool, these guys were the real deal.

"Everyone synced?" Someone asked. They nodded and put the devices away.

They'd said their thanks and goodbyes when Matthew received a call from Rhodes.

"Yes?"

"A private plane is requesting an emergency take-off slot for Russia," he advised, sullenly. "It has to be them."

Matthew, about to straddle his bike, quickly strode back into the shop.

"Want to go on a trip Akash?"

***

A plane landed forty minutes later with the large Mannino 'M' emblazoned on the side in flamboyant royal blue lettering edged in gold. Chase Mannino opened the door and called them all in. A quick refuel and they were flying straight to Pulkovo Airport, St. Petersburg.

"Thanks for coming guys," Matthew said, once they were airborne and settled.

Matthew looked at his cousins via marriage. The six Mannino brothers were Kyle's first cousins and lived in Boston. They weren't really related to him, but his stepmother always said 'family is family'. They were her half-sister's family by marriage.

For them, all to be here with him affected Matthew in ways he couldn't name, and he gulped down the wedge of emotion that had been with him since his father told him he's not alone. The family were coming.

Matthew had been racing to the private airport, the Kawasaki hitting one-eighty, even so, he was too late. Eight damn minutes too late. He'd pulled over and watched the plane Lacy was in fly over his head, so close he could practically reach out and touch the belly of the aircraft.

"No worries, Matthew," Chase said, slapping his shoulder with his massive hand. The Mannino's were half Italian, half Creole all topping six feet two or more. Their grandmother came from the French-speaking Caribbean Island of Martinique. "Tell us what you got," Chase went on, sitting down next to him.

Chase was the second eldest Mannino brother, but the natural leader with his loud, playful personality. Chad was the eldest and quietly watched everything that was going on from the sidelines. Still waters run deep, was how Matthew would describe Chad, seeing him lose his temper on one occasion and the recipient ending up in the hospital. You didn't mess with Chad. King followed Chase, then Jean-Paul and Marco and finally the baby at twenty-four, Delano.

They were a close bunch although it was rare to see them together like this, much less in the confines of an aircraft. Usually, it was the annual family reunion at the lake that brought them all together.

Matthew filled them in with what scant details he had.

"One question," Chase asked when Matthew had finished. "Is she worth it?"

Everyone looked at Matthew, and without pausing, he said. "She's the air that I breathe," Matthew revealed, without embarrassment, looking Chase straight in the eye.

Chase lounged back in his seat with a nod. "Diplomatic incident, guns and false papers aside," Chase joked. "We're going to go get your woman."

They arrived in St. Petersburg eleven hours later.

Rhodes had a 'friend' meet them on the runway with fake passports and with Chad's security connections, they were heading into the city just half an hour later.

They took over one entire floor at the Neva River hotel, which was located in the centre of the city and sat regally beside the famous river.

"Have a rest son," Charles said to Matthew, who was checking the guns Chad had arranged to be waiting for them. The entire table was covered with enough artillery to take out a small country.

"I'm going to look for her," Matthew said, picking up a semi-automatic and turning it over in his hand.

"Rhodes is on it," Charles said. "There's nothing we can do tonight. I'm going to meet a guy I know."

"Who?"

Matthew watched as his father pulled himself up to his full height and tip a silver eyebrow at him. Few people knew Charles used to run a secret British organisation more powerful than MI5, but operated by a select few. Looking on the surface, Charles was a regular English guy now retired and living in America with his Italian wife and all the kids and grand-kids. He wore corduroy and was in the church choir. Below the surface, he was still one of the most highly decorated officers the British Government had ever had. He was a bona fide Sir, shyly Knighted and still called upon by the British Government from time to time.

"Sorry Sir," Matthew apologised, thinking better than to offer to go with him.

Charles nodded, tucked a revolver into the back of his pants and with one of his own retired men, left the room.

Matthew walked to the window and looked out. He'd been to Russia, Moscow, but never this far North. St. Petersburg was a port city and the second largest in Russia. It was said to be more glamorous than Moscow in every way, from the buildings to what people wore. Matthew looked across the rooftops, expecting to see more decorative domes, but instead, a tall glass sphere dominated the skyline.

Lacy was out there somewhere, he thought to himself, closing his eyes as guilt and despair rolled through him.

"I'm coming, sweetheart."

CHAPTER EIGHTEEN

Lacy tried to move, but pain radiated from the base of her back all the way down her legs and she closed her eyes, remembering. She had hurt herself badly and Ulvis–the real Ulvis–had picked her off the asphalted apron at the private airport when she'd tried to run.

She'd hurt her back, aggravated the old injury and could barely stand. As vulnerable as she was, she had no choice but to go with them.

Silently, with tears running down her face, she'd looked into the night seeing the famous skyline of New York and nothing else. There had been no cars, no lone rider on a powerful motorbike coming to her rescue.

Ulvis had gently placed her on a seat and buckled her in, his eyes filled with concern and then anger seeing her bloodied feet.

When his brother had boarded the plane, Lacy had closed her eyes, not wanting to witness the shouting match that had been going on between the identical twins.

Once they were airborne, Ulvis had lifted her from her seat and took her to the back of the plane to a bedroom, where he'd gently cleaned her feet with warm water and silently and patiently picked as much glass from the soles of her feet as he could with a pair of tweezers.

Tears had slipped down her cheeks the whole time. Not from the pain she was in, no, she'd silently cried for the loss. The loss of control in her life. The mess she had made of it. And yes, she'd cried for Matthew.

Ulvis had bandaged her feet and when she'd tried to stand, her legs had failed her, and she fell against the bed. Ulvis had grabbed her arm, intending to steady her, but ended up unintentionally wrenching her back instead and she'd all but fainted from the pain shooting down her legs. Something was very wrong.

When he'd questioned her, she'd refused to speak and looked past him. She still hadn't spoken to him.

He'd left her for a moment, coming back with a packet of pain killers and a glass of water. She'd refused to take them and knocked the foil sleeve from his hand to the floor. She was not going to make this easy for him, she remembered thinking, stealing herself against the rigid offence she'd spied in his usually twinkly eyes that had turned dull, very much like his brother's. Good, she'd needed the reminder. He was not her friend.

Under his watchful eye, she'd inched up the bed and closed her eyes, scared of the pain she was feeling in her back and in her heart.

That had been yesterday.

They had landed to bright blues skies and frigid air early this morning. Ulvis had picked her up and carefully placed her into a waiting black SUV, not unlike the one they had given her to use. Looking out of the window, she recognised the famous domes of the Sunset Church of Our Saviour. She was in St. Petersburg.

Ulvis had placed a thick fur over her knees and watched over her as they drove out of the city for hours. Several inches of snow covered the ground, she saw, as she tried to distract herself from the pain.

She had a bad feeling she may have slipped a disc or something, or maybe a trapped nerve, but the pain was getting worse and sitting up for hours wasn't helping.

They'd arrived at a large regal-looking house about two hours ago and, ignoring Ulvis's help, Lacy had tried to stand, but passed out and reopened her eyes to this opulent bedroom of gold brocade with cornflower blue trimmings, and an English-speaking doctor sitting beside the bed. He'd cleaned and bathed her feet, and she remained silent as he talked.

There was a quick rapping on her door, and the same doctor came in. She didn't remember what he had called himself.

He was tall, with thin blond hair and dark brown eyes. He

was pleasant enough.

"How are you feeling, Miss Dawson?"

Lacy refused to answer.

He went on as though her remaining mute wasn't a problem. "I spoke to Ulvis, and he told me about your back," he explained. "I've ordered a scan, so we can see what's going on. Tanya is not a happy bunny at the moment." He said, going to the bottom of the bed. "May I?" he lifted the sheets and folded them back to expose her feet, where he quickly examined them. "They're coming on along nicely Miss Dawson." He said, peering closely, before straightening, and gently placing a neck brace around her neck.

"Who's Tanya?" she latched on, breaking her vow of silence, having heard Ulvis and his brother say the name several times.

"She's the one we all listen to," he said, looking down at the tablet in his hand. "The scan and then breakfast, you must be starving." He said briskly, opening the door wide and moving back as a hospital gurney was rolled beside her by two men.

She could refuse, but she was hurt. She needed to be sensible. She needed to get herself physically well again to get herself back to America.

Carefully, the two men under the doctor's instructions lifted her gently from the bed to the gurney. Pain ripped through her and stole her breath, bringing water to her eyes. She wriggled her toes and looked down, making sure she hadn't lost feeling in her lower limbs as thoughts of breaking her back had been at the forefront of her mind.

She was wheeled through the house, seeing framed paintings of Russian landscapes and exotic sculptures as they went down corridor after corridor. What little she could see of the house was beautiful, well-kept and about the size of a large hotel, but without the anonymity of overuse.

They rolled her through several sets of double doors, into a large elevator and down more corridors and double doors until the tinge of disinfectant in the air announced the medical facility.

Whatever this place was, it was fully equipped.

"Stay very still please, Miss Dawson," she was told by a pleasant-looking nurse as the conveyor belt moved and she slid into the bowels of the ultra-modern machine.

It was only then that she heard the melodious voice of Otis Redding being piped through the machine.

***

The next day Charles received tip-offs from several contacts. They had five leads but dismissed two of them as, logistically, it was just impossible to be in two countries at the same time.

Lacy being taken by the Russian military was another tip which Charles immediately dismissed. The Russian government had no interest in a single woman who, although she was Special Ops, wasn't high enough to bargain with. The bureau would leave her out to rot if they wanted to, and Russia knew it.

Another tip was that she'd been sold and was already in Latvia. Yet another tip said she'd been taken by a private organisation with conflicting, almost murky urban legends behind it. People referred to it as the BR. When asked what it meant, some said Black Rose, others said Black Russian.

Most people considered BR to be a cult, others said they were a private army that killed anyone who went on their land. Self-sufficient, they had their own homestead about forty miles outside of St. Petersburg and pretty much kept to themselves.

Matthew, the Mannino brothers and Charles, with his men, split up into three groups. Leaving Akash to finish connecting the computers that had arrived this morning, and link up with Rhodes.

In a rented jeep, Matthew with two brothers, went to check out the Latvian angle. If Lacy were sold, there would be no telling which country she could end up in. Russia shared boundaries with fourteen other countries.

***

Chase, with two of the 'veterans' he liked to respectfully call them—because they were almost as old as his father—drove out to the BR, a compound in the mountains. From the intel they'd received, a small convoy had travelled the narrow snow edged road early this morning.

Chase pulled his vehicle off the road, and hid it between thick, feathery conifers and, following the map on his phone, ran to the compound with the veterans, Raj and John, at his heels.

Minutes later, and blending into the foliage, Chase watched the comings and goings. The place looked like an Oligarch's love nest for his favourite mistress. Large, flamboyant and ugly. It was gated, and a high fence surrounded three sides and a dense wall of trees on the other. There was no getting in without being noticed, as between them and the house were several empty fields dotted with islands of melting snow and nothing else. They didn't have time to wait until nightfall.

Chase, always one to just get on with it, decided to head back to the car and approach like an American tourist.

They needed to get inside.

Twenty minutes later he was stopped at the huge, elaborate wrought-iron gates by a giant Russian who greeted him cordially in broken English.

No, this was not a hotel, he answered, telling him to head back down the mountain, clapping and shooing his gloved hands as though Chase was a stray dog.

"Come on man," Chase coaxed, getting out of his vehicle with his camera in one hand, grinning. "I'm travelling around, the architecture of this place is awesome man. One picture up close?" he asked, exaggerating his accent and lifting the camera to take a string of pictures.

The guard stepped in front of him, blocking his view. Chase leaned back and snapped his photograph, knowing everything would go directly to Akash. Hopefully, he was set up by now.

The guard narrowed his eyes at him. "Back," he said, pushing Chase's shoulder. "You go." He ordered.

"Please, man," Chase waved his camera about, bending to look around him. "No harm, one little photograph?" he pleaded.

"No." The guard said, reaching into his coat pocket.

Chase didn't wait to find out what he was reaching for, but could only guess a phone or a radio and he wasn't going to allow that.

He quickly stepped behind the guard, wrapped his arm around his neck and pressed firmly on his carotid artery, lowering him to the ground as he passed out.

Within seconds, Chase put him in the trunk of his car and drove to the house, stopping along the way to take photographs.

He parked in front, got out and took pictures of the enormous round fountain that had water spewing from the mouths of mermaids. It was hideous, Chase thought, taking more photos of the house and getting into the overeager tourist role, by laying on the ground and angling his camera upwards to artfully capture image after image.

No one had stopped him, yet.

He knew the Veterans were watching from the forest and probably thinking what a clown, but being a clown had always got him what he wanted. Chase adapting to any situation is what had made him such a successful detective with his own agency. Unfaithful husbands, Presidents, film stars and even a Priest once, but he always did what was needed to get the job done.

He walked up the stone steps to the arched entryway and, trying the handle first, was surprised the door wasn't locked. He let himself in. The door was heavy but well oiled, and it swung back as though made of plywood instead of solid mahogany.

Chase had to literally rush forward to stop it from slamming against the wall. He laughed to himself, closing it softly behind him.

The foyer was huge, with massive black and gold tiles that lay in what looked like a random design. A twin semi-circle staircase with a red carpet edged in black cupped the foyer on either side and hugged a large open fireplace that could easily roast a pig, or a human, Chase fancied, thinking of the mysterious stories surrounding the place.

The Queen of England would have no problem staying here, he mused, taking more and more pictures.

A harsh command behind him had him spinning awkwardly on his heel, and he jumped, fumbling with his camera, before grinning sheepishly. If he wore glasses, he'd have pushed them up his nose.

The command was repeated by a middle-aged, heavyset man dressed in dark pants, boots and a padded coat.

"Sorry man," Chase apologised, smiling widely and waving the camera in the air. "No speaky Russianski," he said, then looking up at the domed ceiling, took several pictures of the elaborate tiles in blues and white.

"But door was open." He challenged as though an open door was an invitation for anybody, him, to walk in. "This place is awesome," he said with excitement. "Got to take some photos for the wife back home you know," he said, managing to snap a picture of the man and the fireplace before the camera was wrenched from his hands.

More was said, and Chase recorded it all from the device sewn into the seam of his jacket.

He was hauled by the arm to a corridor behind the left set of stairs and pushed into a room. The man stabbed his stubby finger towards a chair.

Chase intentionally tripped on the edge of a rug and stumbled across the room.

"Sorry man," he said as he sat, leaning casually back to look around, wide-eyed. "Didn't mean to offend anyone." He put his palms up before taking out a large tissue to blow his nose loudly. The man wrinkled his nose in disgust before making a phone call.

Chase waited with excitement. This was what he loved, taking them unawares. Walking straight into the lion's den and waving around a piece of raw meat.

The door opened seconds later, and another man walked in, this one much younger and all Russian in height, build and colouring. Bring it on, Chase thought, flexing his hands in his pockets.

"Who are you?" The man asked, in heavily accented English.

"Chase," Chase said, standing to walk over and shake the man's hand. "Sorry to be a pain in the ass, but I couldn't control myself," he shrugged his shoulders. "Impulse it is. The wife always said my impulsiveness will one day get me into trouble." He laughed. He knew the man wasn't buying it. He wouldn't. "But this place drew me like a fly to a bar-be-que pit." His Boston accent went south, straight to Texas, and he hoped they hadn't picked up on his blunder.

He smiled wildly then frowned, hearing the rush of footsteps in the corridor and Chase knew the guard had probably been found.

Time for Plan B.

He grabbed his camera off the old guy and flung open the doors. With a quick glance, he ran up the stairs, clicking away.

"Wallace!" he shouted, slamming doors open along the way. "Wallace!" he yelled, running through the large house. "Wallace!"

"Stop!" he imagined them shouting at him in Russian. "Stop!"

He kept going, up another flight of stairs, shouting for Wallace. This place was a maze, he thought, running down a long corridor that opened up into a sun-filled room, before narrowing and leading to yet another corridor. He was deep within the house, he thought, ignoring the shouting behind him, to leap up a short flight of stairs.

The lighting was softer, and the walls painted brighter in this section of the house. If he had a moment, he would slow down to appreciate the modern artwork on the walls, but instead, there were vivid dashes of colour in metal frames.

The corridor came to an end, so he skidded to the left and burst into the only room.

Inside, Chase came to a stop. The room was bright, cheery and girly.

"Wallace?!" he said, recognising Wallace from the photographs Matthew had shown them all. "Come on, Matthew is looking for you."

Her back was to him, and she looked at him through the

reflection in the mirror in surprise. She was holding an ornate silver hairbrush in one hand and her hair in the other. She was caught mid-stroke. She looked past him before slowly placing the brush on the dressing table.

"Come on," he repeated, breathing heavily, reaching for her and hauling her out of the dainty cream and gold gilded chair she was sitting in.

A wave of intense lust went straight through him, and he snapped his fingers from her smooth skin in shock. The feeling was paralysing, and he knew from the widening of her brown eyes that she had felt it too.

He stepped back and back again, staring at her.

He knew she was beautiful from the photographs Matthew had shown him, but the woman standing in front of him was more than that. Her long hair reminded him of an autumnal bouquet of rich golds, deep reds and browns.

She was wearing some sort of frilly nightwear in white, with lots of lace and ruffles that touched the floor and covered her arms. She was almost completely covered, yet looked more alluring than any woman he had ever seen naked, with the dark circular discs of her areola pressing against the cotton fabric and shallow Vee at her neck, showing off her smooth looking skin. Chase's mouth literally watered. He wanted to suck and run his tongue on that bit of skin.

That was fucked up. Matthew was in love with her.

Chase took a deep breath to clear his head of the crazy thoughts. He'd rescue her, put her on the plane and forget about her.

"Let's go," he said tightly.

He watched her lift up her nightgown slightly and edge away from him. Her toenails were painted a cute shimmery pink, he noticed.

He'd only been in the room mere seconds, but it felt longer. If he'd been thinking clearly, he'd have noticed the men that had been chasing him had fallen back, and now, only two stood frozen on the threshold, watching.

He grabbed her wrist and hauled her towards the sash windows ready to push her out if he needed to, but she wrenched away from him.

He turned back, about to pick her up, only to stumble from the left hook she hit him with to his jaw, taking him completely by surprise.

"Hey!" he yelled in shock, grabbing and pulling her with him as he fell to the floor beside the canopied bed.

He took the brunt of the fall, but rolled quickly to trap her beneath him, pinning her arms over her head and, although her eyes were the deepest velvety brown he had ever seen, he noticed the dilating of her pupils.

The air shifted in the room, and he grew hard feeling her breath on his face.

Forgetting who she was, who he was, he dipped his head and kissed her.

For a moment she softened beneath him, letting him sweep into her mouth and he moved to gather her closer and deepen the kiss when she made the tiniest hum that vibrated around his tongue. He had never felt like this. Ever! She tasted better than the steak and fries he'd had at breakfast. He could go on kissing her for days.

Wedging his thigh between her legs, he swept one hand down her body. She was slight but perfect, and just as he moved up to sample the weight of her breasts, she scrambled out from under him.

Chase rolled onto his back, breathing as hard as she was, looking down at him with her hands going to her slim hips.

What the hell had just happened? He thought in bewilderment, closing his eyes and then opening them again. Holy hell, he'd almost made love to Matthew's girl, and by the look of desire smouldering in her dark eyes, she was still feeling the effects of his kisses too. Holy hell.

Pushing back her shoulders, she looked towards the door and nodded ever so slightly.

From his position on the floor, Chase watched as two men

stepped forward almost reverently. He was grabbed up and because he was still affected by her taste, didn't resist, but watched her, as she watched him, being escorted from the room.

CHAPTER NINETEEN

The doctor walked into her room after a quick knock.

Lacy was tucked up in bed, still in the medical wing of the mansion. The room was nicely sized with all the comforts of a high-end hotel suite. But she still had no idea where she was and the nurse, although pleasant, wouldn't be drawn into a conversation that wasn't related to her health.

An intravenous drip was attached to the top of her hand, and for the first time since New York, she was feeling relaxed and floaty and not in any pain.

The doctor was holding a tablet and drew up a chair beside the bed.

"Feeling better, Miss Dawson?" he asked kindly.

While Lacy had been in the MRI machine, she'd come to the conclusion she needed the doctor if only to get well again. Pins and needles had been shooting up and down the backs of her legs, and her toes curled under as though lacking oxygen. Her symptoms had been getting progressively worse.

"I'm sorry," she began. "I don't remember your name."

He smiled. "Dr Glazunov," he introduced again. "Ready to talk?" he asked lightly, and Lacy read between the lines. Ready to co-operate was what he most likely wanted to say. "How are you feeling?"

Lacy told him about her back injury the previous year and how she had hurt it again yesterday or was it the day before? She thought, in confusion.

He took notes and nodded here and there.

"So you self-diagnosed?" he asked for the second time, sometime later, his disapproval clear in the strong frown he didn't try to hide.

Lacy waved her free hand in the air. "It was nothing."

"A fractured spine is not nothing. You're lucky you're fit and healthy, but one wrong move and in your kind of work," he shook his head. "You could have ended up in a wheelchair." He stated grimly, before adding pointedly. "For life."

"Fractured spine?" Lacy gasped in disbelief. Her back had hurt when she'd wrestled with the head of a paedophile ring, but it had been manageable. My God, she thought, she'd been walking around with a broken back!

The doctor turned so that she could see the screen on his tablet. He pulled up an x-ray image of her lower vertebrae.

"See that thin line there?" he indicated a hairline crack on her lower spine.

"Yes,"

"Another ninth," he put his thumb and index finger close together to show how close. "And you wouldn't be walking." He stated grimly, then he flicked his finger across the screen several times, stopping to show her another image of her spine. "See this?"

He didn't wait for her to answer.

"See how it looks lopsided?" again he didn't wait. "You've slipped two discs, and your nerve endings are pinching between the cartilage."

"What does that mean?"

"It means, your body has been overcompensating and adding additional pressure to other areas of your spine," he held up the tablet. "Here, and here," he pointed. "We'll have to go in and repair the damage,"

"Surgery?"

"Yes."

"When?"

"Ten minutes ago," he said with all seriousness. "You've done a lot of damage, the fracture on your spine has been aggravated. It needs to be repaired and rested. *Properly* repaired. Fixing the discs will be routine enough. No food for you. Do you take any medication?"

They talked some more, Lacy filling him in on what little medical history she had, and the monthly iron shots she was supposed to get but had recently missed, taking prenatal vitamins instead because she couldn't bear to spend a moment away from Matthew to go for her shot. However, she didn't tell the doctor that last bit.

He shook his head at her, his mouth tipping down on one side. "You have a penchant for self-medicating, don't you, Miss Dawson?"

She didn't bother to answer him but asked instead. "Will you be doing the surgery?" Not yet ready to trust anyone else. He had trusting eyes, and her instincts weren't screaming at her.

"I'm a surgeon, just not the kind of surgeon you need. They're flying in specialist surgeons who should be landing," he looked at his watch. "In another five minutes."

"Who are *they*?"

He smiled, and watching closely, Lacy noted how his shoulders seemed to relax. "You're in safe hands, Miss Dawson." Was all he said.

Lacy bit her lip. Unsure.

"General anaesthetic?"

"Of course,"

"Recovery?"

"Depends on you," he went on. "You're fit and healthy."

"How long?" she pressed.

"Depending on what they find. What needs repairing," he listed. "A few weeks to a couple of months."

Lacy nodded, watching as he moved to adjust the drip on her intravenous bag.

The doctor used a syringe, turned a bottle upside down and was about to add whatever it was to her drip.

"What's that?" Lacy asked suspiciously.

"A relaxant," he walked over to her, showing her the bottle with a well-known drug written on the label in English.

She nodded for him to proceed, and within seconds she was fighting to keep her eyes open.

"Do they drug people here? Make them forget?" she asked, the words sounding slow and heavy even to her own ears.

"No Miss Dawson, we rarely drug our own people. Hypnotise maybe. Drugs as a last resort."

"But I forgot Matthew,"

"Maybe you were meant to forget him?" he suggested gently.

"No. Never. I love him, but he didn't come for me," she slurred. "I looked and looked, but he didn't come."

The doctor picked up her wrist, feeling her pulse, before replacing her hand on the bed.

"What is this place?" Lacy asked, struggling to focus on him, "And who is paying for all of this?"

"This place?" He smiled down at her, "this place is paradise, and we look after our own here." He said, as her eyelids fluttered closed. "Welcome home Lacy."

CHAPTER TWENTY

Under the instructions of Rhodes in his ear, Matthew silently opened the front door and went in.

When his father had been chairing a meeting back at the hotel earlier, Matthew did something he'd never done before, he'd walked out and rode his new Kawasaki out to the sprawling compound as he couldn't wait for his father's other men to arrive from England. He had to do something now.

Lacy and Chase were being held against their will somewhere in this beautiful mansion. Although beauty could hide a whole heap of ugliness, Matthew thought, glancing around the opulent foyer which was worthy of a magazine spread.

"You still with me?" Rhodes asked.

"Yeah, which way?" he inquired quietly. Not only was the hearing aid he wore just a hearing aid, when programmed to another frequency, Rhodes, could also track and converse with him too.

A few hours back, with Rhodes and Akash's help, he'd hacked into the Wi-Fi of the compound, although there was a lot of mostly encrypted data, they'd managed to ascertain the place belonged to Dmitri Romanov, a flamboyant Russian oligarch in his early fifties, who always had leggy young blondes with big hair, hanging on his arms. Yet it was widely reported he was only devoted to Tanya.

Tanya. Yet again, the name Tanya. They couldn't find anything on the mysterious Tanya. Not even a photograph. Maybe she was part of the murky Urban Legends surrounding the place, Akash had suggested, and Matthew agreed.

"Take the left stairwell," Rhodes instructed. "There's a party or something going on in the right wing of the house. Everyone is there."

Rhodes could 'see' via Mabel, the high tech drone the size of a bat, he had flying around the compound on the outside and via hacking into the security cameras on the inside of the house.

Matthew quickly, but stealthily, climbed the stairs, keeping to the shadows. However, that was difficult as the entire ground floor was lit by a huge dramatic chandelier, casting prisms of light throughout the foyer, all the corridors leading off it and the stairs. A fire had died down to the embers, Matthew noticed as he climbed.

On the first floor, he opened doors and checked the rooms as he went along. Cameras weren't installed in the bedrooms, they already knew.

"Something is seriously off with this place," he said quietly opening another door, talking to Rhodes. "All the rooms correspond in colour and layout with the one opposite," he stated, closing, then opening another door. "How many people live here?" he asked curiously.

"In the house? Maybe twenty, but there's another compound to the south of the grounds. By the layout, it looks like a typical army barracks or something. I'll check it out once we get Lacy and Chase out of there. There could be five hundred bodies living here easy."

"Shit,"

"Yeah,"

"They have an army or something?"

"Who knows?"

Matthew walked through a dark glass corridor. "There's nothing up here, Rhodes," he stated grimly, coming to a stop.

"There's another short corridor up ahead, check it out before going back down. I don't have eyes, and there's another single-storey wing to the left. I'm picking up a lot of shit."

"Like what?"

"No idea, mate. I'm going to fly Mabel down there and check it out. The roof is red hot, man. They're turning up the electricity with some major machinery down there."

Matthew walked towards the short stairs and noted the change in décor. "Someone important lives up here," Matthew said, climbing the four steps to an upper level with a few doors on each side of the hallway, but which came to a dead end. Directly ahead was a large gilded mirror on the wall with a table full of candles on top of a delicate-looking wooden table.

"Why do you say that?"

"Candles are burning, the carpet and wallpaper are different, and there are fresh flowers in vases." Matthew touched the petal of a white lily looking flower and thought of Lacy as he walked past. She would like that arrangement, he thought idly. Lacy had changed him. He now saw things he would never have noticed before, and smell things like the familiar vanilla scented candles she liked to have dotted around the apartment in New York and which he now smelled here, thousands of miles away in rural St. Petersburg.

Rhodes chuckled. "Sounds like a woman," Rhodes went on conversationally. "Maybe the elusive Tanya–wait, Matthew," Rhodes changed the direction of their light conversation. "Two men have just entered the hall," he blurted. "One is now heading towards you," he said before continuing. "See the door to your left? Go in there."

Matthew silently pushed open the door and went inside, leaving a narrow wedge to look out of. He was waiting to see who the person was and where they went when a slight sound behind him had him looking over his shoulder.

Matthew stilled. Two people were having sex and by the sounds of it, coming to a dramatic end.

He needed to move.

He looked out again, hearing the man on the stairs humming to himself.

"What's going on?" Rhodes asked. Matthew ignored him.

The couple behind him were becoming noisier, the mattress squeaking and the headboard banging against the wall. At least they were having a good time, Matthew mused, thinking what to do. If the man in the hallway didn't veer off into another room or if he came in here, Matthew was screwed. He felt for his gun in his back and flexed his fingers.

To avoid looking at the lovers on the bed, Matthew peered into the darkened room for somewhere to hide. All he saw were large shadows of furniture.

From the candlelight in the hall, Matthew caught sight of the man wearing a fancy red and black silk robe, over black satin pyjamas. He wore a red and black chequered cravat at his neck. Dmitri Romanov, Matthew recognised instantly. Shit! Silently he closed the door as quietly as he could and stepped into the room to hide somewhere.

Dmitri bellowed something in Russian and rapped two times on the door.

Matthew wedged himself into the shadow of a chest of drawers and a chair. Crouching down.

There was a shriek and a scramble of limbs on the bed. Matthew laughed silently, knowing the two lovers had just been caught.

"Dmitri?!" The woman gasped in disbelief.

The door opened, and the room became flooded with bright light from the three-fingered antique-looking chandelier overhead.

Everyone in the room froze. Recovering first, Matthew stood up and stumbled out of his hiding place to stare at Lacy with kiss-swollen lips, hair mussed around her shoulders and a love bite on her neck.

"You fucking bastard!" Matthew erupted in horror, before diving onto the bed in a rage to swing at Chase.

Matthew punched him hard in the face in quick succession, before Chase put up his arms to defend himself. The two men fell to the floor.

"Stop!" Chase yelled, trying to shove Matthew off him, but he was like a demented animal. It looked bad, and Chase was guiltily aware of it.

Matthew didn't fight the red mist over his eyes as he hit out at Chase, unable to believe his so-called cousin actually had sex with Lacy out of all the women in the world. *His* Lacy!

"How the fuck could you do this to me?!" he yelled, punching him in the jaw.

"What's going on?"

Matthew heard Rhodes in his ear.

"Shit! Get out of there quick," Rhodes said urgently. "There's a bunch of men running up the stairs!"

Matthew ignored the warning and revelled in the crunch of Chase's nose, at his punch. The bastard. Chase knew what Lacy meant to him. He *knew!* Matthew grabbed the front of his neck and squeezed. This was how men killed over a woman he thought, not caring. He wanted to see Chase dead.

There was shouting behind him in Russian and still he squeezed, sitting on Chase's chest as he leant over him wanting to see the life die out of his eyes. Chase stared up at him, daring him.

Matthew was yanked off him, and still, he fought to get back at Chase who was being lifted by two burly men dressed all in black.

"I'm going to fucking kill you!" Matthew charged, trying to get to him. "You are dead, fucking dead! I'm going to kill you, bring you back to life and fucking kill you again for the pleasure of it!" Matthew yelled, beside himself. He couldn't get the picture of Lacy looking up at him out of his head. Her eyes wide in shock, as she'd grabbed the sheet to cover her naked breasts.

He was going to kill Chase, he promised, killing him with his eyes until he could get to him. He tried to wrench himself away from the bands of steel holding him, but they only tightened their grip.

There was rapid shouting going on in Russian and Chase was let go and given a towel to cover his nakedness.

Dmitri Romanov strolled into view but remained silent. Matthew didn't know if he spoke English or not, but he didn't care either way.

Chase looked at Matthew. "It's not what you think," he implored cautiously, wiping the blood from the corner of his mouth with the back of his hand, before looking past his cousin.

The room stilled, almost as though a vacuum had pulled the

air out. Matthew felt movement beside him but refused to look. He never wanted to see Lacy again. She was dead to him too.

"You going to be a pussy?" Chase asked after a moment. "Or are you going to see sense?"

"Fuck you," Matthew spat, trying to shrug out of the hold on him. "Get the hell off me!" he yelled, for the first time noticing it was Ulvis holding him on one side. "You!" he sneered. At least The Tree had the decency to look guilty about it, he thought charitably.

Chase stormed up to him and grabbed Matthew's face, forcing him to look at him, to *see* him. Once he had his cousin's full attention, he let go of his face and took a small step backwards. "Look."

Matthew turned slightly, only because he had nowhere else to look. Chase was blocking his view from the front, and he wasn't about to acknowledge the Russian bastard, Dmitri.

To the side of him was Lacy wearing a long silky white robe with large pink flowers on it. It was so her. He felt his breath leave him, and he was thankful he was being held. He closed his eyes, unable to see any more. He couldn't keep the bile from rolling up his throat like hot sludge. He was going to be sick.

"Matthew?"

She said his name.

Matthew kept his eyes closed, refusing to acknowledge her, and breathed in deep trying to control the nausea as sweat broke out on his forehead. He would *not* throw up in front of them!

"Matthew."

This time his name was said more forcefully. A voice used to giving orders.

Matthew snapped his eyes open, finally computing what he was seeing and what he was hearing. He looked at her, touching every bit of her, seeing the delicate polish on her toes, her slender waist, full breasts and hair that hung past her shoulders, way past. He reversed his gaze slowly to make sure.

"You're Lacy's sister," he stated after a moment, looking into her eyes.

Her smile was minuscule. "I'm Lacy's twin."

CHAPTER TWENTY-ONE

"Where's Lacy?" Matthew growled.

"She's safe," Chase answered, stepping forward.

Matthew narrowed his eyes at him. "Don't you fucking talk to me," he gritted. "You should be with her!" The blast of his emotion was volcanic.

"I'm sorry," Chase began guiltily, he *should* be with Lacy, but instead he'd been enjoying the pleasure of her twin. If anything had happened to Matthew's girl, he'd never be able to forgive himself. Yet again, he'd allowed the allure of a beautiful face to distract him from his mission. "I'm sorry."

Lacy's twin stepped in front of him almost as though she could shield him from Matthew's wrath.

"She's downstairs," she said, addressing Matthew in heavily accented English. "I'll take you to her." At Matthew's small nod of agreement, she went on. "My name is Tanya."

"Just take me to Lacy," Matthew snapped, beyond any pleasantries.

Tanya spoke to everyone else in the room and they all melted away, leaving Matthew and Chase and looking to his left, Dmitri. She spoke sharply to the older man, who pulled himself up and silently left the room, but not before narrowing his dark eyes at her, Matthew witnessed.

"I will get dressed," Tanya said, turning away.

"You will take me to Lacy now," Matthew demanded, reaching out to grab her wrist to stop her.

She looked at him, then down at his hand and Matthew was under the impression she didn't get ordered about very much, much less *handled*.

"She is safe," she said.

"You really don't want to mess with me right now, lady," Matthew growled, snapping his hand from her wrist. "And I don't care who the hell you are."

She planted her legs apart, tipped her chin up and looked at him.

Matthew had had enough of the back and forth, and turned to walk out of the room and find Lacy himself.

"Hey!" he yelled, seeing Ulvis talking to Dmitri and another man. "Take me to Lacy." He ordered, noting how Ulvis deferred to Dmitri first before agreeing with a sharp nod.

Matthew followed the big man down the stairs and through long corridors and several sets of double doors.

At the last set, Ulvis stopped and turned to him. "Miss Dawson has hurt herself. She is in hospital."

"I saw what you did," Matthew growled fiercely, remembering the blood on her chest and hands, and the large handprint around her neck. He would see Lacy first, then he would deal with him.

Ulvis shook his head. "I would never hurt Miss Dawson," he said in tight offence. "She is my friend. It was my brother, and he has been dealt with."

"Is he dead?" Matthew asked in all seriousness when Ulvis opened one door and walked through, holding it open for Matthew.

Rhodes had been right, this wing of the house had been converted into a hospital and, glancing around, noted the latest machinery; MRI machines, the X-Ray room and other medical equipment as they walked down the corridor with pristine looking tiled floors. *Who are these people?*

"We have dealt with him our way." Ulvis edged. "You stay, yes?" he indicated a lone plastic chair against the wall. "I will get the doctor."

"I'm coming," Matthew said stubbornly.

Ulvis knocked and entered another room. A man was sat behind a desk wearing blue hospital scrubs.

"This is–" Ulvis began.

"Dr Glazunov," the man stood and walked around his desk with a smile and one hand politely extended. "Matthew, if I were to hazard a guess?"

Matthew shook his hand. "Lacy?"

"Please sit," he invited. "She is in surgery now."

"Surgery!" Matthew yelled, quickly straightening when he'd been about to sit down.

"Please," Dr Glazunov said softly, again motioning to the leather chair in front of his desk. "She is in expert hands. I will explain what happened." He said something in Russian and Ulvis left the two men alone.

Sitting beside Matthew, Dr Glazunov then told Matthew about Lacy's spinal injury, the prognosis and recovery. He even showed him her x-rays and scans.

"She asked for you, you know," the doctor told Matthew conversationally sometime later.

They were in the viewing gallery and able to observe the world's best Neuro and Orthopaedic surgeons and their teams as they worked on Lacy. Matthew was well aware these people had spent a serious amount of money to get the surgeons here, and for that, he was grateful, yet still disturbed.

Something wasn't right. The duplicated rooms, the money, the soldiers, Lacy's twin. Nowhere in her records was there ever a mention of her being a twin and most importantly, why had her twin insinuated herself in Lacy's life without making Lacy aware of their relationship? Knowing Lacy as he did, he knew she would be ecstatic to have a sister, an identical twin no less, but something was off, and Lacy was not leaving his sight until he found out what.

"She did?" Matthew asked, although keeping his eyes glued to Lacy where she lay covered in green surgical sheets, surrounded by twenty doctors and nurses, many of them standing by.

"She said she didn't want to forget you." Dr Glazunov revealed.

Matthew's heart skipped a beat. "What is this place, Dr Glazunov," he asked. "And no bullshit."

"Nowadays?" the doctor shrugged. "We are a charitable organisation. We save people. Men, women, children from war-torn areas across the world. We help them heal and re-settle them in safe places."

"You said nowadays,"

He shrugged one shoulder again. "There has been a lot of evil in this world, greed, cynicism and power making normal men think they are god, yes?" he said. "Once, we were simply an organisation within many, trying to survive the Russian militia, the regime, the wars within Eastern Europe and beyond, now we have come together."

Suddenly, the efficient calm and order below them was interrupted by sharp piercing beeps, and the data on the screen blazed red. There was a flurry of activity and Matthew pressed his hands against the glass in horror. The surgeons issued orders, and surgical instruments passed swiftly between them.

Everyone stopped to look at the monitor, including Matthew and the doctor beside him. After a few seconds, there was a noticeable sigh of relief from the medical staff when the beeping stopped, and the data on the machine settled to a green colour.

A nurse wiped the sweat off the surgeons' foreheads. One surgeon looked up, and Matthew saw the apprehension and panic in his eyes, even from this distance. Again, he thought something was up with this place.

"What just happened?" Matthew asked, forgetting their earlier conversation and trying to still his heart that was beating a rapid tattoo right to his throat.

"It looked as though Miss Dawson wanted to put everyone through their paces,"

Matthew scrubbed his hands over his face, feeling his panic subside like a rolling tide. "Please don't joke."

The doctor placed his hand on Matthew's shoulder. "I'm sorry," he apologised. "Miss Dawson is severely anaemic and hasn't been keeping up to date with her iron supplements. She was taking prenatal vitamins instead. She's a stubborn one, isn't she?" he didn't wait for Matthew to answer. "Ordinarily we would wait, get her iron levels up before surgery, but her spine was in a state, and she was in a lot of pain. Don't worry, we have the best team money can buy working on her and blood at the ready if she needs a transfusion."

That explained the pre-natal vitamins Matthew thought, feeling a chasm of disappointment cut through him. God knows, he'd never thought about having a kid until Lacy had become important to him. That gave him pause, when exactly had Lacy become important to him? Matthew thought back, remembering the first time he had ever seen her. The office door had been open, and Matthew had stood hovering on the threshold with a file in his hand. Lacy had been standing with her back to him, her hands on her hips, and her pants showcasing her cute round ass. She'd been shouting at their superior, Ian Franklin, saying something about not wanting to read any faster and how she wanted to get mud on her hands. Ian Franklin had rolled his eyes, before beckoning Matthew inside and ordered him to take Lacy to the obstacle course and let her 'play in the mud'. Give her an hour, he'd said, then he wanted her back inside. Lacy had squared her shoulders, turned to send Matthew a cool withering look before storming out of the office. He could still feel the chill of that look, he thought with amusement. She'd been assigned to his squad soon after and one night he'd sneaked her out to the obstacle course and together they'd laughed and 'played in the mud'. He'd kissed her that night too. Yep, Lacy had always been important to him even then, and yes, he definitely wanted her pregnant with his kid.

The surgery was over twenty minutes later, and Matthew was led to her room.

"For you," Dr Glazunov told him, indicating the other bed in the luxurious room. "I will order you some dinner."

Matthew nodded his thanks as the doctor left and drew up a chair beside Lacy's bed to hold her hand. For the first time in almost seventy-two hours, Matthew was able to breathe.

***

"Hey sweetheart," Matthew said softly, seeing Lacy's eyelids flutter open and the confusion in her beautiful dark eyes several hours later.

He moved even closer and smoothed one of her slender eyebrows, before leaning over to kiss it gently. "Thirsty?" he asked, turning to pick an ice chip from the glass on the cabinet and pressed it between her lips.

Lacy opened her mouth and sucked gratefully on the slither of ice as she frowned over at him. "Matthew," Lacy whispered, feeling discombobulated. The last time she had seen him had been days ago, looking at her with hatred and disbelief. "You came?"

"Nothing would stop me, Lace," he admitted. In the hours he'd waited for her to wake up, he finally acknowledged his feelings to himself. She was the only woman to ever make him feel the way that he did. He would move heaven and earth, play in the mud and fly halfway around the world to be with her, and he'd do it all again, not that they would ever be apart. He loved her.

"It wasn't me..." she began restlessly, but Matthew pressed his finger against her lips, stopping the tumble of her agitated words.

"I know, and if I'd watched the video to the end, I would have known." He replied guiltily, lifting their entwined hands and smoothing her knuckles back and forth across his mouth.

Knowing where to find the deleted video, he pulled it up and watched the short clip on his phone while Lacy slept. It had been Tanya shooting with cold efficiency into a crowd of people from that roof. When she had stood, her aggressive commands–although he couldn't hear what she said–her body language, the way she talked with her hands, but most tellingly, her walk, he would have known it wasn't Lacy. "I'm sorry for saying what I said Lacy. Please forgive me?" Matthew begged, kissing her fingers.

"But who...?"

"Your sister."

"What?"

"You have a twin. Tanya. That's all I know for now. She brought you here."

"A twin? Here?" Lacy was having a hard time keeping up with the conversation. She was trying to fight the grogginess, but it was getting thicker, his words seemingly coming from afar.

"I won't let her near you until I've checked her out. Rhodes and Akash are working on it. This place is some sort of private army of goodwill or something."

"I don't understand."

"Neither do I sweetheart. But I'll keep you safe," he promised. "Rest, get better, so we can go home." He kissed her fingers.

She smiled groggily. "Okay,"

"I'll never let you down again." Hazel eyes blazed gold as he promised, kissing her fingers again and smoothing them along his jaw.

She fell asleep with her lips tipped into a small smile, and Matthew had never seen anything so beautiful. He was starting to collect her smiles, he thought tenderly, smoothing one of her eyebrows again as he settled back in his chair to watch over her.

CHAPTER TWENTY-TWO

"Why hasn't she come to see me yet?" Lacy mused suddenly, as they turned the corner to continue their slow pace. The wind was brisk now that they didn't have the beautiful building shielding them from the elements and Lacy pulled up the collar of her jacket and snuggled closer into Matthew's side.

It was six days later, and they strolled the last stretch of the gravelled pathway that would take them to the hospital entrance on the right wing of the house. They had already walked the circumference once, all the while with uniformed nurses talking quietly between themselves in softly muted Russian behind them.

Lacy was recovering nicely, the surgery on her back a success, the soles of her feet only slightly sore and already she felt as though she could do several somersaults across a field.

Matthew smiled tightly at the nurses and closed the door in their faces once they'd reached Lacy's suite. The two women were nice enough, but with everything else in this messed up place, he felt as though they were not only here in a medical capacity but also in the guise of guards.

They were never left alone for long.

A few hours after Lacy's surgery, Matthew had heard an alarm sounding deeper in the house and lots of shouting and running. Rhodes was still communicating with him through his earpiece at the time and told him his father Charles, his men and the Mannino brothers had arrived.

Matthew had wedged a chair under the room door and pulled his gun at the ready, thankful they hadn't patted him down, but after several minutes and with Rhodes' running commentary in his ear, a short stand-off had ensued, with Chase talking and calming both sides. Guns were lowered, and his father and his men had entered the house peacefully, then several minutes later, Charles was in the hospital unit and by his side as they watched over Lacy for the rest of the night.

They'd all been invited to stay for as long as they wanted by the flamboyant Dmitri, but Matthew hadn't seen Tanya since that first night and wasn't in any rush to either. Charles came and went as he pleased, although always escorted by someone to 'translate'. The Mannino brothers had returned to St. Petersburg yesterday, leaving just Charles and his two comrades Raj and John, as well as Chase.

Lacy wasn't yet ready to make the long journey home as she was lethargic and sore, although trying to hide it from him. She was extremely anaemic hence the slow recovery. Another couple of days and they'd head out, Matthew planned.

Rhodes was busy using Mabel his bat drone to gather further intel and Akash was doing his thing from the hotel in St. Petersburg. They were making headway.

This place was an army barracks, and it was easy to see why the locals referred to the place as the BR. Forget black rose, Matthew mused, this was all about the Russian, Tanya. Her skin darker than everyone around her. Russian. Black Russian. Her presence was felt everywhere, but she was nowhere to be seen. It was weird.

At least three hundred people were on the compound at any given time. They moved in and out of the grounds at night, long convoys carrying men dressed in black going off in different directions once they got to the main road. During the day, they trained like soldiers. From what Rhodes had told him, there were about five commanding the whole place, with Tanya up there in the ranks. Dmitri played a lot. He went hunting, fishing and horse riding all day, every day. He moved around clapping people on their backs and laughing loudly. What made him dangerous was that Matthew didn't know where Dmitri fitted in all of this.

Matthew was edgy, he felt vulnerable sitting around like this, waiting. Some shit was going to happen or was happening right now, and he didn't like that he didn't know what was going on. He'd been on high alert for days, and he was feeling the strain.

Lacy's twin hadn't made an appearance, but he knew she would come. It was just a matter of time.

Matthew reached for Lacy's hand as she moved to the side of the bed and guided her as she sat carefully on the edge.

She looked at him expectantly, her dark eyes bright and he cast his mind back to what she had asked, ah yes, her damned sister.

"I don't know," he answered.

"Can you go and find her?" she pleaded. She'd been asking him every day, but he wouldn't leave her. "Please?"

"She will come when she is ready, Lacy," Matthew growled. He hated the other woman and everything she stood for. She was a killer and was using Lacy for whatever messed up shit they did in America, and that was a problem for him. Did the bureau know Lacy was a twin? He didn't think so. The implications of all this were huge.

From Akash, he knew there were several sets of twins and triplets on the compound. The identical bedrooms made sense, for kids, but these multiples were grown-ups. Ulvis was a twin, Lacy and Tanya and several more. It was weird. Statistically, there shouldn't be so many multiples in one place. Was there some sort of old Russian experiment going on? It had crossed his mind more than once, but none of them, not Rhodes or Akash, had found anything.

"Does she look like me?" Lacy asked again, eagerly interrupting his thoughts.

Matthew sighed. He didn't want Lacy to become attached. He'd been seeing the wealth of happiness in her lovely eyes from the moment he had mentioned her having a twin. Lacy was a nurturer, a nester. She'd have a Christmas tree bauble with her sister's face in it made specially. Having a family, a real sister, meant a lot to her. There was no way he could keep them separated. But he would try. He needed to get Lacy away from here and onto American soil where he could at least protect her properly.

"No," he answered honestly, then sighed again. "From a

distance, you look alike," he answered, remembering the video on the roof that had fooled even him. "But up close?" he shook his head, his mouth tipping down on one side. "She's harder." He actually shuddered and hoped the questions would end.

They didn't.

"Who's taller?"

"She is,"

"What colour are her eyes?"

"Brown, I guess,"

"Do we sound the same? Is her hair like mine?"

"Lacy," Matthew huffed, shaking his head. He'd had enough of the conversation and walked over to the door, hoping she'd give up on the questions. He had a bad feeling about Tanya and didn't want her anywhere near Lacy. "How are you feeling?" he asked instead.

"Fine," she answered, flicking her hands at him. "Why don't you like her?" Lacy asked perceptively, her head cocked to one side. "How did you meet her again?" she'd asked him before, but he'd managed to distract her and hadn't answered.

Matthew, with his hand on the door handle, turned back to her. "I was looking for you, and there she was."

Lacy frowned over at him, knowing he was lying and glossing over everything with an impatience that worried her. "That's it?"

"That's it." He didn't tell her what her twin had been doing and with whom.

Opening the door, Matthew stepped out, already aware Lacy was the only patient in this area. Isolated on purpose? He didn't know, but there were cameras everywhere. He'd walked towards the main door once, intending to go outside to snoop, but got no further than a few steps before Dr Glazunov and another man walked towards the building, ostentatiously taking an evening stroll.

Now, and right on time, having taken just six strides, a nurse appeared. This one was blonde and beautiful if you liked pale translucent skin and blue eyes. He didn't.

"Is everything all right?" she asked in accented English, she put her hand on his forearm, her thumb stroking his skin as she smiled gently at him.

Matthew shrugged her off, stepping back. "Yeah," he smiled. "Just thought I'd see if the doctor was around."

Her hand was back, but firmer, and he allowed her to turn him around and guide him back to Lacy's room.

"I will tell him you look for him," she patted his arm. "You stay and keep Miss Dawson company, yes?"

He didn't answer but allowed the door to swing shut behind him. Yep, something was seriously messed up with this place.

CHAPTER TWENTY-THREE

Lacy looked over at Matthew's sleeping form across the room. He was on his side facing her, finally breathing deeply enough for her to know he was at least in that third phase of sleep and less likely to hear her sneak out of the room.

Tentatively, she slid from under the covers and with her bare toes skimming the floor, felt for the slippers she knew where there.

She didn't have time to change into the jeans and sweatshirt which had been her uniform these past few days, so, shivering against the cold, and in new pyjamas, she tiptoed towards the door and out into the corridor.

It was almost four o'clock in the morning and, stepping quietly to the entrance–knowing there was a strong possibility she was already being observed–Lacy gently pushed open the doors to sneak outside, to quickly melt into the deep shadows cast by the angles of the house.

She knew where she was going.

From their many walks around the mansion, she had surreptitiously looked through windows and mentally made a note of the layout. They had never used the front entrance, but Matthew had talked about it, the dome, the chandelier, the fireplace and the double staircase. When she'd questioned him about where the stairs led, he'd shut down and for her, that was telling in itself. He didn't want her up there.

Lacy stopped, pressing herself into the brickwork, hearing a faint buzzing sound slightly above her. She heard it because everything else was still. Even the moody clouds stood frozen. Peering into the darkness, Lacy saw nothing except a giant moth or bat flying away. For a moment, she remembered the day at the butterfly sanctuary and how relaxed and happy they were, God, it felt like years ago.

Moving again, she entered the house through a side door she had previously noted, knowing it would lead towards the front entrance. The house was warm and toasty and smelled faintly of birch. She stayed close to the half-panelled walls and stealthily made her way to the brightly lit foyer.

Taking the closest stairwell, Lacy trod quickly and lightly up the steps. With all the physio and walking she had been doing, her back barely twinged.

At the top, she paused briefly to look around, it really was a beautiful house. Very decadent in its lies.

Where to go now, she thought briefly, yet instinctively walked towards a long glass corridor.

Her heart was beating loudly in anticipation. She knew what was happening. Could feel it. This tingly sensation which made the hairs on her arms stand on end and her breathing to become shallow. She had felt like this before as a little girl, she remembered, but more times since she'd begun working outside of the bureau. She recognised it for what it was. Her sister. Her twin. She was picking up twin vibes.

Climbing the short staircase, the smell of vanilla candles scented the air with the familiarity of her home back in D.C. and more recently in Matthew's apartment.

The lighting was softer, the décor not dissimilar to her own apartment, and she knew–just knew–her twin lived up here.

Tanya hadn't come to see her, and Lacy was tired of waiting. She'd dreamt of having a relative, someone who shared her DNA, the history of her beginnings, someone to balance out the chilly childhood she'd had and that someone was mere steps away.

Lacy took a deep breath, knowing the next few seconds were going to change her life. The hall was highly scented now and bathed in romantic candlelight. The door not so far. Lacy stepped towards her future, but just as she was about to knock, a hand covered her mouth from behind, and she was lifted off her feet.

"Shh," she was told quietly in her ear and wilted against the rock-hard body holding her.

Lacy didn't bother to struggle. She knew the warm band of steel wrapped around her waist.

Matthew released her mouth, walked backwards with her clamped to his chest, opened another door and turned on the light before dumping her on the floor.

Lacy squinted against the brightness and rounded on him. But he got in there first.

"What the hell are you doing?!" Matthew yelled. He was furious. He'd finally fallen into a deep slumber after nights of keeping one eye open.

He'd been dreaming of sun, sand and Lacy's soft legs wrapped around his on a beach somewhere. But a voice kept calling and calling, telling him to wake the fuck up, until eventually a loud piercing sound ripped through his eardrum, and he shot awake. Rhodes! His ear was still ringing!

Rhodes, using Mabel the drone, had spotted Lacy leaving the hospital wing and woken him up.

He was not happy, especially as Lacy put her hands to her hips and looked at him through darkly narrowed eyes, before stepping forward to poke him in his chest.

"I want to see her,"

"I know that," he tried to capture her hand, but she flung herself away from him. "But it's the middle of the night," he gritted. "Couldn't you at least wait until morning?"

"Why," she shook her head at him, "what difference would that make?" Lacy, pursing her lips looked at the door, calculating the space between it and him standing there glaring at her.

"Don't even try it," he growled, folding his arms over his chest and catching her quick glance at the door.

Lacy tried not to notice how sweet he looked with half his face lined with sleep creases or how his dark red hair stood on end. She hardened her melting heart. "I want to see her, Matthew."

Matthew scrubbed his hands over his face. He knew Lacy would pull a stunt like this eventually and sighed warily before opening his eyes. "Look around you Lace," he invited with one arm arching around the vacant space.

Lacy shrugged impatiently. "Why?"

"This room is identical to the one across the hall,"

"So?" She looked. The room looked like a typical bedroom. Double bed, dresser, carpet and curtains. Nothing exceptional. She shrugged one shoulder again.

"So," he started, searching for patience, "the room across the hall is exactly the same as this one in layout and colour," he explained. "Something is up with this place, Lace, and I can't have you walking around in the dead of night putting yourself at risk."

"You're being overly dramatic, Matthew," she chided. "My sister is here,"

"Don't you get it?" he was done with playing nice and took a step towards her. "Your *sister* is a fucking murderer!" Forget patience. "She's dangerous!" he threw at her. "These people, this place," he listed savagely. "Is dangerous!"

"You don't know that!"

"Oh yeah?" He rocked back on his heels and crossed his arms over his chest again. "Was it you shooting into a street with civilians? Hmm," he asked tightly. "Three men shot dead, right there in the open, with the whole of fucking New York City watching!" he yelled with derision. "Was that you, Wallace?" He challenged.

Lacy felt the tingling of tears. She knew he was right and answered quietly. "You know it wasn't."

"We don't know her," he said grimly, seeing Lacy's shoulders droop. He knew she would get attached to the idea of a twin sister. Of family. He got it. But Tanya was no sibling in the Brady Bunch. "We don't know what she is capable of, sweetheart, and what she wants from us. From you."

"But–"

He sighed and pulled her over to the bed. He was smashing her dreams of a happy family reunion, he knew that, but she had to understand.

Over the weeks he'd been watching her lose her edge. That

166

judgement call which should have been second nature to every operative at the bureau had disappeared like a puff of smoke in a rainstorm. Lacy was a soft heart. A sweetly feminine homebody trapped in a screwed-up government system she had no business being in. She should never have been recruited, and he wondered, not for the first time, why she ever was. Yes, she had memory skills, but in this digital age, her skills weren't essential.

How she looked now, glancing forlornly towards the door as though her sister was about to materialise and prove him wrong, wrenched at his heart and he hated Tanya, hated her, for giving Lacy a glimpse of a family that was not meant to be.

Seeing her bottom lip wobble and the glimmer of tears, Matthew took her hand and laced their fingers together. She had such pretty fingers.

"We'll be gone in another day or two," He explained gently. "This place isn't safe for us, Lace. It has too many unknown variables." Using his free hand, he turned her chin, so that she was facing him. What he saw in her lovely eyes broke his heart. "I need you to keep yourself safe, if not for you, then for me, baby," he appealed earnestly. He couldn't handle it if anything happened to her.

He kissed her softly when she finally nodded, but tears overflowed and, using his thumbs, he swept them away and kissed her trembling lips.

After a moment of just holding her close, Matthew walked to the bedroom door and pressed his ear to it, before turning back to the room.

"Is it safe to come out?" he said out loud.

Lacy looked around. "Who are you talking to?" She asked, watching him now stride over to the window and move the thick curtains aside. He smirked over at her, tapped his ear before nodding at someone or something outside. Which made no sense to Lacy as they were at least three floors up. Then it all fell quickly into place. The faint buzzing sound she had heard earlier must have been a high-tech drone. High tech, because of its size. And he was obviously corresponding with someone–probably his friend at the bureau, Ronald Rhodes–in his ear. She chuckled. His hearing aid wasn't just a hearing aid.

"Yeah," Rhodes said in Matthew's ear. "They fell back about three minutes ago," he revealed. "Tanya was watching, and they have ears in the room."

Matthew shook his head, not the least bit surprised. He'd been feeling stalked from the moment he'd walked onto the damn compound. Every move they made, every conversation, he knew was being recorded somewhere.

Matthew looked over at Lacy, who was watching him keenly and, with a small, encouraging smile, held out his hand. "Come on."

When she placed her small hand in his, he opened the door and guided her out with his hand gliding to the centre of her back.

Before they left the corridor though, Matthew paused, looked over his shoulder and smirked as he raised his middle finger and insultingly stabbed the air knowing they were being watched.

"Oh, very mature," Rhodes drawled, chuckling in his ear.

"It wasn't for you," Matthew snickered, walking nonchalantly down the wide staircase.

"I know," Rhodes answered with amusement. "She flicked one back at you."

CHAPTER TWENTY-FOUR

It was the next morning, and after a light breakfast of fruit and yoghurt for Lacy, and steak and eggs for Matthew, they walked over to the gym.

The whole place was fully equipped, and since being shown its existence, three days after Lacy's operation, they worked out together.

"The floor?" Matthew enquired, watching appreciatively when Lacy began to rotate her slim hips in a circle and then raise her arms over her head as though reaching for the ceiling, to reveal a sliver of warm brown skin on her stomach. Matthew licked his lips in anticipation. He'll be licking that soon, he thought hungrily.

"Sure," she replied, ignoring his hungry look and cupped her left ear with her right arm to pull gently on her neck, then reversing the manoeuvre before moving to the padded blue mats in the middle of the gym floor.

She went into position with a mischievous smile, remembering the early days of the two of them in training and pairing up to spar. It used to get hot and sexy very quickly.

They hadn't made love since being here, and Lacy was feeling the frustration. Matthew still slept in the double bed beside hers and wouldn't be moved. Tonight though, that was going to change, she thought with a bemused smile, pressing her breasts forward and liking the way his eyes dropped to her chest, and his whole body stilled for several seconds before he dragged his hot gaze away. Oh yeah, Lacy thought, tonight he was hers.

Lacy had trained in Krav Maga, and Matthew had several belts in the usual martial arts. They faced off and to indulge him, Lacy bowed and waited. Matthew grinned with confidence, knowing she usually went for his head with the heel of her hand, but in three seconds flat, he was on the mat, with the wind knocked right of him.

"Hey!" he yelled as she looked down at him, before dancing on her toes and punching the air as though she was pummelling him to the ground.

"Come on, Edwards," she said over her shoulder. "Let's fight."

They sparred for almost an hour. Both of them sweating, although Matthew was completely aware she was still mending and watched her carefully for any signs that he was hurting her.

"Is that all you got?" Lacy taunted, frustrated he was still playing with her.

"That's all you're getting," he grinned, sidestepping her kick. "Not too high Lace," he advised. "Mind your spine."

"I'm fine."

He narrowed his eyes in warning.

A warning she ignored and went for him.

He sidestepped her again, and she growled, swinging around to grab his arm and twist, which sent him flying through the air. Again.

He landed with a thud on the mat.

"That," he huffed. "Was cheating."

"That," she parried. "Was me showing you I'm not a China doll."

She reached down, offering her hand, although wise to the playful glint in his eyes now swirling in greens and browns.

Just as Matthew was about to pull her down to him, the door slammed, and they both turned to see who had entered. At first, the two nurses had stayed with them. Nowadays they were left alone, although looking at the cameras dotted around, they were never really alone.

From the dry twist of his lips on the other man's face, Lacy recognised him straight off and stalked towards him, tightening her loose ponytail on the way.

"Wallace, no," Matthew called expecting her to stop, but she kept going.

As he trotted past her, he said. "I got this." He owed this bastard a fist to his god-damn face! "They said you have been punished," he stated softly to the twin, remembering the marks he'd left on Lacy. "But the way I see this," he went on reasonably. "You're a dead man walking."

Ulvis's twin brother tipped his chin up but looked past him with a sneer.

Reaching Matthew's side, it was plain for Lacy to see the last bruising and small round puncture wound on the side of his thick neck.

"You want to fight me, yes?" the big man snarled. "You Americans are all alike, thinking you can have everything with a snap," he snapped his fingers in the air. "It is all about you, yes?"

"Yes, it is," Matthew confirmed with breezy arrogance, taking a step that took him into the other man's personal space. "You hurt my woman."

They were toe to toe, but the twin was so tall; Matthew's head came to his chest.

"One round," Lacy challenged the twin, trying to nudge Matthew out of her way.

The twin looked over Matthew's head, the sides of his mouth going down as he addressed Lacy through cold blue eyes. "I do not hit women,"

Lacy laughed and raised a single brow. "Since when?"

The beefy twin had the decency to flick her a guilty look, which incensed Matthew even more.

"One round, on the mat." Lacy invited softly, refusing to look at Matthew.

"No," Matthew stated automatically, putting his arm out to stop her from getting in the giant's face.

He knew Lacy wanted to fight the big man and settle the score, but he was too big, rough and nothing like his more honourable brother, not to mention, she'd had back surgery not even ten days ago.

But the fighting gleam was back in her eye, and she looked contrary to how she had been these past few weeks back in New York. If he didn't know any better, he would think Tanya was standing beside him, and that was a fucking scary thought. "No."

He repeated adamantly.

"It's not up to you," she said, but she was looking at Ulvis's twin. "Want to settle the score big guy?" she invited. "Have another go at the girl who kicked your ass and left you with scars?" She taunted, looking pointedly at the pucker of skin on his neck. "Every time you look in the mirror, you remember me, don't you?" she laughed. "Now isn't that a lovely thought?"

He smirked and flicked a derogatory look down her slender frame. He had been ribbed when he'd returned to the compound. Ribbed? He'd been humiliated. Laughed at and called a *zanudnyy*. A wimp! He now had a scar on his neck and would forever remember she had almost got the best of him. Almost.

She wanted to fight? He would fight. He didn't care what Tanya, or his love-struck, sissy brother said. Lacy Dawson had made a fool of him. Yeah, he'd be banished to the outer compound. The one with nothing but a log hut, but so what, he'd had enough of this place, anyway. He would leave. His brother wouldn't miss him. They hadn't bonded over the two years they'd known of each other's existence. He'd go back to Lithuania and run drugs like he used to. He didn't need this place or his so-called brother. He didn't need any of this.

He nodded towards the mat and pulled off his T-shirt.

"What the hell, Lacy?" Matthew demanded, grabbing her arm as she made to move past him. "I'm not letting you fight."

Lacy narrowed her eyes at Matthew. "Leave me alone, Matthew." She was already distracted, watching as the giant man rolled his shoulders and frog jumped three times.

"You're not doing this Lacy,"

"It's not up to you," she challenged, swinging her dark eyes back to him and shaking off his hand. "He manhandled me."

"I get it, but you're too soft." As soon as the words left his mouth, he realised his mistake. Yes, Lacy had lost her edge, but she was still a trained operative. To call her soft was to insult her and by the lift of her chin and the steely glint in her dark brown eyes, he knew he had. But he would apologise later.

The big man snarled something in his language that didn't

sound like he was offering to make them a coffee.

Without another word, Matthew turned and walked to the mat.

His opponent smirked and gave Matthew a left hook before he had even faced him.

Shit! Matthew thought, stumbling backwards from the force of it and shaking his head to clear the Tweety birds flying overhead.

He wanted to fight dirty? He was going to fight dirty. Matthew ran for him.

The fight was brutal. Lacy grimaced as Matthew was punched several times in his abdomen and then kicked in his side before he even managed to lay a single punch.

The twin was too big and used his height and weight to his advantage.

The men grunted as they fought. Blood and sweat went flying, and fists flew, connecting with slaps and thumps to leave glaring white marks that settled into deep mottled red.

Lacy flinched as the twin landed a vicious blow to Matthew's face, making his head snap back and stagger to his knees. She was about to run to him, but with a deep-throated war cry, Matthew charged at the giant.

For a moment they were locked together, going in tight circles as neither man let go of the other. There was nothing professional about the fight, nothing honourable. This was dirty, dirtier than a back-alley street fight.

"Matthew!" Lacy yelled in distress when he went down, hitting the mat hard.

"Stop!" she rushed, going to his side and holding her hand out to stop the twin from attacking him. "Enough,"

The twin snorted and spat on the floor beside where she knelt.

"*Suka.*" He sneered, wiping his mouth as he turned to leave.

Lacy was glad to see the swelling mess above his right eye, his split lip and blood dripping from the corner of his mouth. Good, Matthew had got something in.

When he neared the door, Lacy repeated what he'd just said.

He turned, his blue eyes stormy with stiff offence and she knew, just knew, this was not over. He was an enemy for life.

CHAPTER TWENTY-FIVE

Matthew was mad. Mad that he'd let his emotions get the better of him, making him lose focus and crash out of the fight the way that he did.

"Are you okay?" Lacy asked him again, as they made their way to her suite in the hospital wing.

He grunted his response while plotting his revenge and holding his side. His insides felt as though they'd been put through a mixer.

He slowed his pace and held his hand out to her before dropping a quick kiss on the lines of worry dissecting the patch of skin between her eyebrows.

"Yeah," with his fingers, he playfully nudged her chin before walking on again. "Next time–"

"There won't be a next time Matthew," Lacy said sternly. "I love you, and my heart can't take it."

Matthew stopped mid-stride and turned to her.

Because she was busy gazing at an old flatbed truck filled with cabbages, ambling along a road she hadn't noticed before, Lacy bumped into him.

Matthew placed his hand on her shoulders to steady her. "Your heart can't take loving me?" he asked fiercely.

"Huh? What?"

Matthew bent at the knees to look directly into her eyes. "You said you love me."

Lacy frowned, scrambling backwards over the conversation in her head. Did she actually say what she was thinking out loud? By the way, his lips were tipped up she had.

"Maybe I did," she whispered and waited. And waited some more when he continued to look at her without a flicker of emotion in his hazel gaze. "Then again, I was actually talking about *my* heart." She stated, biting the corner of her bottom lip when the silence stretched.

Matthew shook his head. "Nah," he rejected lightly. "I don't think so Lace," he tipped her chin up in the gentlemanly way he'd been doing of late with a loosely curled fist. "My heart has accepted. You love me, Lacy Dawson, and I think I love you."

"You *think* you do?"

He chuckled at her look of outrage. "It's not like I've ever been in love before," he explained casually.

"Well neither have I."

"Well, all right then. This thing we have must be love because I can't not be where you are Lace. Ever."

She smiled at his angry expression, his hazel eyes were swirling again in a mixture of confused emotion, before settling to warm sable. He was content. He was happy.

Lacy stepped forward to smooth her fingers along his silky, but sweaty left eyebrow. "Well, all right then." She repeated with a confirming nod.

Hand in hand, they walked on, both silently amused at the pivotal moment they had just navigated through.

***

Sometimes Charles joined them for their evening meal, but today he'd gone off to the other end of the compound to eat with some men he had befriended.

Charles had earlier informed Matthew of a rumoured government experiment involving Russia and America that had taken place over sixty years ago, before and after the cold war. It was all very hush-hush, and gleaning information was difficult, although his father believed it to be true and had gone off to find out more.

After their meal, accompanied by shy smiles from Lacy and a strong sexual pull from Matthew, he ran her a bath.

"How's the water?" Matthew asked Lacy, watching when she dipped her toes into the water. She was wrapped in a large fluffy towel, and her hair was stuck on top of her head, showing off the lovely lines of her neck and shoulders.

"Just right thanks," she told him and waited for him to glance at her, before dropping the towel. But instead of stepping into the water, she slid onto his lap, curling her arms around his neck to kiss him hungrily.

He moaned against her lips and stood up, allowing her to wrap her legs around his waist.

They kissed long and deep, and Matthew gently bent at the waist for her to jump down. If he didn't stop this now, he'd be deep inside her in the next few seconds, he knew.

"Lacy," he mumbled against her lips. "We have to stop,"

"No,"

"Babes," he tried to slide her arms from around his neck, but she wasn't having it. "Lace," he tried again. "Cameras."

"No," she buried her fingers in his hair, angling his head where she wanted him. "Don't care."

They already knew the entire suite was rigged with cameras, which was messed up enough, but they weren't aware of any in the bathroom.

"Yeah," his brain went to mush as she moved to tongue his ear. She knew what that did to him.

To hell with the cameras, he thought, going between their bodies to undo his shirt buttons. When she realised what he was doing, she helped him with a giggle and released his belt buckle, pulled down the zipper tab and went inside to release his hard length into her hands and squeezed.

In a rush, Matthew stepped out of his pants and with her naked body glued to the front of his, arranged the towel around her shoulders to hide her nakedness, stepped into the bath and placed her on top of him.

This was her show, he thought lovingly, watching as she eased down onto him, taking him inside her body and gliding her tongue over her bottom lip as she tipped her head back. God, she was just so beautiful, he mused, placing his hands on her smooth hips when she moved.

***

They were dozing on her bed after making love in the bath

until the water cooled when a siren blasted throughout the house.

"What the hell!" Matthew asked, sitting up suddenly. "Stay here," he ordered when Lacy moved to get up.

"Rhodes," he said, pressing his ear. His friend tuned in and out. Mostly out these days, as nothing was happening and there was nothing to report. "Ronald?" he said urgently, finding and pulling on his pants, before reaching for his phone.

He punched in the number for his dad, but the screen was blank. "Shit," he said with dread. "Get dressed Wallace," he ordered, mad at himself. He'd let his defences slip these last couple of days.

They were both heading out of the door when they heard heavy footsteps rushing into the building and seconds later the door swung open to reveal men, clad entirely in black, station themselves at all four corners of the room.

"What the hell is this?" Matthew demanded, pushing Lacy behind him and then looking on in astonishment as Tanya marched in.

Lacy's twin was dressed in black military gear like her men. Her hair was pulled back into a tight ponytail.

"I don't have time to explain," she said, looking at Matthew. "The Americans are coming for you."

He frowned. "What Americans?"

"In eight minutes, they will be here and either arrest you or kill you," she said. "You are a loose end; they cannot afford to have."

"What the fuck are you talking about, lady?"

"Here," she held out a phone, and he took it automatically. A black knapsack was handed to her, and she shoved it at him. "Inside is money, passports and keys. Your motorbike is parked against the south wall," she advised, all the while keeping her eyes steady on Matthew. She looked nowhere else.

"Get to the ports and out of Russia, now." She instructed fiercely. "Do you understand?"

One man said something to her.

"Where's my father?" Matthew asked.

"Avoiding arrest," she answered, holding his gaze. "You have six minutes."

Lacy had moved to Matthew's side, hearing her sister's voice. Her senses had gone haywire.

Lacy looked at Tanya for the first time. She looked familiar, like looking at an angry, cynical version of herself. Tanya didn't look her way, not once, although Lacy was very much aware of her twin's tension.

With a minuscule nod, Tanya spun on her heel and left.

Matthew breathed in deep, not sure what to do. Did he believe the other woman? Where was his father? Could he leave here?

Lacy voiced her own concerns that echoed those in his head. "Should we go?"

"We can't stay here," he admitted after a moment. No matter what, Tanya had been looking out for Lacy. He had to take the chance that she knew what she was talking about and that she wasn't playing games. "Grab whatever you can," he ordered. "You have twenty seconds."

They slipped easily into their operative roles and collected their coats, her pain killers and boots. They got it all with seconds to spare, before leaving their sanctuary and making their way to the south side of the compound.

All around men were running with guns slung over their arms and positioning themselves. Matthew looked into the hills behind them and saw a long thin line of vehicle lights bumping along the road.

"Come on," he grabbed Lacy's hand.

"Over there," she pointed a moment later, seeing the motorbike parked where Tanya had said. "How do we get out of here?" Lacy asked the question Matthew had been silently pondering, knowing the only route he knew was by the front gate and that, he looked there now, had just been breached. He shrugged, jamming his helmet on her head.

"There's a track at the back over there." she pointed over his shoulder. "It leads around the back and veers off into the woods," Lacy said, remembering the truck filled with cabbages this morning.

Matthew didn't stop to question her, she was a genius after all and roared the bike to life and sped off into the cold night.

CHAPTER TWENTY-SIX

Lacy clung to Matthew's strong back as they rode through the night. It was cold and the coat, although heavy-duty enough for morning strolls, was nothing against the harsh wind and rain that periodically lashed through them.

Pulling over at one point, they turned on the phone Tanya had supplied and pulled up the Maps App.

They were heading for the coastline, where a choice of small villages and docks were located. From there they hoped to catch a freight and sail out of Russia.

The road they were travelling on was winding and bumpy. Lacy was feeling the effects of each jolt up her back and hips. It was too much for her, but they couldn't stop because of her sore back. Matthew himself would be sore from the fight earlier today too she remembered, turning her head to snuggle into his body when sheets of rain fell hard.

None of it made any sense, Lacy thought when she could think past the aches in her body. Which Americans were after them? And what were they chasing them for? She knew Matthew was thinking the same thing, but they had to put as much distance between themselves and the supposed threat before they could even decipher what it all meant.

Tanya. She had seen her sister.

Lacy felt the sting of tears, adding to the miserable night. Tanya hadn't looked at her once, not once when she'd issued those orders like a general. Granted, there had been an urgency about the whole situation, but even so. A glance of interest maybe? Or even a hug. What if tonight were the last night they would ever be in the same room? There had been nothing. Lacy tried to swallow past the hurt but gave up, letting her salty tears mix with the drops of rain on her tired face.

Matthew hit a pothole hard, and she couldn't smother the

groan of pain that ripped up her throat. He took one hand off the bike handle and pressed his palm against her arm, wrapped around his waist in apology. She squeezed him back, and he rode on.

She was cold, sore, disappointed and miserable, but there was no one else she would rather be in this situation with. Matthew. The only bright side to this whole sorry mess was that she was with him. They hadn't talked about their feelings, but with the childish declarations of love they'd made this morning– my God, was it only this morning?–they had moved one step closer to something organic. Deeper. She'd stopped thinking of him as just the man she had sex with. These past few weeks had changed their dynamic. This morning's proclamation confirmed it, and she couldn't help thinking about their future.

To distract herself from the ache in her lower back and the cold drops of icy rain seeping through her coat, Lacy gave her imagination free rein and designed her wedding dress.

It was definitely going to be ivory to complement her skin tone, with plenty of beads on the bodice and a flare of traditional lace from her hips downwards, but with a modern low back.

Matthew hadn't got it all right, she mused with an affectionate smile. Yes, she liked to go into baby stores, but wedding dress shopping was another one of her pastimes when she needed to decompress after an assignment.

She tried on dresses and veils. She knew the silhouette that suited her best, she even had her favourite designers. When they got to America, she couldn't wait to start shopping. Albeit, he hadn't asked her to marry him yet, she might even ask him herself, she thought, then immediately vetoed the idea. Nope, she was too traditional for that. No living together for years on end without a ring on her finger. She had always wanted to be a wife and a mother throughout high school until she'd found herself railroaded into being an operative. Not being an operative when the bureau had come calling had made her feel like she would be betraying her country. Her parents and Ian Franklin had even said as much. But not anymore. She was getting out. She'd find a way. She wanted to start her own family and soon.

She felt Matthew's un-gloved hand squeeze hers and, berating herself for not thinking, pulled off the leather gloves he'd given her to use and nudged them to his chest.

When he shook his head, she held them in one hand and buried her other hand in his jacket pocket.

Understanding, she felt him squeeze her hand gratefully, slow the bike slightly to pull them on, before roaring off again.

This was one of the worst nights of her life, but there was no-one else she would rather be with.

***

Matthew cast his eyes downwards for the fifth time in what seemed like the last second, if that could even be possible and yep, the bike stuttered and coughed as the red warning light went from flickering to steady. They had run out of gas.

He swore colourfully in his head. They were in the middle of nowhere with not even a twinkling light of civilisation in the distance.

The bike eventually sputtered to a stop, and Matthew glided the dead vehicle over into the shadow of trees and pulled down the scarf he had covering most of his face.

Lacy slipped tiredly off the back of the bike, took off the helmet Matthew had forced her to wear and went to lean against a tree. The ground was soggy with mud and leaves, the air sharp. The only light came from the motorbike.

"We ran out of gas," Matthew said grimly at her enquiring look once her helmet was off. Lacy had been holding his waist with increasingly frantic grabs as she tried to hold on.

They'd been riding for hours. The rough, little-used road, that more times than not became a track of deep ridges of frozen mud, which, with a trailer bike and daylight, would have been great to ride on, but in the dead of night, no lighting or signage, was hazardous. Matthew had driven as fast and as carefully as he could, but even with his skills, he couldn't make the ride any smoother for her.

Lacy sighed and looked around seeing exactly what he was seeing, and that was nothing but tall, dense woodland outside the circle of light from the bike.

"I guess we'd best hide the bike and walk." She suggested, trying not to flinch while pressing her back into the tree trunk. It hurt. It hurt bad.

Matthew would have done anything to make this easier for her. "Do you need your pain killers?" he asked, watching her carefully.

Lacy took a step here and another there, testing her lower limbs. She rotated her hips slowly and shook out her legs before answering. "I'll be okay," she looked around again. "Which way?"

Matthew looked down at the phone in his hand. He would have preferred to keep it off, knowing the phone could track them, but he had no choice.

"We can take the road," he turned the screen for her to see. "Or we can–"

"No," Lacy shook her head in the darkness. "We should go through here," she ran her finger down through the solid green patch on the screen. "It'll be faster."

"That's forest, Lace," Matthew warned.

"So? You've never been through a forest before, Edwards?" she teased.

Matthew laughed at her joke. They'd been through many a forest while on assignment over the years. This was serious, but he loved her for lightening the moment. They weren't likely to get lost because it was practically a straight route north to get to the coastline. But it was bitterly cold, minus something and the raindrops were getting denser and likely to turn to snow. They didn't have the right gear to go trampling about in the forest, not to mention they could be a potential meal for the wildlife, Matthew listed silently.

"If there were anyone I wanted to get eaten by wolves with, Lacy," he said, pushing the bike deeper into the undergrowth. "It's you."

Lacy helped him pull branches off trees and laughed. "I think this love business is getting to your head, Edwards," she joked, covering the bike, "all this flowery language is making me swoon."

He laughed outright at her fake Southern accent.

"You wait until I get you to a hotel, Dawson," he warned, stashing the motorbike helmet in the undergrowth, "then you'll really see how I can make you swoon."

Together they turned to face the wall of trees and bush in front of them. "Ready babes?" he asked, putting the gloves on her hands.

"When we get to the other side, I want a hot bath, a massage and a stack of pancakes." Lacy listed.

"Got it,"

"And a large hot chocolate with marshmallows,"

"It's yours."

"And kisses from a red-headed man with a beautiful body and hazel eyes that make me melt."

Matthew stopped, placed his hands on her shoulders and kissed her. "That's the prelude of more to come."

"Hmm, okay." She flung her shoulders back. "But as our dear superior, Ian Franklin likes to say," she saluted Matthew and grinned, "get it over with operatives!"

Matthew laughed, grabbed her hand and together they fought their way through the forest.

***

The sun was just easing over the horizon when, three hours later, the trees thinned, and the air became slightly warmer.

It had been hard. Lacy was in agony, but she kept up with him, knowing he had adjusted his stride to ease her way.

They stepped onto a high ridge of shovelled snow, paused on the top for a moment to gather their bearings and together they climbed down the other side to the road.

There was an old man throwing salt onto the street in front of his house. He stopped and watched openly as they passed, but quickly dipped his head seeing Lacy, Matthew noticed. That wasn't good, he thought, tugging her closer and hoping she hadn't noticed as he rushed them down the street.

Twenty minutes later, he spied a hotel from a popular European chain and, leaving Lacy hidden behind a van, checked them in, before finding the employee entrance and letting her in.

CHAPTER TWENTY-SEVEN

Matthew watched Lacy settle into a deep sleep before moving towards the window. Wisps of smoke slithered from chimneys from only a few houses, as the small town hadn't yet woken properly. He looked at the time on his watch, barely five-thirty.

Knowing there wasn't much he could do; he ensured the mobile phone Tanya had given them was turned off, and he removed the SIM card.

Moving warily because his body, battered from the fight and then frozen from the long ride had become stiff, he ensured the door was bolted and added the extra security precaution by wedging a chair beneath the handle before he allowed himself to relax just a little and have a quick shower.

He was tired, confused and angry with himself for forgetting the reason they were in Russia in the first place. Tanya, the Black Russian, had kidnapped Lacy and practically rendered her immobile with the back surgeries. Forget that Lacy had needed them, he should have insisted she recuperate in the city or be flown somewhere else. He'd messed up, and he was angry with himself. He had no idea what Tanya had been talking about, what Americans? Who wanted to harm them? Why?

His friend Rhodes hadn't really been communicating with them because things were quiet. There was nothing to report, no intel, no movement, nothing. Tanya was in Russia, at 'home' training like a soldier and ordering people about. Dmitri had left to continue his playboy lifestyle in Moscow and Charles, his men and Chase had spent most of their days in St. Petersburg city, and Matthew had stupidly allowed himself to relax like he was on a fucking vacation!

Shit, he had even planned to leave here in two days. They all had. Lacy was fit enough to travel, and he was itching to get back on American soil.

He looked over at Lacy sleeping peacefully, although he could see the lines of fatigue below her eyes. She'd been a champion. He'd been wrong all along, she hadn't lost her edge, she just chose when to use it, and he was more than okay with that.

Using the remote, he turned on the TV and flicked through the stations. All Russian, but he knew enough to keep skimming as the BBC would have a station even in this remote place. When he found it, he made himself a coffee from the small station on the side table and after another glance out of the window, settled in to watch World News.

***

Matthew must have dozed off because it was feeling Lacy gently shake his shoulder that woke him.

"Hey," she said, slipping onto his knee.

"Hey beautiful," he leaned in to kiss her neck. "Sleep okay?"

She nodded before saying. "I think we should scope out the area," she began. "I've been surveying the place and noticed a milk van parked off to the right that hasn't moved in fifteen minutes. The driver keeps checking his watch."

"Shit," Matthew grumbled. He should have been the one watching, but knowing he had to give Lacy being an operative a whole re-think. She still had her instincts. It wasn't all dead and buried under property websites and venison recipes.

He nudged her up and strode over to the window, slowly pushing the curtain aside. "Dark green van with the yellow writing on the side?" he asked over his shoulder.

She came up beside him and peered over his arm. "See the guy leaning against the wall?" she asked and went on. "He was the passenger then he got out, had a cigarette, talked on his phone and is still there. The driver hasn't moved. What do you think?"

"We'll give them another five minutes. We're sitting ducks in this place, and I don't like it." He wanted to ask why hadn't she woken him sooner, but she had this, and he trusted her to look out for them.

"Not really, Matthew," she countered, moving away to pour herself a glass of water. "You checked us in. You didn't use your real name, did you?"

He snorted. "Course not,"

"And the receptionist was too sleepy to pay much attention to anything."

"Lacy, anyone would pay attention to a stranger walking in from off the street at four in the morning? Use your head."

Lacy lifted her chin at his sarcastic tone. "So okay, what's your next plan?"

"I'm sorry I didn't mean to snap," he dropped the curtain and scrubbed his hands tiredly over his face. He needed a shave. "I don't have a plan aside from moving from here."

He looked out. "The receptionist is leaving. He's her boyfriend." He noted, seeing the young lady and man kiss by the wall and then watched as he helped her into the truck. It drove off without either of them glancing at the hotel.

"I'm going to order some breakfast and then take a walk. I need a phone and an internet cafe."

"I'll come with you."

"No," he said. "You stay here." At the flash of defiance in her dark eyes, he strolled over and tugged gently on one of her curls. "It'll be easier to melt in with the locals if you aren't with me." He said carefully, not wanting to offend her.

"Because I'm black?"

Trust her to get straight to the point. "And beautiful." He tacked on with a smirk.

"Nicely done," she teased up at him.

"I have my moments," he dropped a kiss on her nose. "Another half an hour and I'll go, okay?"

"Okay."

***

Lacy watched from the window as Matthew melted in with the locals. He'd hunched into his jacket and pulled the collar up, but his hair shone bright auburn, and his skin looked tanned against the pasty white locals. He looked like a foreigner. She waited until he had disappeared down the street before moving to finish her breakfast.

He came back within two hours, with a new phone.

"The internet cafe doesn't open until midday," he explained.

"Do you think you should turn that on?" Lacy asked, looking at the smartphone.

"It's a burner,"

"Wait until we really need to," Lacy warned.

Matthew looked at her properly, finally noting the pallor to her skin and the pinched look around her mouth. She was lying flat on the bed. "What's wrong?" When she didn't answer, he walked over to the bed. "Lacy?"

Opening her eyes, she looked at him from beneath her lashes. "My back," she admitted with regret. "It has seized up."

Matthew, placing one knee on the hard mattress, pushed aside the blankets and gently rolled her over. Her back looked smooth and subtle. The tiny puncture wounds from the keyhole surgeries, fully healed.

Matthew covered her again. "I'll run you a bath," he said grimly. The ride had been too much for her, he thought, testing the water with his wrists. At least the warm water would help ease her pain.

They stayed holed up in the hotel for three days before Matthew felt confident enough to leave her alone for a while to go to the internet cafe. She was able to walk if only slightly bent over. The gentle massages and warm towels on her muscles helped with the healing process, alongside the stretches and exercises every morning and evening.

***

Matthew quickly hacked into the bureau's portal for any information and followed the digital footprints Rhodes had left for him.

He scoured the info but came up with nothing new that Rhodes hadn't already told him. He was about to switch off when picture after picture of him and Rhodes came up. They had been friends for a long time, and Matthew watched and waited. There was something his friend was trying to tell him, and it came in the form of a Christmas party photograph.

Neither Matthew nor Rhodes had been at the office Christmas party. Matthew had been about to enjoy a leggy brunette when Rhodes had called, in need of help at a club. He'd been beaten up. Matthew had spent the entire night hunting down the men who had beaten up his friend. It was a memorable night for all the wrong reasons.

Matthew froze the photograph and, flexing his fingers, worked on the encrypted data behind the image.

It didn't take him long. He and Rhodes spoke the same IT language. Their minds worked on the same wavelength.

And what his friend told him, sent him cold. Shit!

CHAPTER TWENTY-EIGHT

"We've got to go!" Matthew rushed, as soon as Lacy opened the door after his signal of one, two, then another single sharp rap on the door.

"What did you find out?" She asked, stepping back.

"I'll explain on the way," he said, looking around and then finding the bag Tanya had given them. He up-ended it again, searched all the pockets and crevices for the second time since she gave it to them; he couldn't risk the other woman hadn't put a tracking device in there. He should have left the damn thing with the motorbike, he thought with regret, not for the first time, but he hadn't been thinking. He'd just wanted to get Lacy out of the elements that night and then the bag had somehow ended up under the bed out of sight.

Shit, where the hell had his wits been?

Lacy had everything packed and was ready to go in under a minute.

"Here, put these on," Matthew ordered, holding out the black woollen hat and thick scarf he had purchased for her and watched as she pulled the hat down low and wrapped the scarf around her neck and face until only her eyes could be seen. That would have to do, he thought grimly.

"They're looking for me?" she asked, with another flicker around the beige and brown hotel room that had been their brief sanctuary, before closing the door and moving in sync to the stairwell.

"No, they're looking for us," Matthew stated, throwing the backpack down the garbage shoot.

Lacy fell silent as they made their way down the dimly lit flights of stairs. Matthew had been using them to come and go.

She followed silently as he skimmed the rim of the foyer, went down a dark corridor and through a door marked with the silhouette of a man. The male toilets.

Once inside, Matthew entered a cubicle, stood on the toilet seat and opened a rectangular window with frosted bevelled glass.

"Up and out, Wallace," he ordered quietly, moving to make room for her.

They didn't speak again until they were both standing in a darkened alleyway with large garbage bins pushed against both walls.

Matthew grabbed her hand, knowing he was going to make his way to the docks. They needed to get out of Russia, fast. He knew best to go via the small market, busy with shoppers.

The docks were nothing more than a glorified fishing port. A cargo ship was moored out to sea, and several fishing boats were beached haphazardly on the pebbly sand. It was not picturesque with the rotting boats, open crates with fish scales and guts beside rubbish from the market stalls.

Matthew turned to Lacy, grabbing her face to peer into her eyes. "Remember our plan?"

Matthew had sat her down and made a contingency plan if they were to get separated just last night. Lacy hadn't thought they needed one and had paid little attention to what he'd said, but she nodded, recognising the urgency and panic in his eyes, now flashing gold.

"Whatever happens," he went on. "Make your way there, and you'll be safe. Got it?"

She nodded again, trying not to let him down and cry.

Matthew put his forehead to hers and slipped a folded piece of paper, money and phone into her pocket without her noticing.

"Stay here. If I'm not back in ten minutes, leave me."

Lacy grabbed his waist. "I won't lea–"

"You will," he interrupted harshly. They had already gone over this. She was to leave him and get herself out of Russia. He pulled down her scarf and kissed her tenderly before replacing it.

"I love you, Wallace." He whispered, kissing her again

through the wool. His eyes were swirling with a mixture of sadness and love. "Come on."

At the market, they separated. Matthew to the left. Lacy to the right. Lacy looked at the fruit, picked up an apple, replaced it and walked on.

Matthew strolled past a stall with brightly coloured plastic buckets, smiled at the pretty woman sitting on a wooden bench feeding the birds and walked to the other aisle. They were directly opposite. Lacy looked at him over the leather handbags but frowned when he looked over her head. He turned his back on her and picked up his pace.

Something was wrong. Something was off.

Matthew walked to the pale ribbon of concrete that sectioned the market from the beach. Lacy held back, something telling her to wait.

She turned her back to look at the magazines stacked on a carousel. They were all in Russian, but she recognised Dmitri and Tanya on the front cover of one. Lacy peered at her sister, who looked more like her, in a long black velvet ball gown and white satin gloves to her elbows. She was wearing diamonds, bright red lipstick and smiling serenely up at Dmitri. They looked like a couple. Lacy looked over her shoulder at Matthew, but he had walked quite a distance. He was too far away. She was about to follow him, when a bunch of uniformed men ran past her, almost knocking her over as, with guns raised, started shouting at Matthew, who turned, saw them coming and then ran towards the pier. She knew what he was doing, he was putting distance between them and her. Lacy watched in frozen horror when a shot rang out, and he went down.

"N–" her screamed was muffled behind the large hand that caught her words, and she was lifted off her feet and rushed towards the back of the stall.

"Shh," she was told and felt the steel of a gun pressing into her neck.

They stayed like that, cocooned at the back of the stall, while men yelled at each other, and she could feel the heavy vibration of their footsteps as they ran through the market.

Her captor held her tight, his large frame covering and pressing hers into the rough wood. She could barely breathe. He was giving her no room to manoeuvre around him and escape. Lacy had never felt so useless or afraid.

After what felt like hours, there was excited chatter and more footsteps, but this time, slower. They were leaving. Matthew was dead, and they were leaving. Lacy felt her body wilt and the burn of tears, remembering his last words.

Her captor moved slightly and said a few words in gentle Russian. Then a folded handkerchief was held out to her, and she looked at it and then into the face of her enemy that wasn't her enemy.

Ulvis.

CHAPTER TWENTY-NINE

For the sake of travelling via train up to Helsinki, Norway and flying into mainland Europe, before waiting a day for the all-clear to cross into Great Britain, Lacy was called Natalie Adams by the passport Matthew had somehow slipped into her pocket along with some money, phone and written instructions. She had no idea when he'd written the note, but she was grateful.

Ulvis was with her, and wouldn't leave her side. She was so worried.

All they knew was that Matthew had been shot by the Russian military police. She didn't know if he was dead or alive, but she followed his instructions to the letter.

Change your appearance if you can, he'd said. She'd dyed her brown hair auburn to match his. Blend in, she'd bought clothes at a charity shop. Keep a low profile. No tech or smartphones and get to a village in England called Frecknor Green and wait.

They had been here two days already.

Frecknor Green was a long drive up to Derbyshire in a beautiful area called the Peak District. And Frecknor Green was a tiny village with no hotel, only the B and B he had told her about.

With Ulvis dodging her heels, because she'd tried to shake him off more than once, being as Matthew's instructions hadn't included him, she'd knocked on the door to the charming but very old house.

She told the owner, Sylvie Watson, her name and was met with a blank stare and then Lacy had expanded when the seconds ticked by on the doorstep, saying Matthew Edwards and the older lady's face lit up and they were ushered into the most mind-boggling living room Lacy had ever seen in her life. The Queen's image was everywhere, even the curtains.

They'd stayed the night, and the next day, Sylvie walked them around the corner to another house that had ivy growing up the walls. It was a postcard in the making. Low grey stone walls and a narrow path that sliced the front garden in exact halves to a quaint front door with a brass knocker. Lacy fell in love with it.

They were met by Stewart, who apparently owned the place, shown around, asked questions in that polite, yet direct way the British were known for, and then left alone.

She and Ulvis had been waiting ever since.

The gate creaked, and Lacy walked quickly to the window, beating Ulvis. She was testy. He was testy. Neither of them good at waiting.

It was Stewart.

Lacy opened the door before he could knock as he was holding a basket.

"Morning, Miss Lacy, it's a pleasant morning like, isn't it?" he said with his broad Derbyshire accent.

"Good morning, we're yet to go out," she answered, stepping aside and following when he went straight to the narrow kitchen at the back of the house.

There, he placed the basket on the counter, removed the red chequered table cloth that, to Lacy, screamed country life and proceeded to unpack a loaf of bread, bottles of jam with handwritten labels on them and a white tub of what Lacy presumed to be butter.

"All local like," Stewart revealed with pride. "This here," he tapped the tub, "is from my farm just over the next field. My friend Camille–"

"Camille?" Lacy looked up quickly from where she was leaning against the door frame.

"Aye, Camille, you know, Camikara the actress?" he went on as though knowing the mega Bollywood actress was as normal as knowing the postman. "This here came from her cow." He chuckled obviously remembering Camille with fondness as his eyes twinkled.

"I know Camille," Lacy revealed.

"Aye," he touched his flat cap, "we know."

"How?"

"We are all family here, Miss Lacy," he said simply, looking directly into her eyes and holding her gaze, "we look after our own. You never mind anything out there. We will keep you safe." He turned to look over at Ulvis who was watching with his arms folded over his chest and his blue gaze unwavering. "With his help, of course." He tacked on with a chuckle.

"Do you know when we can leave?" She asked.

Stewart shook his head and moved his mouth from left to right. "Never mind that like, but things are happening." He picked up his now empty basket. "Sylvie and I do a spot of clay shooting in the evenings, you are both welcome to come along. I know this place can be too quiet for some people like." He offered kindly.

Lacy's smile was small, well aware he knew more than he was telling.

"No, I like it," she said, and she did, only wishing Matthew were here to share it with her. He obviously knew these kind people and the area well enough for her to stay here. He trusted them. "And yes, we would love to go clay shooting."

Stewart moved to the front door, and Lacy trailed behind him again. "Camille is a good shot. Eighteen in a row she got once. Can you beat that?" he challenged.

Lacy grinned. "I'll double it."

With another tip to his cap, he left.

CHAPTER THIRTY

Clay shooting was enjoyable enough, and she did shoot twenty-six clays in a row, but Lacy wasn't about to become fanatical about it. However, it broke the monotony of long wintry afternoons with nothing to do, except plan for a Christmas she may never see. There wasn't even a TV in the cottage.

With Ulvis by her side, Lacy, wearing clothes Sylvie Watson had loaned her, walked into the one-street village.

There was a small grocery store, a cafe with quaint metal chairs that reminded Lacy of Paris and a sixteenth-century church with a modern hall attached to it. That was it. For anything else, the villagers had to go into either the neighbouring much larger villages or the major cities of Derby, Manchester or Nottingham.

They walked down a grass lane, through a field to Stewart's dairy farm. He'd told her he was going to either change from dairy or sell completely. He wasn't making any money.

It would be a shame though, Lacy mused, as they jumped over a stile and plodded through the field, careful of the cow-pats along the way.

Stewart saw them approach and waited for them in the yard.

"Morning all," he welcomed.

"Morning," Lacy parroted, jumping the last fence and walking towards him, "we just thought we could come over, maybe watch TV, go on the internet or something?" she asked hopefully. She really wanted to scour the internet for anything she might find, try to contact Charles Edwards and even Rhodes if she could. Not knowing if Matthew was dead or alive was killing her, and she was willing to expose herself to find out. She'd give it all another three days and if she didn't hear anything, if no-one contacted her, then she was going back to

America, whatever the consequences.

Lacy watched curiously as a shallow tide of red crept up the older man's neck. He coughed once and then cleared his throat before answering.

"I can't go inside just yet," he answered, looking over Lacy's head, avoiding her eyes. "I've got me a pot of jam that needs stirring," he lifted his hand, showing the large metal spoon, "you can come and help me like." It wasn't a request because he turned to walk towards one of several outbuildings that dotted his property.

Lacy spent all day with Stewart, learning to make plum jam from the plums and damsons he'd picked and frozen over the summer.

Then the farmer showed her the mechanics of the dairy farm and where he made the butter. He kept them busy, enlisting Ulvis's help to move things around and by the time they'd returned to the cottage exhilarated yet exhausted that evening, Lacy hadn't realised she hadn't gone online.

For days, Stewart kept her busy. Putting her in charge of the jam-making for the village winter fête later that month.

***

"You hoo. You hoo!" Sylvie Watson called out, waving her arms spying Ulvis. He was about to enter the cottage. He turned to watch her approach. "Sorry I'm running late young man," she said huffing along with two bags filled with old Home and Garden magazines, Lacy had shown an interest in over tea at lunch today.

"I'll just leave these here on the doorstep like, and we can go," she placed the bags on the step, threaded her arm through his and guided him towards the back garden, where there was a low gate that led into the fields behind the cottage. Lacy was shooting with Stewart again.

They crossed the fields, and Sylvie chatted away about the goings-on in the village. He was a big bloke, very quiet and obviously devoted to Lacy.

Walking over a small rise, they could see Lacy shooting the

clays, splitting them into pieces as they whizzed across the evening sky.

"Great shoot," Sylvie cheered as they approached clapping her hands.

Lacy turned with a smile on her face, froze and then aimed her gun at the giant.

"Lacy? What on earth are you doing, dear?" Sylvie exclaimed with wide eyes.

Lacy ignored her, keeping her eyes trained on Ulvis's twin. She recognised him straight away. Ulvis had just walked towards the farm in the opposite direction and not only that, his build was thicker, his face meaner and of course the scarring on his neck that he didn't bother to hide.

"Leave her alone," Lacy stated coldly.

He sneered over at her. "No boyfriend now to hide behind," he drawled, grabbing Sylvie's arm and pulling her closer.

Lacy was dismayed to see Stewart saunter over. He'd been too far away to hear what was being said. "Stay where you are Stewart," she ordered. "He's not welcome here."

She saw Stewart stop in her periphery, not daring to turn to him.

"You and me," Lacy challenged, keeping her eyes steady on the twin. He was a bully, didn't want to be beaten by a girl, not that he and Matthew had fought, no, this was between them, and he wanted her beaten, bloodied and probably dead.

"Leave Sylvie alone," she said reasonably, lowering her rifle and then throwing it onto the grass. She raised her hands. "See? Just you and me. No guns."

The giant turned and slapped Sylvie so hard in the face, her whole body turned with the force of it before she hit the ground. She looked as though she had lost consciousness, Lacy thought, hoping the older woman would stay down.

"You!" The twin stabbed a meaty finger at Stewart. "Down, down!" he ordered, pointing to the ground beside Sylvie.

"I've got this Stewart, do as he says," Lacy warned. This was a replay of the incident back in New York with the young shopkeeper, Akash.

Stewart took his time, keeping his eye on the other man, before going down on one knee, touching the underside of Sylvie's neck checking for a pulse, before sitting down beside his friend and lifting her head to gently place it onto his lap.

"This! You do this!" the giant pulled a zip-tie from his back pocket and held it out to Lacy. He wanted her to tie up her friends.

"They won't move," she said.

"This!" He snarled. "Or they die!"

Lacy snatched the zip-tie from him and knelt beside her new friends.

"I'm sorry," she whispered, tying them loosely together.

The twin yanked at her ponytail, pulling her up before kicking her bottom and sending her flying. But she stayed on her feet and turned to him. His fists were already raised, his eyes narrowed and trained on her.

Lacy took him on. She could tell he was surprised, and she used every trick she had to get him flat on the ground. He would stumble, but always remained standing. She was nimble and wasn't afraid to dive between his legs or skitter to the side.

If he grabbed her, she would go down. She couldn't go down.

The fight wasn't ending. They were both tired, and she could see her frustration echoed in his eyes as she dived to the left, avoiding his meaty hands again when he tried to grab her shoulders and throw her down.

Lacy doubled back to kick him in his side, but he grabbed her ankle and twisted it to the left. Lacy twisted her entire body with the movement, flinging herself forward to roll on the ground or she'd end up with a broken ankle. Lacy landed hard, but before she could move, the twin slammed his booted foot into her lower back. Pain shot up her spine and down her legs, and she couldn't help the scream that burst up her throat.

Dazed, she rolled again and again when he tried to stamp on her.

He was smiling now, he saw through her tears of pain, and he picked up her feet, dragged her forward and sat on her chest.

Lacy tried to buck him off, but he laughed and leaned forward to press his thumbs into her windpipe.

He pressed harder, smiling tightly. She tried to twist away, but the darkness was creeping. Creeping as the air disappeared. She tried to fight it. Fight the darkness. Snatch at the air. But he was too heavy, too solid and too evil.

The surrounding scenery blurred into a mass of faded green, like a fudged painting, going darker and Lacy said goodbye to Matthew, her parents, even Ian Franklin. She said goodbye to Sylvie and turned her head to say goodbye to Stewart. Such awesome people.

"Get up, operative!" Stewart yelled. "Fight!" he ordered as his face faded and blurred away. "Fight!"

Lacy wilted against the heavy weight on top of her, then with uncanny precision and renewed strength, twisted and slithered from under him. She skittered away as he slipped sideways and raised her booted foot to kick him square in the face. His head snapped back. Blood flew through the air, and he wobbled on his knees.

With a roar, the giant raised his head and with death in his eyes stumbled to get up.

"Run, Lacy!" Stewart shouted. "Run!"

But Lacy wasn't going to leave her new friends, people who had opened their home to her and protected her without even knowing her.

She positioned herself and, before the twin could stand properly, high kicked him in quick succession in the face. He stumbled backwards, three, four steps, but still, he kept coming. Lacy was exhausted. She had nothing left.

They squared off again. He was breathing deeply. So was she, but she needed to end this. Remembering the word he had used back in Russia. "*Suka*," she sneered and spat on the ground much like he had done. "Come and get me you bastard."

Lacy braced herself, but before he reached her, a loud shot rang out. He spun on his heels to face the other direction.

Stunned, Lacy looked over his shoulder before falling to her knees, the adrenalin ending as though shut off by a tap.

"I'm sorry, Ulvis," she whispered, knowing his brother was dead.

Ulvis said nothing, but went to Stewart and Sylvie and, using his hands, snapped the zip-tie as though it were cotton thread.

"I need to take care of this, yes," he stated grimly, looking at his brother a moment later.

Sylvie groaned again and opened her eyes. Stewart pulled her head into the crook of his neck, not wanting her to see the dead man.

"I'm sorry," Lacy said again to all of them. She had brought this on these lovely people. She needed to leave.

They were all silent for a moment. Overwhelmed with all the emotions swirling around them, friendship and hatred. Loyalty and dishonour. Brothers.

"Let's go," Stewart said eventually, pulling Sylvie to her feet. The older woman had a huge bruise already forming on her usually unlined cheek.

Lacy stumbled to her feet. Her back hurt, but she could walk.

"I'll go and get some shovels," Stewart said to Ulvis, leading Sylvie away.

With a glance at Ulvis and his nod of acknowledgement, Lacy followed.

Not long after, they were all sat quietly in Stewart's kitchen, thinking between themselves.

"I'm leaving," Lacy said suddenly into the silence.

"No," this from Stewart. "Ace and Charles asked us to take care of you."

"Oh yeah?" Lacy challenged, "they didn't ask you for this, did they?" She slammed back. She was angry. She had lost all control of her life. She didn't know if Matthew was dead or alive. She was hiding out in England, and she didn't even know who she was hiding from. It was time to finish this.

Lifting her chin, she turned to Ulvis. "Tell me everything."

***

They entered the United States via Canada. Lacy didn't ask where Ulvis got the money from, but he had it. She just needed to get to the States and would ask questions later. Much later. They'd flown into a small airport in Ontario and hired a car to cross the border.

He drove through the night, saying little. She had little to say, ever since he had told her about his early life and what he knew about hers.

The night before they'd left, Lacy, deaf to Stewart's pleas, went online, searched for and found information on any killings on or around the time she'd been in New York. She'd found several and one where three men had been killed while trying to rob the Bollywood actress Camikara. Her friend Dirk had also been killed. An absconded female Government agent had been implicated in the killings. Stunned, as without being named, Lacy knew they were referring to her. There was an international warrant out for her arrest!

It was then that Stewart admitted he'd known of the warrant from Charles who was now in America. She was supposed to stay in England until he could clear it up. Lacy wasn't about to leave anything up to a man she barely knew, and where was Matthew? There had been no mention of him anywhere, and she worried over the lack of information, hoping no news was good news in this case.

They all knew she was innocent. It had to have been Tanya, but to prove that, they had to find her twin and *she* was missing.

Stewart and Sylvie hadn't wanted her to leave but knew they wouldn't have been able to convince her otherwise. So with tears clogging up her throat, she'd waved goodbye to them and the little village that had given her a brief spell of paradise. Life outside of the bureau. A simple, tranquil life. She'd wanted to promise and say she'd be back. But that was a lie. She knew it, and so did they. They had secrets now the four of them. To see her, would be to relive the horror of a single evening. No, she would never go back to Frecknor Green.

CHAPTER THIRTY-ONE

Matthew didn't think the nightmare would ever end.

He was sat in the loaned Q7 his brother Ace had given him to use for the night. He had a massive headache pounding the front of his head and huge knots of tension extending along his shoulders and across his back, adding to his distress and lack of sleep. He'd been like this for six whole days and counting.

From the docks in Russia, he'd been blindfolded and bundled onto a large aircraft. Nobody had spoken, not even when they'd taken care of the flesh wound to his shoulder where he'd been shot.

They'd arrived in the States, and he was taken to an empty house on a street busy with heavy traffic. He'd been locked in a room with an en-suite, fed decent meals three times a day and that was it.

Nothing happened. No demands were made from him, nothing, which made it more fucking frustrating. Rhodes had been silent too, and he could only assume something had happened to his friend.

Then this afternoon they'd bundled him into a car and dropped him off in front of Ace's fancy building. Inside, he'd connected with Akash–who was back in the States and working freelance for his father–and been informed Lacy had made it to Frecknor Green with Ulvis. He'd been finalising his flight plan to England when his father had issued an alert. Kyle, his cousin, needed their help. Someone had been killed at his girlfriend's Camille's house, and she had gone into labour.

He'd gone to help, knowing Lacy was in the safest place she could be, while he helped with this new family crisis.

Only things hadn't been that simple. Camille wouldn't meet his eye when she'd looked at him and refused to say who had killed the man. She was hiding something. Everyone knew she was hiding something, but for now, his father and Kyle could deal with her and that messed up situation. He needed to get to Lacy. The Mannino plane was on standby waiting, and he just needed to collect some stuff from the apartment.

He was about to alight when his new phone rang. It was his father.

"Sir?"

"Lacy has been implicated in the murder of Camille's brother," he stated grimly.

"What the fuck?!" Matthew yelled, forgetting who he was talking to. "She's in England!"

"We know that son," his father said soothingly. "Your friend at the bureau found a way to get a message to Akash. It can only be Tanya."

Matthew rubbed his head. The knots of tension tightened along his neck. This was bad.

"What do I do?" Matthew asked fiercely, yet already forming a plan in his head. He was going after Tanya.

"I will see if I can track Tanya down," Charles said. "You stay where you are and rest. Nobody knows where Lacy is, and it's safer to keep her out of the way."

"But–"

"We need to find Tanya," his father interrupted calmly. "With her running around shooting people in the name of your girlfriend, well," he reasoned. "I need to shut her down and find out why they wanted you out of the way."

"Kyle, okay?" Matthew thought to ask, to get his father off the scent. Rest? He was going hunting.

"Kyle has never been better."

Matthew felt a shiver of envy for his cousin. He'd had a messed-up year, losing his sight and everything, but at least his woman was under his own roof. Lacy was out there in danger.

Matthew hung up, used the key fob to lock the car and walked to the elevator. At least his computers and everything was still there, he thought, planning.

***

Matthew entered the apartment and knew immediately that he wasn't alone.

"What the fuck are you doing here?" he asked viciously once his mind had registered it was Tanya and not Lacy who was standing in front of him pointing a weapon at him.

"Are you alone?" she asked harshly, looking over his shoulder.

He kicked the door shut and walked into the room.

There was only one lamp on, and the rest of the room was cast into gentle shadows.

"Don't make me repeat myself, lady," he drawled and frowned down at her gun. "And get that damn thing off of me now!"

Tanya lowered the gun and tucked it into the waistband of her jeans, before quickly striding to his computers.

Keeping his eyes on her, Matthew strode over to see what she was doing.

"Where is Wallace?" she asked quietly, tapping away without looking at him.

"Safe from the likes of you,"

She turned to him; her eyes narrowed. "I am not her enemy."

"Oh yeah," he folded his arms on his chest, then thought better of it and with a single stride that took him to her side, leaned in close, placed both hands on each arm of her chair and got in her face. "She's under arrest for a murder you committed!" he pointed out savagely.

Tanya's dark gaze didn't so much as waver. "I had my reasons,"

"Fuck your reasons!" Matthew snarled. "How the hell did you get in here, anyway?" He looked around as though seeing the room for the first time. "And what the hell are you doing?"

She stared at him, daring him to move. He did so on his own accord, only because looking at her was like looking at pure evil. She was nothing like his Lacy. Nothing at all.

"Ulvis tracked you to the village docks," she told him, talking while running her own programme on his system. "He was there when the Russian military grabbed you on my orders. He travelled with Wallace and kept her safe. They've developed quite a friendship, don't you think?" she asked casually.

"Your orders?"

"The Americans were closing in, I thought it best to grab you first."

"It was you who kidnapped me? Had me shot?"

She flicked her hands at him, turning back to the screens. "Never mind that. Ulvis and Wallace are in America,"

"What? No!"

Tanya turned to his computers and pulled up a map. A red dot was moving.

"Ulvis," she stated simply, pointing at the dot.

"You have a tracking device on him?" Matthew asked, already knowing the answer.

"His twin found them in England."

"What?!" he yelled. "How?"

"The same way I knew he'd gone rogue," she shrugged. "It happens with some of us."

"Lady, I don't know what the hell you're talking about," Matthew blazed in confusion. She was talking in fucking riddles, and his tired brain couldn't keep up.

She didn't look at him, but tapped away, pulling up a map of England. "He was there, but his digital pulse disappeared," she explained. "We are all chipped."

"Digital pulse?"

"We are all chipped," she repeated, pulling forward the cuff of her sleeve, before thinking better of it and letting the fabric settle around her wrist.

Matthew grabbed her arm, shoved her sleeve back up and peered at her skin.

He'd heard the bureau had started micro-chipping the latest operatives, but not that any other organisation was doing it. He ran his index finger along the underside of her forearm and felt the tiny rectangular chip just beneath her skin, about two inches from the crease of her elbow.

She tugged her arm away before saying. "His digital pulse died with him."

"Are you saying Lacy killed him?" Matthew scoffed. Lacy couldn't kill a flea, but then again, the Lacy of late had regained all her survival skills when she'd needed to. Like him, she had been trained to kill. They all had. But still...

Tanya shrugged and zoomed the map closer. "By the looks of this, I think they're heading to D.C."

"Why?" Matthew asked.

She spun around in her chair and pinned him with an innocent look. "To clear her name, of course."

Matthew looked at her for a full five seconds not believing her audacity, before yanking her out of the chair and away from the computers, to march her to the nearest wall where he caged her in.

Things started falling into place all at once. Tanya was hiding in plain sight. He hadn't meant to come here tonight. He should have gone straight to the airport and on to England.

There was something else bugging him, and he asked outright.

"What happened to your accent? Why did you ever get into contact with Lacy? What the hell do you want?"

He'd pinned her against the wall with his forearm across her throat and was disgusted to see her looking bemused by his actions. He let her go and spun on his heel. He was so out of sorts he didn't know where to begin.

"You love her?" she asked quietly.

Matthew spun back to her in disbelief. She could actually ask him that!

"What the hell do you think?"

She shrugged one shoulder; the move was so like Lacy.

"You would kill for her?" she asked casually.

"Without a doubt," he looked at her. "Starting with you."

Throwing back her head, she laughed outright.

She laughed like Lacy too. Damn it!

She looked at the large watch around her wrist.

"In a little over two hours, I'm guessing Wallace and Ulvis will get to the bureau. You need to be there."

"You, lady, are coming with me." He charged darkly. Tanya went where he went from now on.

She shook her head. "No,"

Matthew was about to get in her face again when she suddenly paled and closed her eyes as though about to faint. He stopped himself from reaching for her.

"You okay?" he asked reluctantly.

"Yes," she whispered, but the hand she used to touch her mouth was trembling.

She didn't look okay, Matthew thought. She looked bewildered and noted her hand going to the base of her stomach. She closed her eyes again, and when she opened them, she looked different. Softer, if that was at all possible.

Matthew went to the fridge for some water. He might hate her, but she was obviously sick.

"Here." He handed her the bottle.

She twisted the cap and drank half before looking over at him. "You didn't answer me," she said.

"What?"

"Do you love her?" Tanya repeated.

He laughed in the face of her seriousness but played along. "I love her.

"Good," she drank more water and moved towards the door. "We need to get to D.C. before she does." She added chirpily.

Matthew stood frozen. Was she playing him again? He couldn't trust her, he wouldn't trust her, but she was right. He needed to get to D.C., and *she* was coming with him.

"Wait," Matthew jogged to his bedroom and rummaged around for Lacy's security pass before they left.

CHAPTER THIRTY-TWO

Rhodes saw her coming and timed the security override perfectly. For a split second and only because he was looking, did he see her flicker of relief, but she kept going, confidently striding down the corridor as though she wasn't about to start a war within the bureau.

If he didn't have to wait, he'd map her progress, so instead zoomed back outside, seeing the shadow of her Russian bodyguard in the car, before scanning the rest of the car park.

With only her smile and a small wave, Lacy walked past security, flashing her expired badge as she went along. She nodded at the colleagues she recognised and made her way further into the depths of this horrible place.

It was all very grey and clinical. The lighting harsh. People glanced and then quickly looked away as though to maintain eye contact was to give away state secrets. She hated it. Hated everything about it.

She didn't knock on the door but strode straight in.

He was waiting for her. She could tell by the steely glint in his eyes. He wasn't the least bit shocked.

"I want to know what the hell you're doing?"

Her superior had the gall to laugh.

"If it isn't my favourite operative," Ian Franklin drawled, leaning forward to place his elbows on the uncluttered surface of his desk.

He didn't even pretend to not know what she was talking about and picked up his black mug which said, *Best Dad* in a red scrawl, he took a sip, grimaced into it, before placing it down and leaning into his cracked chocolate leather chair.

"Do you know how old I was when the bureau came courting, Wallace?" he asked pleasantly instead, steepling his fingers before looking at her.

212

Lacy shrugged, this was not how this interview was supposed to be and stepped right up to his desk. "I really don't want to go down memory lane with you," Lacy sneered. "I want to know why you thought you could play with my life!"

"But to know that," he reasoned casually. "I have to start at the beginning, Wallace." His smile was slight. "You know you're like a daughter to me." His glance was telling, and he moved his head to the side. "I was young and ambitious," he tapped each of his fingertips together, "it was easy to play both sides."

"You're a traitor," she seethed, her mouth pulling down in disgust before tossing at him. "A disgrace to this country,"

"*Au contraire*," he countered with a fake accent. "I had the backing of everyone. Russia *and* America. Fifty years ago, they were sworn enemies to the outside world, but really? A group of Russian and American scientists worked together in harmony. Perfectly. It was beautiful."

He looked off into the distance as though seeing the Russian and American Presidents holding hands and playing in the damn sandpit! Lacy thought, disturbed.

"You want to arrest me!" Lacy slapped his desk to bring his eyes back to her.

"Your sister and her merry men are ruining my experiment." He delivered tightly, the mocking glint in his eyes gone.

"I didn't shoot anyone, you know that," she charged. "You know me!"

"It is what is it, Wallace," he tapped his fingers again. "There will always be casualties in war. You are my favourite though, and I really didn't want it to come to this." He picked up his phone and turned the screen to her. "See? I was still counting the time you had been away from me." He placed the phone face down and sighed. "Only now I'm going to have to arrest you."

"You're crazy." She sank into the chair behind her and faced him. The way he said that made the hairs on the back of her arms and neck stand on end. How had she never felt this before? His look was disturbing, not sexual, no, more territorial. "You can't arrest me." Lacy threw at him tipping her chin up and searing him with her dark gaze.

"Watch me."

"I'll tell everyone what you did. Go to the papers. Everyone above you."

He laughed. "And you think they would believe a disillusioned operative like you? I have images of you walking around Mother World with a dazed expression on your face!" he laughed, seeing the colour leech from her face. "You think I would let you walk out of here?"

Lacy stood.

So did he.

He pulled his gun from the back of his pants and pointed it at her.

"You won't shoot me," she challenged, remembering as a little girl, him pushing her on the swing in her back garden and their laughter.

"I don't want to, Wallace, and it will pain me, but you've given me no choice, I've got a bigger picture to consider, and I can't let you leave." He sounded almost regretful.

"This is playing out like a 1950 movie *Uncle* Ian."

He chuckled, tipping his head at the title she used to use until she'd started working at the bureau and she'd deemed it inappropriate. "I will kill you, Wallace."

"And ruin your little experiment?"

"It is what it is," he said again lightly. "You are only one of many."

"How many?"

He shrugged impatiently. "It's hard to keep up with the multiples having multiples."

"You were playing God."

"Still am." He admitted without remorse.

"I don't know you like this," she whispered, shivering. He was so cold and detached. She had never seen him like this.

"Come on now Lacy," he checked his watch, then went into his desk drawer. Looking directly at her, he pulled out the silencer for his weapon and began slowly screwing it on. "I can't let you leave here. You know that."

She didn't think, and he didn't see it coming.

Lacy jumped across his desk and kicked the gun out of his hand. It went flying and hit the black and white print with an elaborate Gemini symbol. They both went crashing to the floor. Lacy quickly jammed the heel of her hand into Ian Franklin's throat and as he gasped for breath, ran for the gun and pointed it at him from across the room.

Ian stared at her first in shock and then with lazy humour.

"Don't make me kill you." She whispered.

He took a step forward. Lacy pulled the trigger.

CHAPTER THIRTY-THREE

The vase of flowers to his right shattered.

Lacy was just about to shoot on his other side when she was suddenly hauled off her feet by a band of steel hooking around her midriff and the gun yanked from her surprised hands.

"What–" she gasped, then she was turned and rearranged against the one body she wanted to be closest to. "Matthew?" Her eyes immediately filled with tears, and she clasped his face with hands that shook. "You're alive?" she said in wonderment, letting the tears fall. She'd been praying and hoping and willing him to be alive. Now he was here, the tip of his nose was red and peeling, he had lines of fatigue around his eyes, but his eyes were warm and swirling, no doubt echoing the relief in hers.

Lacy was overcome with emotion. Going from cold hostility to tender relief in the space of seconds and her throat closed. "Please tell me you're okay?" she whispered against his lips and wrapped her arms around his neck. She wanted to stay in that exact place forever. Never mind the one man she thought looked out for her wanted her dead and was standing behind her. Ian Franklin was dangerous. But right now, all that concerned her was that she was finally with Matthew. He looked unhurt, although his right arm was in a sling again.

"I'm fine," Matthew answered, giving her a quick hug before setting her down on her feet. He'd been beside himself these past few days, hell, he'd been beside himself these past few months. Lacy sure came with a lot of drama, he thought tenderly. "You planning on doing something with this?" he inquired, looking at and turning the gun over in his hand.

"Yes," she answered, gazing up at him. He was the most beautiful man she had ever seen. She'd missed him, had worried for him and now he was here. She turned in his arms, keeping her back pressed to his front. "I was about to kill the bastard."

Ian Franklin's rough laugh bounced off the walls.

"You're too much of a tender heart to shoot me, Wallace," he stated with confidence.

"She might be," a voice behind them said. "But I'm not." Tanya stepped around the loved-up couple.

Lacy watched as her twin, dressed very much like herself in black jeans and long-sleeved T-shirt raised the Glock–her Glock– at Ian Franklin.

"Tanya, I presume?" Ian Franklin asked with a raised brow.

"You know who the hell I am." She replied tightly, watching as the old man moved behind his desk to sit in his chair.

"I wouldn't if I were you," she said conversationally watching as his hand dipped beneath the edge of his desk, sliding under the rim to no doubt press a button for security. He stopped, entwined his fingers and rested his hands on the desk in studied casualness.

"You can't leave here Tanya," he said, leaning back in his chair, "in fact, neither one of you can, and now that you're here too Edwards..." He left that sentence hanging before glancing at Lacy. "There's an arrest for killing three men in New York, and one for killing the brother of that famous Bollywood actress, Camille–Camikara, something or other," he derided. "*Both* of you will be going away."

Lacy, not wanting her sister to be arrested, stepped forward. Well, she tried to, but Matthew hauled her back into his arms.

"Tell him," he said to Tanya.

"I killed them all," she admitted, watching the smile creep onto Ian Franklin's face. "But then you already knew that didn't you?" She queried.

The older man looked as though everything was going his way, and it was. Admitting to the killings was what he wanted.

"You're making this very easy for me," he rocked back in his chair, his pale eyes mocking. "Tanya, the notorious Black Russian in the heart of the bureau, imagine that?"

"I don't know *Ian*," she stepped forward, careful to keep herself between Wallace and Matthew. Ian Franklin looked like a soft-hearted easy-going American. But he was one of the deadliest people she knew. A true psychopath. Smiling while killing you softly. "I think it's about time the world knew what a modern-day Frankenstein you really are."

He sat forward now, narrowing his eyes before flicking to Wallace and then back to Tanya.

"You at least owe Wallace an explanation," Tanya insisted. "The adoption, the experiment." She listed. "Did you tell her what you actually do behind the security of your desk, hmm? Taking advantage of your position? Your seniority within the bureau."

"She already knows,"

"I don't," Lacy shot back. "Not all of it."

Her sister had yet to look at her, but without turning, she spoke.

"Almost sixty years ago, during the height of the cold war, a bunch of scientists thought to make superhumans," Tanya explained to the entire room. Lacy and Matthew listened keenly. Ian Franklin with pride glowing from his eyes. "But things didn't go as planned. The women they impregnated in the laboratories had twins and triplets, multiples, with distinct personalities. With the first crop of babies, one twin was obviously much weaker, and they were experimented on like lab rats before being fed to the dogs.

"Then a certain young recruit new to the bureau, an egotistical hot head, thought to separate the babies and place them in controlled environments. Taking the experiment one step further. He had the weaker twins placed in normal homes, with families in first world countries, like America, West Germany, Australia. The dominant twins raised in Russian children homes that were run like military camps. Or made to struggle on the streets of Syria, Iraq, Third World war-torn countries. No love. Killing to survive."

"For years, it went on. Hundreds of multiples born across the world, but the lies really began in the womb." She leaned closer to Ian. "How am I doing so far?" she asked, although not waiting for an answer. "The birth certificates said Germany, England, Canada, France and Italy. The babies living as siblings until the dominant twin was established and sent to the roughest orphanages or parts of the world for the training to begin. They were turned into killers. *I* was trained to hate."

Lacy gasped and was grateful for Matthew's arm around her.

"You can arrest me Ian Franklin, but how would that look?" She sneered at him. "You can even try to arrest Wallace and all the others, but we are products of your perverted vision. We are of your blood."

"What?" Lacy said, seeing his face pale.

Still, Tanya kept her gaze on Ian Franklin. "How does it feel, *father,*" she snarled. "Coming face to face with your children?" she asked with a tilted eyebrow. "Any fatherly protectiveness coming out for your daughters?" She laughed, stepping around the desk and tilting her gun to the underside of his jaw.

She pushed back on his chair with her foot, forcing him to look at her.

"When you look at me, what do you see?" she tipped her head to the side. "A woman with your eyes? An experiment? A killer? Your daughter?" she asked lightly. "You must be so proud."

She stepped away and flicked her sweater up.

"See this?" she indicated the wire taped to her chest, the microphone between her breasts. "I can either erase this right here, right now and you let us walk, or you can arrest us, and my new friend Kev Taylor will have this conversation on the news within five minutes."

"You're bluffing," Ian Franklin said, swivelling his chair to look at Wallace. "She's lying," he said.

"Why would she lie?" Lacy asked.

"Because she's jealous, always wanted what you had. A family." He blustered. "I'm your father, Wallace. I've always looked after you." He appealed.

"You're my father?" she scoffed. "My father lives not six blocks from here," Lacy answered, thinking of the man who'd raised her. She may not have had a lot of cuddles growing up, but she had parents who cared about her.

"It all makes sense now," she thought aloud, thinking back over her childhood. The extracurricular activities, the mental training. Ian Franklin had always been in her life. Visiting her parents on a Sunday, always keen to know what she was doing, how she was progressing. "Did my parents know?" she asked on a whisper, not really wanting to know, but knowing she had to. He was her father!

"No."

"You have two seconds," Tanya went on menacingly, bringing the conversation back on track. "Make the arrests go away. Leave us alone for the rest of your miserable life and retire with dignity and our silence, or,"

"Or?"

"Or I press this," she held the device the wire was attached to in her hand. Her thumb over a tiny button. "And the life that you know will be ruined."

CHAPTER THIRTY-FOUR

"At least Dmitri has redeemed himself," Tanya was on a roll, her mouth twisting in displeasure, knowing she now had his full attention, and he wasn't sneering in superiority at her any more. It was a relief to get it all out.

"You know what your problem is?" she didn't wait for an answer as she glowered at him. "You actually thought you could get away with it," she chuckled. "Start killing us off as though we are nothing but lab rats for political experimentation, used, abused and discarded when things didn't turn out how you wanted them.

She laughed. "Oh, how you must hate Dmitri for publicly owning us and showing me off to the world as his open secret, Ian," she sneered. "Me, living an open life," her voice quivered, just a little, with the clogging emotion of her distress. She had waited a lifetime to say this.

"You panicked, didn't you? Your living secret brazen enough to be out in the open and *you*, egotistical psychopath that you are, showed your hand. Dmitri was funding the project to find and protect us all from the campaign you had to kill us off." She stabbed the air close to his face. "You and your evil cronies almost got away with it. You are a disgrace to your country!"

She glanced at Lacy then shifted her gaze back to him. "Look at us, *father*," she spat. "Two of your children in the same room. In the same country. How does it feel? Hmm. What would your wife think? The children you share with her, carve a turkey at Thanksgiving. What would they think?" She asked, not expecting an answer. "How many children have you fathered? Hmm, ten? Twenty? Fifty? More? I don't know," she shrugged one shoulder. "Do you? You're a psychopath, worse than the scientists. You did this for no other reason than because you could! You are worse than the filth on my boots!"

Ian Franklin stood up then, his face purple with rage, his mouth working quickly before the sound came out in a growl.

"Go near my family, Tanya, and I will kill you myself." He warned coldly.

Tanya casually reached over and picked up the heavy silver frame perched on his desk, scowling at it before throwing it face down with scorn.

"You get to have a family," she breathed chillingly. "What did I get? What did *she* get?" she tossed over her shoulder at Lacy. "What did any of us get? You played God, and you're still playing God. But not anymore. I'm going to expose you for the scum that you are. You are ruined, finished and all of your cronies with you! And I don't care if most of them are now dead. I'm going to name every single one of them. I'm going to name all the children you fathered, the grandchildren and all the names of those you've already killed!"

Lacy watched this once larger-than-life man deflate right in front of them.

"What do you want?" he'd sunk into his chair, beaten. He knew that. The scandal would be too big to contain. Fifteen years ago, Professor Sokolov had stupidly begged for forgiveness on his deathbed, to his priest, with a junior nurse in the room, they'd had to pay her off before eventually killing her when she got too greedy.

"I want you to leave us alone."

"You are already in America, the deal was for you to remain in Europe, Tanya. You never should have come here."

She laughed then, a rusty sound that tore across the room and slapped him down.

"You think I would let you kill her?" she tossed her head in Lacy's direction again. "She has always been protected."

Lacy gasped in confusion and watched as her superior actually smiled knowingly.

"The missions you sent her on," Tanya began again. "The *unnecessary* risks to her life?" she smirked. "She was the experiment within the experiment, wasn't she? Normal upbringing but taught to be an operative. Taught to kill. You sick bastard!" She got in his face. "But there was something else wasn't there, D*ad*?" she sneered. "The screwed-up fascination of knowing your child, your daughter, was near and nobody knew it but you?" she revealed with a huff of disdain.

"She is my daughter, as are you," he pointed out, with a twist to his lips as though acknowledging Tanya would poison the air.

"Sperm donor," Tanya clarified, running out of patience. "You leave us alone, call off your dogs, and I will forget you ever existed."

"Or?" Ian Franklin dared to ask.

"Or the wire I am wearing, the files that we have, the monitoring of your calls and whereabouts, every time you touched Russian soil when you told the bureau you were elsewhere for the last thirty years will become public knowledge." Tanya pulled out her phone and showed him a black-and-white image of himself holding a newborn with two other babies in cots behind him, before putting her phone in her back pocket.

"And if anything happens to her," she said over her shoulder. "I will hunt you down and kill every single person on that photograph," she flicked a glance at his desk. "And that, *father*, I can promise. After all, I am the product you always wanted aren't I. The evil twin. The deadly soldier."

The air in the room was fraught with tension as the seconds ticked by. Nobody moved.

Ian franklin's nod was minuscule, the anger mixed with defeat, palpable as it rolled off him and he took a step back to slump into his chair.

It was silent.

Lacy watched on with tears that stung the backs of her eyes, her heart squeezed tight with cords of mixed emotions. Ian Franklin was their father? The Gemini Project, and Tanya protecting her all these years?

Matthew, feeling Lacy's shoulders tremble, pulled her tighter into the security of his arms.

Tanya had told him some of it on the flight up here, but this? This was…? He couldn't find the words. This was what happened when psycho's with too much power and egos cooked up crazy ideas. There wasn't a novel out there like this reality.

"Come on," Matthew said, as the silence continued. He wanted to get them out of here.

Tanya turned to look at him then, almost as though suddenly remembering he was in the room.

"Do it," Tanya turned to Ian Franklin, holding his subjugated stare. She wasn't done with him yet.

His pale eyes narrowed, knowing what she wanted him to do and with a defeated sigh, reached up, pulled off his tie, unbuttoned the top two buttons on his crisp white shirt and pulled out a silver chain. He pulled it over his head and held it in his hands, looking down at the Gemini pendant almost reverently.

Tanya turned to his laptop and started typing as he watched.
"No!"

"This is your resignation," she smiled with cold malice. "See what a perfect daughter I am? So very helpful." She pressed a key, and the printer on a side table jumped to life, and the printed A4 slid out.

"Sign it." Tanya helpfully held out his pen to him.

He grabbed it, sprawled his signature across the bottom and slid the page across the desk.

Tanya smiled. "This is for me to take home." She folded the letter and tucked it inside her jacket. She tugged the chain out of his hand and looked down at the symbol. "The Gemini experiment," she jeered. She'd already collected six others, and there was another one out there. She put it in her pocket. "It is finished."

She stepped backwards. "And anything those two want, they get," she stated adamantly. "Have you got that?" She commanded at his bent head. When he didn't answer, she grabbed the front of his shirt, forcing him to look at her. "Have you got that?" she asked softly. Too softly.

Lacy watched in awe as her sister held the gaze of the man who had fathered them both, until his eyes, now blurry with tears nodded.

"Good."

Tanya let him go and walked out of the office without looking left or right.

When she had gone, Ian Franklin looked at Matthew and Lacy, searing them with what could only be called a pathetic look.

"We're quitting," Matthew said into the silence and with his good arm over her shoulders turned them both towards the door.

"With the bureau's blessings," Lacy added, as they crossed the threshold and strolled casually to freedom.

***

Matthew and Lacy walked out of the building and were just in time to see Tanya moving towards a dark blue Sedan. Lacy looked at the car, remembering all the other times she had seen it and not just these past few months.

"Wait!" Lacy called out, but Tanya kept moving. "Tanya wait!" Lacy yelled, running to catch her. "Please," she begged.

Tanya paused, about to lower herself into the vehicle and slowly turned to look at her.

Lacy's breath left her. This was the first time Tanya had ever made significant eye contact.

"Will you come for dinner?" Lacy asked quietly.

There was a flare of something in her sister's dark eyes, but Lacy didn't know what it was. Maybe sadness, maybe joy. Maybe even relief.

The smile Tanya bestowed on her was more of a soft twitch to her lips.

"One day."

CHAPTER THIRTY-FIVE

Matthew pulled Lacy close and rested his chin on the top of her head when she returned to his side, and together they watched the convoy of eight vehicles leave the bureau car park. The dark blue Sedan leading.

Tanya had ensured she had reinforcements in case they were needed, he mused, still stunned by her revelations. On the flight over, although wary of each other, they had the welfare of Lacy in common, and that was a bond they both respected.

He'd been surprised when she'd opened up like she had, informing him what Ian Franklin was to her and telling him about The Gemini Project. When he'd asked why all the subterfuge regarding the children Lacy looked after, she'd explained the need for secrecy. They had snatched the children moments before they were to be killed. They were barely ahead of Ian Franklin's assassins.

Everything slotted neatly into place now, he thought, as he remembered the stuff Rhodes had gleaned, the international babysitting. Tanya and her team had been saving those kids in more ways than one. She needed a fucking medal.

Tanya had known of her sister's existence from her early teens and at first via social media and pretending to be somebody else, she had kept tabs on her. When Lacy joined the bureau, Tanya had been closer, much closer, protecting her and shadowing her missions. Matthew always knew Lacy wasn't meant to be an operative and thoughts of her being deliberately placed in harm's way by Ian Franklin sent a fiery fury racing through his blood. He'd wanted to kill him outright.

Lacy turned in his arms and crept her hands around his waist.

"You okay?" he asked.

Lacy sniffed. "Hmm-mm,"

"Back to yours?" Matthew suggested, looking over her head

and into the building. He never wanted to set foot in the place again.

She buried her nose in his shirt and breathed him in. "Sure." Stepping out of his embrace, she looked at him properly.

"You're definitely okay?" She repeated, sweeping her deep gaze over his blue jeans, simple shirt and jacket.

He smirked. That single bracketed line around his mouth deepening and she traced her fingers over his lips. She couldn't get enough of simply touching him.

Matthew caught her fingers. "It was a graze, Lace," he reassured her yet again. "Come on."

As the convoy pulled away, a door slammed, and they turned to see Ulvis walking towards them.

"You are fine, yes?" he asked with concern, looking Lacy over.

She didn't know why, but her tears finally overflowed seeing her friend. Like her, Ulvis was a victim in all of this. Good twin, bad twin. What a joke.

She went on tiptoe and hugged him. He remained stiff for a moment before his arms went around her.

"You are safe now, Miss Wallace," he said with his version of a smile, patting her head.

"What happens now?" she asked, pulling away and turning to Matthew.

Before he could say anything, the double doors swished open, and a good looking, tall, dark-skinned man walked casually towards them with his long, knee-length dreadlocks swinging behind him.

Matthew grinned and embraced his friend Rhodes.

"Good to see you, man!"

They slapped each other's backs as men do and Lacy winced at the sound.

"Yeah yeah." Rhodes grinned. "Got a bit hairy for a while and the boss had me locked up when he realised I was communicating with you."

"Sorry about that."

Rhodes laughed. "I could hear everything you were doing, so I knew you were okay." He winked knowingly over at Lacy.

Lacy felt the heat soar into her face. Oh God, he'd heard them making love. She pressed her face into Matthew's chest and felt the vibrations of his chuckle. Men!

Lacy had never had a long conversation with Rhodes, just the regular colleague-to-colleague-from-a-different-department kind of chit chat.

"Well, hello there," Rhodes said.

Lacy turned her head to see Rhodes smiling brightly at Ulvis.

"So, I'm finally meeting the massive hunk looking out for my best mate's girl." Rhodes winked and stepped closer to Ulvis.

Lacy watched in astonishment as a delicate pink touched the top of Ulvis' cheeks. Well well, she mused, watching as the two men shook hands. Hands that stayed clasped longer than necessary.

"I've got the rest of the day off," Rhodes said, eyeing Ulvis. "Where are you heading big guy?"

Ulvis looked down at Lacy who was smiling with encouragement and then over to Matthew whose look was more cautious. "Wherever you are, yes?" he answered, eventually.

Lacy tried to hide her shock and quickly re-evaluated her opinion of Ulvis being shy.

Matthew slung his good arm over Lacy's shoulders. "Catch you later." He said to the men before swinging her around and walking to the direction of her car.

"She didn't even look at me, Matthew," she said despondently getting into the passenger seat. "I mean, not properly."

"It's hard for her, Lace, you have to realise that," he secured his seatbelt and turned to her. "But she loves you and has been protecting you all these years. When Franklin started killing the multiples to save himself, she willingly exposed herself to him, using herself as a bargaining chip and the rest you know." He patted her thigh, then started the car. "She is what she is, not by choice, but she has a good heart, Lace. She'll come round."

"One thing is bothering me though," she said.

He pulled out into the line of traffic. "What?"

"What was she doing at Camille's house that night?"

Matthew remained silent, and she turned to him.

"Do you know?" she asked.

"No, I don't." He confessed. It was one of the things he didn't want to know.

CHAPTER THIRTY-SIX

"So, what are you going to do now that you're unemployed?" Lacy asked Matthew a month later, where she lay naked on top of him.

His wide hard body easily accommodated her petite frame, and this was fast becoming her favourite place. Another one. He was slowly running his fingers up and down her spine as their heart rates settled after another marathon session of lovemaking.

"Something will come up," he answered casually with his eyes closed.

Raising her head, she settled her chin on his chest and looked up at him expectantly. That had been the same answer for weeks now. But it really was getting a little ridiculous.

After they'd both resigned, with the bureau's version of blessings by awarding them plaques for 'exemplary service', he'd vetoed any visitors and the bank of computers had vanished. They'd stayed holed up in his brother's apartment making love, trying new recipes and watching movies.

"We need to look for our own place," Matthew said suddenly into the contented silence.

Lacy raised up slightly to look into his handsome face, smoothed her finger down his nose and then outlined his lips. He nipped at it, and she jumped.

To his chuckle, she asked with a raised slender eyebrow. "Is that your way of asking me to move in with you?"

He smirked and tapped her bottom. "You live where I live." He stated simply.

"What?" Lacy sat up to look down at him and scoff. "No flowers or how about; *Lacy as you are the love of my life, and I can't live without you; will you move in with me?*" she chastised with a huff. "Or could you even look at me?"

Matthew tumbled her onto her back and straddled her body as he looked down at her with hazel eyes alight with laughter, seeing her adorably petulant expression.

He breathed in deep before saying. "Lacy Dawson, as you are the love of my life, and I can't be without–"

"Live," she interrupted.

Matthew rolled his eyes but swept his palms soothingly over her chest. "Live without you. Will you move in with me?"

She pursed her lips. "Depends,"

His eyebrows lowered, not expecting that response. "Name it, and it is yours."

"I'll tell you another day," Lacy said, watching through her lashes when he reached forward to palm her breasts. "I can't–" He strummed her nipples almost roughly, "think..." Lacy tried to remember what she'd been about to say and not to surrender under the pleasure of his gifted hands.

"I'll do anything you want," he encouraged, bending to run his tongue between her breasts, tweaking her hard nipples between his fingers.

Lacy couldn't help undulating her hips, trying to concentrate on his words. Something about doing anything she wants. "Anything?" She asked suggestively, her voice dripping with the passion he'd already stirred. She watched, liking how his hazel eyes blazed gold and he touched his tongue to his bottom lip. A bottom lip already swollen from her kisses. "At my beck and call?"

Matthew moved down her body, pushed her legs apart and blew on her sex.

"Always." He confirmed, opening his mouth to flick his tongue over the tiny nub before sucking it into his mouth.

"Well all right then," she whispered, echoing the words they'd used all those weeks ago in Russia.

***

Lacy looked out across the water. The lake was still, with only the odd ripple where a fish had come to the surface disturbing the glassy surface like a silent hiccup.

The air was frigid, too cold to snow, and she felt the chill deep into her bones. She wrapped the blanket tighter around her shoulders, remembering the last time she had been up here. So much had happened since then. She wished she had got to know the hairdresser, Dirk, more than just those two days they'd had right here on the lake. She smiled, remembering the day they'd all gone fishing, the fun they'd had and the campfire later that night.

She had yet to meet Camille again and didn't want to intrude now that she had a newborn.

Lacy sighed into the night, tightening the blanket as though to keep out her maudlin thoughts. It was a wasted task.

Matthew had asked her to move in with him but not offered a happily ever after. At first, she'd been okay with the arrangement, had even enjoyed apartment hunting with him. But was it the exciting mixture of being with him and the normality of the task over the weeks that followed, that was weakening her principles as she gushed over yet another city apartment? Yes, it was. She'd always wanted a garden, and no matter what, she felt rejected as a person.

She was a wife. She was not a girlfriend. She loved him, but this didn't feel right. None of it. Was it unfair to remember the day he'd kicked her out of his life with chilling ease? She didn't have any security where he was concerned, and she'd vowed never to put herself in that situation again.

They were great together in every way. He was a good man, and she was lucky to have him, but still? Was she foolish wanting more? What was a ring anyway? Many couples lived together for years without that one piece of paper and that ring which proclaimed to the world they were committed to each other forever.

She closed her eyes, trying to imagine a life without him and couldn't. She wanted to wake up to him every morning. She wanted to make love with him and watch when the colour of his eyes blended and swirled when he was overcome with emotion. With a deep sigh, she opened her eyes again. She would do it. The empty feeling of him not being in her life trumped that of a bare ring finger. She would live with him.

"Hey,"

The man of her thoughts came up behind her and wrapped his arms around her stomach, drawing her into his strong embrace.

Lacy leaned into him and covered his bare arms with her blanket.

"Everything okay, Lace?" Matthew asked, nibbling the side of her neck. Feeling her sigh, he turned her around to face him.

He'd known something was up when, with her head bent low, thinking he was sleeping, she'd wrapped herself in a blanket and crept outside. It was five in the morning, no good thoughts ever happened at five in the morning. He'd spent another five minutes thinking about what could be wrong with her and came up with her sister.

Lacy wanted a relationship with her twin. Family meant everything to her. He'd met her parents, and she insisted they visit his family every Sunday. Lacy was about family.

"Hey," he said gently. "Talk to me," he urged, not liking the way she avoided his eyes. With a finger under her chin, he lifted her head, even so, her lovely brown eyes slid to the ground.

On his own sigh, he picked her up and walked over to the cabin, where he sat on the porch swing and rearranged her until she was nice and snug on his lap.

"Do you want to go back to Russia?" He asked grimly.

She gasped, not expecting that question. "You would take me back?"

He kissed her temple. "It's what you want, isn't it?"

"I guess." She admitted. Actually, she hadn't really thought about it. She and Tanya had video chatted several times, and their relationship was progressing. But to go back to Russia?

"Okay," Matthew conceded, satisfied he'd guessed right. "I'll make the arrangements." And with a silent nod to himself, snuggled her in even closer and together they watched the sun rise slowly over the water.

CHAPTER THIRTY-SEVEN

"Do you know where she is?" Matthew asked impatiently, with rough reluctance, knowing there was one other person who looked out for Lacy besides himself.

"What have you done?" Tanya asked sharply, narrowing her eyes at him via the laptop screen.

"Nothing," he griped reluctantly. "Not a damn thing."

He'd used all the resources available to him up at the lake. Only he still hadn't found her. Contacting Tanya was the last resort.

"She left," he admitted, barely stopping the 'me' from tumbling out of his mouth. He thought things were going well. She loved him. Just last night she'd held his face when he was deep inside her and told him so. They were looking for a place to buy together, and then she suddenly ups and leaves? It didn't make any sense. Then a thought struck him.

"Do you have anything to do with it?" he charged suddenly.

Tanya didn't bother to answer him but turned slightly so that he could see only half of her body but could hear her tap away at her computer.

"If you are not the right man to cherish and look after her, tell me now," Tanya warned in a voice so cold Matthew actually shivered. What was it with these sisters? Both of them messed with his emotions, taking every single one to the extreme.

"You know I would fucking die for her, so don't mess with me lady and tell me where she is!"

She looked away, did something on her computer and then turned back to him. She held his gaze for several seconds, looking for what, he didn't care to know.

"If I were you," she warned eventually, reaching forward. "I would make dinner."

The screen went blank, and Matthew painted the air blue in

frustration until her words finally resonated.

"Dinner?" Matthew repeated before understanding dawned, and he chuckled.

***

Matthew sat on the front porch with his booted foot pushing the swing into motion while he waited for Lacy. He should be mad at her twin for still keeping tabs on her as though he wasn't up to the job, but he'd get back to Tanya later.

He tipped his head to the side, picking up the sound of a vehicle approaching.

Rhodes had made him a new hearing aid, and he could hear better than ever. The world was so loud he was getting a headache with all the trees creaking. He laughed at his ridiculous thoughts. He'd woken to a cold bed, had a hellish day, didn't know if he was coming or going, had to deal with Tanya and now? Now, his life with Lacy was in the balance.

He watched her park and their eyes connected for a moment before he saw her take a deep breath as though preparing herself for a fight. She wanted to fight? He wasn't going to give her one.

He watched her saunter towards him, her shadow long and narrow in the late afternoon. Her eyes were red and puffy, two of those knot things in her hair had come loose, and she was wearing his sweats and T-shirt. She was a beautiful dishevelled mess.

"Hi," she signed nervously at the bottom of the steps.

She was holding a plastic bag, he noted, and she looked miserable as she moved from one foot to the other.

Matthew wanted to take charge, kiss her forever and demand that she stay with him for always. But this was her show, so instead, he folded then unfolded his arms and waited.

"Hey," he said, wondering why she was using sign language.

She licked her lips.

They looked at each other.

"I bought milk," Lacy signed again, diving into the bag she

was holding to pull out the carton of semi-skimmed. She'd messed up today and using sign language somehow made her feel closer to him.

She hadn't meant to leave Matthew this morning but had intended to go to the store, pick up some milk for porridge and then head back to make breakfast. Only she'd driven right past the small cluster of shops and headed for the city, barely able to see through her tears.

Matthew stopped the swing and reached forward. "Thanks." He uttered, taking the carton from her, being careful not to touch her and waited for whatever she was going to do or say next.

She moved the bag from her right hand over to her left and placed one sneakered foot on the step. Her bottom lip was being mauled by her teeth, and he continued watching silently, waiting for her to explain why she had disappeared for ten hours and seventeen minutes.

"I was leaving you," she stumbled, quickly reverting to speech. She'd almost reached New York City, but seeing the famous skyline through her tears and realising several things all at once, turned around as soon as she could and drove back.

His heart tripped. Forget being shot, the pain of her words killed him outright. But he was determined not to show a reaction and folded his arms high over his chest but remained quiet.

"But I couldn't do it," she admitted, feeling the sting of tears that were never far from the surface today. "I love you too much." She declared and waited for him to pounce. He always pounced and kissed her whenever she told him she loved him, but instead, he tipped up a single eyebrow and set the swing into motion.

She breathed in deep and bravely went into the bag again, this time taking out a square gift box wrapped in silver paper and tied with green and yellow ribbon. She held it out to him. When he made no move to take it, she pushed her shoulders back and climbed the shallow steps to the top.

Matthew looked at the box in her hand and reached for it. Their fingers touched, and he felt that telltale flare of recognition of his lover charge through him.

"For goodness' sake, Matthew, unwrap it!" Lacy burst out impatiently when he continued to look at her, and not what she had given him.

Silently, Matthew pulled one end of the pretty bow. The knot was tight, so he slipped the ribbon off one corner and then the other, happily drawing out her discomfort. Good, he thought meanly, she'd put him through hours of hell today. What were a few minutes to her?

The paper off, he took his time placing it on the seat beside him and with the box balanced in his open palm, lifted the lid and pushed aside the white tissue paper with a finger that shook slightly.

For a moment, he stared at the contents, not comprehending what he was seeing. His hearing was messed up, but there was nothing wrong with his eyesight. Socks?

With a deep, heartfelt breath, he put the box down beside him, reached forward to grab her hand and pulled her onto his lap.

"I love you, Lace," he said simply, completely overwhelmed.

"I love you too," she sniffed, crying into his neck. "I'm sorry."

"You came back."

"I couldn't leave you," she cried, as though him hearing that was okay. "But I drove along, getting further and further away and missed you all the more. I don't care if you don't want to get married. I just want us to be together for always." She wailed, holding him tightly.

Matthew let her cry and murmured sweet words he didn't even know he had while looking at his gift.

Sometime later, he heard a buzzing sound coming from inside the cabin and after a moment realised what it was.

"Lacy sweetheart?" he cajoled, trying to move her off his lap, but she wasn't moving. "I need to get this, or your sister will probably use a drone or something and shoot me." He pulled her clinging arms from around his neck.

"What?" she gasped, wiping her eyes.

Matthew kissed her, scooted her off his lap and then, clasping her hand, dragged her inside to his laptop already open on the table.

Tanya looked at them both, her dark eyes alight with amusement Matthew noted with annoyance. It was the first time she looked more like her sister and not the hard equivalent.

"What did you make for dinner?" she asked Matthew.

Matthew smiled, hugging Lacy close. "Ratatouille with poached eggs,"

Tanya frowned suddenly. "Not runny eggs,"

He shrugged. Why? What did runny eggs have to do with anything and asked.

Tanya looked knowingly at her sister.

Lacy gasped, comprehending what Tanya's question meant. "You know?" she charged.

"We're twins," her sister said by way of explanation. "Suddenly, I don't want my morning espresso." She frowned, obviously not appreciating the lack of caffeine in her life. "And I feel like I want to throw up all the time. Remember when you had your appendix out?"

"You felt that?" Lacy had been twelve.

"Everything." Tanya smiled, and Lacy smiled. They connected, really connected, at that moment.

Tears drenched Lacy's eyes again. "Thank you," she whispered softly with a wealth of feelings.

As was normal with Tanya, Lacy watched when her twin suddenly lifted her chin and sat straighter in her chair. She flung her shoulders back as though not appreciating, she had forgotten herself and become soft.

"No runny eggs," Tanya warned Matthew. "It is not good for pregnant women." She rang off.

CHAPTER THIRTY-EIGHT

Later that evening, Matthew, holding Lacy's hand, dragged her out to the pier.

She had wanted to laze around in the bath, but he had plans.

To her grumbles, he'd bundled her into one of his thick sweaters and sweat pants, pulled a hat down low on her head, and with a blanket draped over his arms, sat down at the edge of the pier with her back to his chest and them both dangling their legs above the water.

"Really? I don't see a blood moon, Matthew," she scolded. The moon was out but looked like it always did partway through its cycle. The fullness had already come and gone days ago to leave that funny misshapen shape that made you wonder if you knew your shapes or not.

"Oh, maybe I got it wrong," he said, looking at the face of his watch to count down in his head.

After a moment, and foreseeing disaster, he heaved them both backwards away from the water.

"What–?" Lacy grumbled, but he silenced her with a finger to her lips.

"Lacy?"

"Hmm,"

"If you had waited just twelve hours, you wouldn't have needed to put yourself, our baby or me through the distress of us not being together."

She looked at him, not understanding, and said as much.

"Wallace Lacy Dawson, will you marry me?"

Lacy looked down at the pear-shaped diamond he was holding out to her.

The ring was set in what she could make out to be dark yellow gold, very antique looking and so her.

"When did you get this?" she asked, peering at it.

He chuckled uncomfortably. "Before Russia,"

"That long?"

"Yeah," he admitted. "I knew a long time ago I wanted to spend the rest of my life with you."

"But–"

"I know, shit happened," he declared. "Are you going to marry me or not?" he charged as she still hadn't taken the ring from him.

"I will,"

But just when she held her hand out, the sky exploded with red and green fireworks, making her jump. Just as well he'd moved her from the edge of the pier, he thought tenderly.

"Oh my goodness," she exclaimed, looking in awe as rocket after rocket shot into the sky, adding sparkling splendour by reflecting off the dark lake.

Matthew grabbed her hand and shoved the ring onto her finger. "There," he declared, kissing her fingers. "The best place for it."

There was a break in the display, and she held her hand out and looked at the ring. "It's beautiful."

"I'm going to spend the rest of my life loving you and our baby, Lacy," Matthew promised, looking down at her beautiful face, just as fireworks exploded overhead bathing them in flashes of pink, white and green light.

Lacy smiled gently, reaching up to touch his face. "Well, all right then."

***

When the display had finished, they walked down the pier and, to Lacy's surprise, were met by her parents and Matthew's family. His stepmother, Greta, was smiling and had tears in her eyes. One arm was looped around Matthew's aunt, whom Lacy had met briefly and adored. She'd found a kindred spirit in his aunt, she knew. At Greta's other side was Kyle, Matthew's oh so handsome cousin. He smiled and, releasing his aunt, walked over to Lacy with sure steps.

"Welcome to the family, Lacy," he said, enveloping her in his

240

arms.

After that, the congratulations rained down on them. Camille holding baby Luna, Ace with his lovely family, and the Mannino brothers. All six of them. Lacy had never seen so many handsome men in her life and had to drag her gaze away. Ulvis and Rhodes, clasping hands with each other, engulfed her in a bear hug.

And then, just as Lacy thought she had hugged and accepted kisses of congratulations from everyone, the crowd parted.

"Tanya?" she said in confusion. "You're in Russia,"

Tanya didn't quite smile, but it was close. "Technology, I can be anywhere."

Lacy held out her arms and waited for the one moment she didn't know she needed.

Her sister walked towards her and into her arms, and they hugged for the very first time.

"Congratulations," Tanya said, pulling away after the brief hug. "Look after my sister, Edwards," she warned. "Or I'll shoot you." She declared, and everyone except Kyle's mother and Greta knew she was dead serious.

CHAPTER THIRTY-NINE

It was the next morning, and Matthew, Ace and their cousin Kyle were standing on the porch at the main house. It had been several months since the three of them had relaxed together like this.

Growing up, they had been more like three brothers, all close in age, with Ace just a few months older than Kyle and Kyle spending every vacation and practically every weekend with them.

"So is everything settled?" Matthew asked Kyle, who was holding his baby daughter Luna, snuggled close to his chest and rocking her gently within her swaddling to lull her to sleep.

Kyle squinted across at the water, seeing his wife walk towards Lacy and Tanya who were practically opposite them across the lake. He dropped a kiss on the patch of skin visible between the rim of Luna's woollen hat and layers of blankets on her face before answering. "I've never been this happy in my life," he answered with gruff honesty. "Who knew?"

The men looked at each other but didn't acknowledge the smug expressions they all had in common. They didn't talk *feelings*.

"Yeah, who knew?" both Matthew and Ace parroted.

"You'll get one hell of a sister-in-law with the Russian there bro," Ace said to Matthew with all seriousness.

"Yeah well, Tanya would do anything for Lacy and has proved it. So yeah, it could be worse."

"Chase seems to be sniffing around her," Ace went on with amusement. "This morning, he saved her a place at the breakfast table, and she ignored him to sit with Dad and Uncle Mitch. You should have seen his face."

Matthew didn't tell them Chase had already gotten a taste of his soon to be sister-in-law. But it was funny to see their burly cousin looking all puppy-eyed and trailing devotedly behind Tanya who acted as though he didn't exist.

Just then Chase walked from the side of the house, and without noticing them, looked out across the water, zipped up his thick coat and started to walk towards the women.

Matthew, Ace and Kyle chuckled but remained silent as they watched his long stride eat up the pebbly terrain cushioned by inches of snow.

"So what's the plan?" Ace broke the contented silence a moment later, "when's the wedding?"

"As soon as I can plan it," Matthew answered, meaning every word. "Lacy showed me pictures of our wedding cake last night–"

"Last night?" Ace exclaimed. "Didn't you just get engaged last night?"

Matthew narrowed his eyes at his brother in warning. "You think I'm going to let her slip out of my fingers for ten years like you, dip shit?" he reminded him, knowing it took Ace ten years for him and Sabrina to re-connect. "So yeah, last night. A Christmas wedding is what we want."

"Aunt Greta won't be happy, that's just weeks away," Kyle warned.

"Simple and chic is how Lacy wants it and what–"

"Lacy wants, Lacy gets." Ace and Kyle finished for him with a grin. They had both found the loves of their lives, and what their wives wanted, they would move heaven and earth to get it for them. It was a given fact. A wedding in two weeks was nothing.

They continued to talk amongst themselves, contented and making plans for the wedding while behind them, the house was noisy with laughter.

***

"Are you going to tell me how you two know each other?" Lacy asked eventually.

Camille had now reached them, and they continued their stroll around the lake and had reached the group of privately owned cabins directly opposite the Mannino compound where she could see the distant figures of Matthew, Ace and Kyle on the porch. She waved and blew Matthew a kiss only to laugh out loud, seeing him dramatically catch it and put it in his pocket. The two men beside him were obviously poking fun at him, because of the playful pushing she could see going on.

When they settled, she turned to Tanya and Camille with a raised brow and a hand on her hip, watching the silent exchange between the other two women before they looked at her.

"Camille is a patron of our cause," Tanya revealed, folding her arms high across her chest.

Lacy gasped, looking at the famous actress, also known as Camikara. Camille was so beautiful and elegant it was hard to imagine her doing anything but walk the red carpet draped in jewels, much less be involved with the sordid evils of the Gemini Project. "You know about the Gemini Project?"

Camille re-wrapped her orange scarf around her shoulders before answering. "India was a dumping ground for a lot of the twins," she revealed. "And it was easy to hide them away in the slums. I run several charities and orphanages in India and Sri Lanka, and we noticed babies being dropped off, which wasn't out of the ordinary, but what was different was these kids came to us clean and healthy. They'd been cared for. Suddenly, they started disappearing or turning up dead. Throats cut. Shot. Brutal deaths," she listed, her unusual grey eyes glistening with tears. "It didn't make any sense. We looked after them, they went to school. Yet they ended up dead years later." She shook her head. "We got suspicious, and I started looking into it."

"She got too close," Tanya continued, seeing the distress in Camille's eyes. "Ian Franklin and his cronies were planning to assassinate her. So, I stepped in." She admitted, tipping up her chin.

Lacy looked at her sister, who looked defensive for saving Camille's life. "How long have you known each other?" She asked, curiously, as things slotted into place. Tanya and Camille were friends, which was why Tanya had been at Camille's house the night of the shooting and in New York. Tanya had been protecting them both.

"About eight years or so," Camille answered.

"Did you know she was connected to Matthew's cousin?" Lacy asked her sister.

"That came later," Tanya answered. "When he showed up here." She pursed her lips, remembering all the trouble Matthew Edwards had caused her before he'd revealed his feelings for Lacy, and she let him live.

"So you didn't know at first?" Lacy challenged.

Tanya's eyes, so like her own, narrowed as she looked at her. "If I'd known," she explained with measured, cultured tones, unused to being questioned. "I would not have made arrangements for you to do a pick up at the cabin, and all the trouble that followed would not have happened."

Lacy echoed her sister's stance for a moment before sticking out her left hand to admire her engagement ring, turning it this way and that to catch the light. Tanya called it trouble. Lacy called it fate. What were the chances of bumping into Matthew up here? "Well it's a good job you didn't know, isn't it?" Lacy stated with a smidgeon of annoyance. She was sick and tired of being manipulated. Granted, it had ended well, but that was beside the point.

Sensing the tension and seeing Chase walking towards them, Camille looped her arms through both of theirs and steered the sisters down the same pier, where she had said goodbye to her dear friend Dirk all those months ago.

"I see you have an admirer, Tanya," Camille teased, watching Tanya's face flood with embarrassment when she spied Chase striding towards them.

Lacy giggled. "Who knows? there just might be another wedding and we can double up."

"Never," Tanya sneered. "I'm going back to Russia and don't have time for stupid American jocks, who think they are God's gift!"

"The woman objects too much methinks," Camille joked,

reaching the edge of the pier. She snuggled them closer, a barrier against the cold wintry breeze that skittered across the water as they all fell silent, deep into their own thoughts.

Lacy was thinking about centre-pieces for the wedding reception. Camille was considering where to hang the portrait of the baby Kyle had recently painted, and Tanya was thinking about adding more semi-automatics to her arsenal back in Russia.

***

With plans for the wedding in full steam, Kyle, Ace and Matthew were about to go inside, happy with progress, yet knowing they were going to have to gang up and convince their stepmother Greta, that they wanted the wedding by Christmas.

Kyle put his hand out, stopping Matthew. "Did you see that?" he asked, looking into the snow-dotted trees in the distance.

The brothers turned to look.

"What?" Matthew squinted, not seeing anything but acres of pines.

Kyle shrugged after a moment before pushing up his tinted glasses to rub his sensitive eyes. "I thought I saw a flash or something." He replaced his glasses. "Must be my eyes playing tricks again."

Just then, a shot rang out, startling the birds from the trees, breaking the silence of winter, to echo across the water like thunder.

"Shit!" Matthew exclaimed, seeing Chase look over his shoulder and then break into a run. "Shit!"

Another shot rang out, and they watched with horror, Chase zig-zagging across the packed snow, frantically waving his hands at the women as he ran.

"Kyle, get inside! Look after the family!" Matthew shoved his cousin into the house and on Ace's heels jumped over the porch rail and started running.

Another single shot and Chase went down.

"Fuck!"

Frantically Matthew ran, overtaking his brother, as a barrage of now automatic gunfire rang out.

Life slowed.

He could see himself. He could feel the tight pull of each breath, hear the crunch of icy snow under his feet. His chest was on fire. The air frozen. They were too far away. He passed one pier, two more to go before he would reach Lacy.

He was shouting, he knew he was. *Run!* He yelled at the women. *Run for cover!* They were out in the open, exposed.

More shots were nipping at his ankles where he shadowed his cousins' footprints. He ran on, passing another pier, fear powering him on. Chase was just up ahead out in the open. Still.

The snow was stained with spots of blood and Matthew rolled his cousin over to check for a pulse and relief scaled through him as Chase groaned and opened his eyes a moment later.

The shooter was letting off another round of gunfire and ducking, Matthew, now with Ace's help went to move their cousin behind a narrow log, but screams ransacked the air and when they looked up the pier was empty.

Life froze.

"No!"

CHAPTER FORTY

The water closed over him, sealing him in like an icy tomb.

He could barely make out Lacy in the depths of the lake, a blur of colour, sinking deeper and deeper, without life.

Matthew screams her name, hearing himself inside his own head and powers towards her, pushing into the icy depths, deeper and deeper and deeper into the darkness.

Almost as though she'd heard him, she looks up, *Lacy*! Her eyes are darker than he has ever seen them, wider, the whites smothered. Her hair floats all around her, and her blue-tinged lips stretch into a small smile when their eyes meet. Relief floods through him. She's not dead.

His lungs feel like over-inflated circus balloons about to burst. The cold water is slowing his heartbeat to almost nothing. He can feel the coldness seeping under his skin, his clothes heavy, dragging him down, yet he's barely moving. She's sinking faster than he can get to her.

She reaches towards him, her movements graceful like a ballerina with one arm arched over her head, her fingers elegantly tapping into the current like a wordless song. Her smile still in place.

Their fingers touch once, twice, and he grabs her wrist, pulling her quickly towards the surface. The sun is bright and welcoming, the water clear and tranquil. But silent missiles suddenly whizz past, piercing the surface. Bullets! Countless bullets slicing the water like underwater fireworks.

Matthew feels her jerk away from him, and he looks back in horror. Blood is pouring from holes all over her body, turning the water scarlet.

She looks at him, her eyes resigned, and her smile fades. *I love you*, she mouths, closing her eyes.

No! Stay with me Lacy, he silently begs. *Stay with me!* He can feel his breath leaving his body. The sun is blood red overhead. He needs air.

He sees her hands go to her stomach, cupping the precious curve. Their baby! The baby!

She's sinking further and further away from him, the water swirling beneath her, sucking her into the darkness. She's leaving him!

His lungs fill with water.

***

"Matthew?"

He didn't move.

"Matthew," Lacy tried again, gently shaking his shoulder. "Wake up, honey."

Hearing Lacy's voice, Matthew grappled towards the surface of sleep, pushing the darkness away to look into the concerned eyes of Lacy.

"You had another one?" she asks gently, smoothing her fingers over his sticky brow.

Ever since he'd rescued her from the lake all those months ago, Matthew had been gripped with night terrors. He told her they were always the same and instead of hauling her out of the shallows, as what really happened, he'd run up the pier and dived into the lake.

Matthew reached over and touched her face like he always did after the nightmare. She knew he was checking to see if she was alive and silently gave him a moment to collect himself and waited for the fear to clear from his hazel eyes.

"Yeah," he admitted gruffly, sitting up and pushing his fear away to focus on her. "Sorry for waking you."

"I wasn't sleeping," Lacy arranged the pillows behind her shoulders and watched indulgently when Matthew splayed his fingers to sweep over the large firm swell of her belly.

"How are you feeling?" he asked.

"Ready for a birthday party tomorrow." Lacy rolled her

shoulders and moved the pillows again, trying to get comfortable.

They were in the VIP maternity wing at Mercy General Hospital in New York, which had been her home for the past seven months. The night of the shooting, she had started bleeding heavily, and due to other complications was immediately put on bed rest.

It had been a terrible, chaotic time, with Chase wounded and the whole family vulnerable in one remote location. The Mannino brothers had chased the shooter, but he'd got away leaving a crude Gemini symbol painted in red on the road. Thankfully the bullet had missed all of Chase's vital organs, and he'd made a full recovery. But still...

"Don't think about it," Matthew warned, seeing that familiar flicker of fear cross her face again ever since the shooting, and he kissed her fingers to soothe her. He was now lying on his side facing her on the king-sized bed, watching every flicker of concern in her eyes. He wished he could do something about it, make her feel safer, but he couldn't. Everyone he knew, plus Tanya's small army, were out looking for the shooter.

"I can't help it."

"They can't touch us, Lace," Matthew soothed. "And you know I won't let anything happen to you."

She lifted a single brow and smiled. "You mean anything else," she teased, lightening the mood. He was right, no-one could get past the extra security, not to mention the medical staff had all been vetted and flown in by Tanya, including Dr Glazunov and his twin, another doctor.

Matthew chuckled, cuddling her close before re-arranging the pillows under her knees, knowing the position helped ease the pain in her lower back. "And you wouldn't have it any other way," Matthew insisted, winking. "Birthday party tomorrow." He promised. "Now get some rest," he leant over to kiss her cheek goodnight.

"Okay," Lacy replied, however, too excited to sleep. "Movie?" she suggested instead.

Matthew rolled his eyes, unsurprised, being as this had become their new normal, so he reached over for the remote to start the next Bollywood movie featuring the mega superstar Camikara, whom they both knew as Camille.

***

The birthday party spilt out into the corridor. The entire family were here, including the Mannino brothers, Matthew's uncle and aunt from the lake, Camille and Kyle, Ace and Sabrina, not to mention all the half-siblings and his best friend, Rhodes. Even Dmitri from Russia came as a surprise.

It was loud, and champagne corks were still being popped as everyone celebrated. Every spare surface was covered with brightly wrapped presents, teddy bears, and large bouquets of balloons touched the ceiling.

Lacy wasn't the least bit tired, but only a little sore. The scheduled caesarean went without a hitch this morning, and she and Matthew had had a few hours alone with their children before the rest of the family descended.

Lacy smiled at the sight of Charles holding baby Theo. All she could see of her son was his tiny hand clenching his grandfather's finger.

Ulvis was still wearing a stunned expression, gazing down at little Chloe. And Tanya, sitting beside him, was quietly singing a Russian lullaby to Kit.

All three babies had bright auburn curls like their daddy.

"Are you ready, Lace?" Matthew asked quietly, coming to her side and taking her hand gently kissing her knuckles.

"For what?" she tilted her head to look at him. He looked so serious, gazing down at her with eyes blazing with emotion. It was as though it were only the two of them in the room.

"For the rest of our lives."

She turned their hands over and pulled him closer to kiss his knuckles.

"Well, all right then."

The End

I usually leave it here, but please consider leaving a review as I'm seriously lacking.

Thanks!

Scan Me

Join Caroline's influencer list for more fun reads and freebies.

Read an excerpt of **Love To Belong** below.

LOVE TO BELONG

Chapter One

She was beginning to dislike it, but plunged ahead.

"Okay guys, I'm super excited. I'm at St. Pancras train station and finally on my way to Paris. Got my portable chargers, my favourite bag with all the pockets. Remember, it's about convenience when you're travelling," she advised, with a swiftness she was famed for. "And look at this beauty," Chilli aimed her camera to showcase the furry pink, totally impractical suitcase at her feet. "How cute." Angling the camera back to her face, she fluttered her freshly in-filled eyelash extensions and giggled. "See you on the other side."

With a sigh of relief, Chilli swivelled the camera screen into its housing, signed off and carefully placed the expensive camera into her bag, before grabbing the outrageous suitcase, entering the train, and making herself comfortable in First Class.

Ten minutes later, she was joined by her friends and fellow influencers, Candace Mason, and Vinny Sang.

They'd been friends via cyberspace for years, but had only met physically two years ago at a media conference in Berlin.

Fortunately, although beauty vloggers, Candace took the healthier, hemp, aloe vera, au natural approach, and Vinny's content was wild and theatrical.

"So, what's the deal?" Vinny asked, re-arranging his bucket hat on his head. His clothes were loud and vibrant, his hair shaved on one side from the left temple, right around the back of his head to the opposite ear and he sported a chin-length fringe tipped in platinum blonde. Last week it had been deep purple.

"We have the fashion shows and the after-party at the hotel." Candace explained, checking her emails.

They talked about fashion, influencers, designers, who they

wanted to interview and definitely what they'd hoped to be gifted.

For the three of them, content creation was big business. They each had followers in the millions. Two years in a row, Chilli was voted Social Influencer of the Year.

Yep, life was good, and she revelled in it.

"Love the hair, Chilli Pepper," Vinny teased, using his nickname for her and reaching across the table to tug the strands sweeping over her shoulders.

Chilli leaned back out of his reach and shook her head. "You know the rules, Vinny," she scolded seriously. "Don't touch the lace front." She wagged her finger at him in warning. She was wearing a prototype for a collection they had approached her to endorse from an American wig manufacturer. It was a shoulder-length brown bob with a deep parting on the left. Apparently, if she sprayed a little water on it, the bone straight strands would turn into a tousled wavy beach babe look. She was going to try that later when she changed for the party, although she had a long wavy lace front wig as backup in case it didn't work.

Chilli had been creating content for years and covered everything from fashion trends and makeup to talking about her daily life and pop culture.

She collaborated with large, well-known brands. Wearing their clothes and using the products that had been sent to her. And also shopping in their brick-and-mortar shops. Almost everything Chilli did was documented via video, and she shared her views publicly and was paid handsomely for it.

Anything Chilli endorsed, sold out and her last makeup tutorial had received over three million views in a few days. She was liked and in high demand.

She was aware she couldn't rely on content creation as a stable income. The money was good but influencing fickle. Trends came and went. Popularity could disappear like a puff of smoke. It was becoming saturated, and Chilli was missing the enthusiasm she had had when she had started out. With the help of her staff, she was looking at other ways to monetise her brand.

Born in England, Chilli, whose real name was Chillitara Laurent, was bi-lingual and as comfortable in France, where her beloved grandmother lived, as she was in Britain and frequently travelled between the two countries.

"How's life with the boyfriend going?" Candace asked, interrupting the pleasant thoughts of her grandmother, whom Chilli intended to visit before she left France in a few days.

Chilli sighed, thinking of Paul. He'd lasted all of three weeks and was only a boyfriend on paper. She couldn't get past his large sweaty hands, much less have him kiss her. Besides, it soon became apparent he'd wanted to use her for her contacts for his T-shirt business.

"It's not," Chilli answered without remorse, barely concealing a shudder.

Vinny laughed. "You go through men like I go through–"

"Men," Chilli finished for him with a teasing wink.

"Oh, *touché*," he waved his hand about.

"Who knows, maybe we'll both find somebody rich to snog at the after-party tonight," Vinny declared.

Chilli laughed. "That's right, we're only snogging rich men from now on," she proclaimed.

They high-fived each other as they laughed. None of them had much luck with relationships. Candace flittered from man to man. Vinny was continuously looking for a lover who could support his extravagant lifestyle and Chilli wasn't looking to be in a relationship at all, but played along, contributing to their outlandish list of what Mr. Rich Man should be like.

***

Arno Tournier cringed and swiped his finger across the surface of his tablet a little too aggressively. The passengers in front of him laughed and talked loudly about their love lives. Generation Z, he thought, knowing he'd just about escaped that label being thirty-four himself.

Arno couldn't concentrate on the blog he was reading and with a huff, put his tablet down and glared at them. The Generation Zs were gossiping with no consideration for the other passengers.

He was tired. He'd been in England for a nine o'clock appointment, and because of the lateness of one of his suppliers, the meeting hadn't started until after eleven, ruining his entire day.

Arno slumped in his seat to rest his head against the headrest and closed his eyes. He wanted to return to the vineyard. He was a vigneron at heart, but with his grandfather's steady decline in health, there was no one else to manage what he liked to call the sterile side of things.

Arno hated it. Hated life in Paris and couldn't wait to head home. But his beloved grapes had to wait because of a conference in the morning.

A loud burst of laughter captured his attention, and there was nothing for him to do but look and listen to the conversation going on not three feet from him. Unfortunately, he'd forgotten his headphones so couldn't tune the world, *them,* out.

The girl directly opposite was beautiful in a lanky blonde sharpness kind of way. She was probably a model or something, seeing the long willowness of her arms. Her shoulders protruded rather sharply from the cut-outs of her black top, and her breasts were small. She did nothing for him. Paris was full of women who looked like her.

He shifted his gaze to the girl sitting beside her. She was smaller, wearing a hot pink felt hat placed at a jaunty angle on her head. Her features were soft, and her face was round. A dimple played by the side of her mouth. Her complexion was dark gold, and the hair poking out from under the hat was slightly darker. She was wearing a long-sleeved black, V-necked, T-shirt thing, and the hands that she waved expressively about were tipped in hot pink too.

He mentally rolled his eyes. High maintenance was stamped all over her. And as for the vicious way she dismissed her boyfriend, Arno knew the poor bastard had had a lucky escape.

He closed his eyes and didn't open them again until jolted by someone landing on his lap.

"I'm so sorry," Chilli apologised in a rush, trying to get up. But between the table at her back and the hard-muscular chest at her front, not to mention the arms now holding her, she couldn't move. "I tripped on something." She explained, trying to wriggle free.

Arno looked at her. Up close, her skin was flawless, her eyes the darkest brown he had ever seen. They could even be black. Her eyelashes were very long and thick and her lips full and tempting. He had to force the inappropriate urge to lean forward and run his tongue along her succulent bottom lip from his thoughts.

"I'm sure that you did," Arno drawled, gritting his teeth when his body reacted to the soft cushion of her bottom. She was well within her rights to slap his face and call him a pervert, knowing she couldn't help but feel the hard ridge of his lengthening arousal beneath her. He'd gone too long without a woman and couldn't remember the last time he'd enjoyed the smoothness of a woman's thighs locked around his waist.

Chilli gasped at his harsh tone and heaved herself up. Or she tried to. She'd noticed him earlier as she'd waited for her friends. He was hard to miss with his deep olive skin tone, and dark wavy hair she'd had the mad compulsion to touch and remembered curling her fingers into a fist to control the tingling.

From a distance, she hadn't been able to make out his eye colour, although they hadn't looked run-of-the-mill brown. Now, with only inches between them, Chilli was fascinated to see they were deep forest green. Funny how the colour reminded her of the dream she'd had this morning.

It was weird, and she knew there was some psychobabble explanation about it, but she dreamt in one colour. She thought it was some kind of premonition or something, so whatever colour it was, she'd always wear it close to her skin that day. The dark green of his eyes matched the colour of her satin bra and panty set perfectly.

His shirt was unremarkable, plain crispy white. She glanced down to see what colour his trousers were. Please don't be black, she prayed silently to herself and looked down to stare at the patch of cloth between her legs. His trousers were dark. Black, or maybe navy, she mused curiously, but with a stripe running through it and she peered to discover what colour the line actually was.

"Do you mind?" Arno barked. The girl was practically looking at his crotch. Did she have no shame?

"What?" Chilli looked at him wide-eyed.

Arno all but growled. "Get up!"

"Oh, I'm sorry," Chilli declared, with an embarrassing gasp, "you see I have this thing about colours," she explained quickly. "I wanted to see what colour your trousers were, if they were like your eyes or boring like the rest of the suits on the train." She tipped her head towards the businessmen in the carriage, clear by their white shirts, generic ties, and black trousers.

Chilli, feeling the heat still scorching her cheeks and thankful her skin was dark enough to disguise her embarrassment, wriggled about, trying to lever herself up without touching his chest or wrapping her arms around his neck.

"I'm really sorry," she repeated with difficulty. It was as though he'd sucked in all the air surrounding them and her heart was struggling to beat. He continued to stare into her eyes as though she were a crazy person, before dropping his gaze to track all over her body. "Can you at least help?" she ordered eventually. Everywhere his eyes touched sent tiny flames of awareness through her. If she could, she would fold her arms over her breasts to cover her peeking nipples.

Chilli wasn't fat, but half-African genes ruled over her figure. She had curves. Curves that when growing up had been embarrassing, especially beside her petite French grandmother. Now she embraced them, but unfortunately, they were still the first thing men noticed.

Arno opened his legs, and she slid between them. He didn't

dare look at her, having already lost the battle with his body and just wanted to move her on as quickly as possible to save them both further embarrassment. He'd seen the heat in her eyes, the brazen sexual awareness as her nostrils flared. Her scent had changed, reminding him of the shift in the air when a summer storm was coming. He was close enough to see a flush of red gently touch her cheeks to sweep down her neck. He wanted to map the enticing colour with the tip of his tongue, knowing she was as aware of him as he was of her. The ever so slight rocking of her hips told him so. But this was neither the time nor the place. He did not pick up loud young women on trains.

Turning to his left, Arno twisted away, placed one hand on the back of the seat, the other on the table, and hauled himself up.

Chilli quickly scrambled out and stood to face him.

"Thank you, and again, I'm really sorry," she said, hoping she didn't sound as breathless as she felt. She didn't know what this was, but wow.

"Think nothing of it, *Mademoiselle*," his tone was formal, icy, and unpleasant.

Chilli gasped and stepped back in indignation. He made it sound as though she had intentionally fallen on him, and she wouldn't be surprised if he checked his pockets for his wallet. Forget the wow, she thought, pursing her lips. She wanted to smack that arrogant sneer off his face, and she wasn't a violent person.

Instead, Chilli tipped her chin up and spoke to him as he towered over her. He was tall, with broad shoulders she didn't want to think about. He could be an athlete, she guessed, trying not to notice the distracting broadness of his chest. "I really did trip," she defended tightly.

They both looked down, staring at the pale blue carpet with a narrow red line running through it. There was nothing to trip on.

"Run along," Arno said, sitting down to pick up his tablet in a blatant display of dismissal.

With a chilling look, completely wasted as it landed on the

top of his head, Chilli straightened her spine and went to the bathroom.

On her return, instead of sitting in her old spot, she sat beside Vinny. Her back to the rude Frenchman.

It was almost one in the morning.

After a late meal in the hotel restaurant, Arno made himself comfortable in the foyer. It was a beautiful space, decked out in creams, golds with deep red trimmings, that reminded him of the full-bodied Cabernet he produced.

His mouth twisted, and he shook his head at himself. He was such a wine freak and was precisely what one past lover had called him.

Five, no, six generations of prized winemakers coursed through his veins.

One past relative had planted vegetables with the vines and they had lost much of the vineyard to disease, and it had taken another generation to recover.

A sexy server walked over to him in a tight black skirt and white shirt that strained across her breasts. She flirted outrageously with him, and the thought of asking for her number almost tumbled from his lips. Paris was perfect for a one-night-stand.

Once he went home, it was long days in the vineyards and even longer nights in the office, doing the sterile admin things that bored the life out of him.

His last girlfriend had left him months ago, or was it a year now? He mused, trying to recall what she looked like. He clenched his fists. The server, although pretty, wasn't doing anything for him. He'd gone about his business with the girl on the train skirting the periphery of his mind all day, distracting him. The subtle scent of her perfume had clung to him. He'd felt the whisper of her breath across his skin when he should have been listening to one of his distributors. And he definitely remembered how her luscious bottom had felt pressing against him. Added together, and the memory of her had kept him in a state of semi-arousal all day. He wanted her. He should have got *her* number.

Arno declined the server's invitation with a polite smile and ordered a glass of red wine. Hell, if he was in Paris when he wanted to be home, he may as well check out the competition, he thought, relaxing into the plush armchair.

The server walked away with a swing to her hips, and a look over her shoulder to let him know her offer was still open.

Arno pulled out his phone and checked his messages instead. There were plenty of emails, and he steeled himself, hating all the paperwork, and thought about hiring a firm to manage it all. Although felt like he was betraying his ancestors.

Tournier Wines was one hundred percent family-owned. He and his grandad were the only ones left. Past generations had killed off his workforce by not reproducing enough, Arno mocked, saluting them with his glass.

The elevator doors opened with a soft ping, but it was the raucous laughter skittering across the polished porcelain tiles that made him look up with annoyance, and his breath caught. It was the girl from this morning with her loud friends. Did they never shut up? He thought with irritation, watching them and then *her* as she tipped her head back in laughter.

Her dress was sexy as hell, electric blue and soft looking. It looked complicated to put on. Much less take off. Rope-like things crisscrossed her otherwise bare stomach, connecting the top half of the dress to the skirt.

The rest of her body was covered from the hip down. Tight sleeves billowed at her wrists, covering her fingers. It was dramatic and seductive, and he found himself wanting to lick those patches of skin on display at her waist.

Her hair was longer than this morning, and he frowned, knowing he'd thought it to be shoulder length on the train. Maybe it wasn't her. Perhaps it was someone who looked like her? he thought, watching her closely. But no, her laugh was the same, her lips ripe and as kissable as he remembered, and, oh yeah, her bottom was definitely the same, peachy and pert, he noticed with a smirk appreciating her curves as she turned to link her arms with her friends when they made their way to the bar to his right.

He had been tired, but Arno suddenly felt excited, like when his grapes were ready to harvest.

The server brought his glass on a dainty brass tray, hovered for a moment, then, realising he really wasn't interested, walked off without a wiggle to her bottom. Women. Arno laughed to himself, how fickle is thee, he misquoted.

With the glass held loosely in his hands, he looked at the colour, swirled it around, sniffed and then tasted, letting the wine slide along his tongue and fill his mouth. The flavour was good. His was better. Without thinking, he walked towards the bar with his glass, his tiredness gone.

**

Chilli saw him enter the dimness of the room and her heart skidded to a halt.

She was still on a high because style icon Annika had said her name in greeting and that high now shot to mega heights.

After pausing in the doorway, the man from the train sauntered over to one of the semi-circular seats and sat down, sliding to the centre. He was directly opposite to where Chilli was standing at the bar with her friends. She moved, turning her back to the room, knowing she could watch him openly via his reflection in the mirror behind the glass case.

The soft lighting from the five-fingered brass chandeliers scattered here and there lent a romantic feeling to the intimate room. It was a new modern hotel, yet the bar had a quaint 30s feel about it. A white piano with an enormous vase of red roses on top dominated an elevated stage, but Chilli didn't see any of that. She was locked on him.

He was beautiful. Definitely French by the aristocratic angles of his cheekbones and jawline. His hair, brushed back from his face, was thick and glossy, but it could do with shaping, she noted.

Funny how this morning she took him to be a boring businessman, probably an accountant. Watching him now, his long fingers slowly smoothed up and then down the stem of his wine glass, she would say he was an artist or something else, passionately creative.

He could do with a makeover, though. His clothes were as boring now in dark trousers and a plain shirt as they were this morning. Yet there was an exciting restlessness about him. Chilli could feel it. The sleeves of his shirt were rolled up in defiance of rigid formality. He didn't want to be here.

Their eyes connected via the mirror and Chilli could not look away. Neither acknowledged the other, and Chilli was grateful when the shots arrived, and she had an excuse to escape his intense gaze to pick up her glass.

Only she couldn't help herself and watched him surreptitiously under her lashes, very much aware of him staring when she clinked her glass with her friends, toasting the success of the day. She spilt some and licked it from her fingers.

Almost defiantly, Chilli did another shot, even though her first drink still scorched a trail of fire down her throat. She raised her chin, noticing a single dark eyebrow lift ever so slightly as he watched on.

Chilli loved Vinny and Candace, but after twelve hours of togetherness, they were rattling her nerves. Thankfully, they were returning to England in the morning. However, she was staying on.

Tomorrow she was going to an all-day AXP Centennial Conference, a foreign exchange programme she had taken part in a few years ago. She was a guest speaker. Afterwards, she was going to spend time with her grandmother.

"Okay," Chilli suddenly turned to Vinny and Candace, "I'm going to do a quick update, and then I'll be back," she promised, digging into her designer bag shaped like a gold cherry tomato and pulling out her beloved camera.

Chilli was looking for a quiet corner to film when she spied him. Boosted by the alcohol, she straightened her spine and walked over.

She really needed to call him something else 'the man from the train' made him sound like a serial killer, she acknowledged, giggling to herself before stopping in front of his table.

"*Bonjour*," she greeted in French, "remember me?" she finished in English.

Chilli hovered by the table and licked her suddenly parched bottom lip. Now that his dark green gaze was trained on her, she'd lost her nerve. The tiny amount of alcohol she had consumed had rapidly evaporated under his sizzling stare. He was intense, his regard giving nothing away, although the fingers skimming his wine glass had stopped.

"I remember you," Arno replied.

Chilli scooted in beside him. "Can I borrow your table for a moment?" she asked.

He canted his head to one side, then looked around the room before pinning her with his gaze, his forehead pleating into a puzzled frown.

"What for?"

Chilli beamed. "I'll show you," she invited. Opening her handbag, she carefully pulled out her beloved camera she called Frankie.

Knowing exactly how her camera worked, she adjusted the settings to facilitate the dim lighting in the room. She fluffed her hair and angled the camera just where she liked it–slightly above her–before turning somewhat. Then, clearing her throat, she smiled into the lens.

"Hi guys," Chilli said, then talked excitedly about her evening and everything that had happened throughout her day.

Arno listened as she talked into her camera. She was talking about herself and reeling off names and details of her meal as though she were writing a diary.

She talked and talked and said something about rating her foundation ten out of ten.

Then repeated everything in French.

Arno found her speech fascinating as he listened keenly and

deduced she didn't live in France. Her pronunciation, though perfect, was accent-less.

"And finally," Chilli turned towards the man from the train, "I'm going to find out his name," she angled her camera at him for a split second, "And then ask him to buy me a drink." She winked. "When in France...?" Chilli left the rest unsaid.

"Thanks," she said, placing her camera carefully on the table.

"What was that?" Arno asked.

"I'm a content creator," she explained, but at his baffled look went on. "Vlogger."

"Blogger?" he'd heard of the stuff people wrote on the internet were called blogs and read many articles on the winemaking industry, but he didn't delve much further than that.

"No," Chilli explained. "Vlogger. I don't write about things so much anymore. I film myself talking instead. It's more exciting."

"Isn't that how you say?" he cocked one silky brow at her. "Pretentious *oui*?"

"What's pretentious about giving people an honest diary of my life?"

"The fact you are giving people a diary of your life?" he shot back.

He didn't quite sneer, but it was there, hovering in the corner of his well-shaped mouth. Chilli really hoped he would not disappoint her and be an arse, she thought. Good looking, but still an arse.

"Everyone loves my content," she defended, losing the excitement of the day to his moody disapproval. "I have my own YouTube channel." She announced, tipping up her chin.

His dark eyebrows dipped, and he reached over to pick up his glass. He swallowed down his wine disrespectfully–wine was supposed to be honoured across the palate–before turning to look at her.

"Is that what you will do?" he inquired. "Put it on YouTube for people to watch?"

"Yes."

"With me on it?"

Oops. Chilli should have seen where this conversation was leading.

"Not necessarily," she hedged. But by the tilt of a single eyebrow, knew he knew she was lying.

Time to go. He was an arse, she thought, fighting her disappointment and scooting across the seat, but he grabbed her camera and put it on the other side of him, out of her reach.

Available Now

Join Caroline's influencer list for more fun reads and freebies.

ABOUT THE AUTHOR

Caroline Bell Foster

Caroline Bell Foster was born in Derby, England, and went on a six-week holiday to Jamaica with her family. She stayed for years!

Ever the adventurer, Caroline bought her first pair of high heels in Toronto, Canada and traded her pink sunglasses for a bus ride in the Rift Valley, Kenya by the age of 18.

A self-proclaimed cat person, Caroline is looking forward to one day being called 'The Mad Cat Lady. She enjoys writing sweet or spicy romances.

The multi-award-winning writer is also the author of the Amazon Bestselling Call Centre Series, Call Me Royal and Call Me Lucky, where she pays tribute to all those who work the night shift in call centres as she has done.

With themes of substance, Caroline's latest novels defy convention and celebrate modern-day Britain with several titles set primarily in the East Midlands. Caroline has been listed as one of the most influential creatives in her region.

Caroline has come full circle and lives in Nottingham, England, just twelve miles from where she was born. She married her college sweetheart David (Mr Sunshine) and they have two children.

If you would like to keep up to date with Caroline's new releases, please sign up to her twice-yearly newsletter via her website.

www.carolinebellfoster.com

BOOKS BY THIS AUTHOR

Sweet & Spicy Books For Every Mood.

Love To Belong - How could one little lie cause so much chaos?

Distracting Ace – (International Heroes Book 1) It took thirty-six hours for Ace to fall in love. But longer to find it again and keep it.

Convincing Kyle - (International Heroes Book 2) First, love and family interference spelt disaster for Kyle and Camille. Years later, they tried again, but even more, interference threatens their love.

The Pussycat Trap: 3 stories in 1. Who knew the pitter-patter of tiny paws could melt the hearts of these powerful men? (Sweet Romance)

The Cat Café. London banker Blake enters the cat café by mistake. Not only is he shocked to see so many cats in one place, but to also fall in love with the mad cat lady, Trinity Peters.

Amazon bestselling Call Centre Series:
Call Me Lucky. Teddy could not believe the foul-mouthed girl he once knew had changed so little. He needed to show Felicity the world could be better and brighter with him.

Call Me Royal. Della now lived her life by one word, safe. Could long lost love Spencer remind her how it used to be?

Spicy Tropical Romances:

Saffron's Choice. Engaged to a man she hadn't seen in 5 years. Saffron gives in and falls in love with the man that had always been in front of her.

Caribbean Whispers. Could Merrissa escape her past and take a chance on Alex, or does her past continue to haunt her?

Ladies Jamaican. Three friends, three kinds of love. Could they make it?